THE BITTERSWEET VINE

The Bittersweet Vine

THAMES RIVER PRESS
An imprint of Wimbledon Publishing Company Limited (WPC)
Another imprint of WPC is Anthem Press (www.anthempress.com)
First published in the United Kingdom in 2013 by
THAMES RIVER PRESS
75–76 Blackfriars Road
London SE1 8HA

www.thamesriverpress.com

A CIP record for this book is available from the British Library.

ISBN 978-0-85728-094-7

This title is also available as an eBook

THE BITTERSWEET VINE

Marissa de Luna

THAMES RIVER PRESS

For James

1

Pulling the duvet around her, Maria takes comfort that it is a Saturday and she can stay in bed for as long as she likes. A smile forms on her lips. The thick duvet protects her from the draughty skylight. Then, in an instant, Maria becomes aware of reality. Feeling a sense of foreboding in the pit of her stomach, she knows something is wrong.

Squeezing her eyelids together, fragments of Friday afternoon return to her: Sitting at her desk in the office, Tina talking incessantly about her impending wedding—her yellow mug filled with calming camomile tea, feeling tired, drowsy even. And then nothing. A blank. Her wrists feel sore, her head starts to pound and her body aches like she is coming down with the flu. She can hear music. The same music that has played in her bedroom from the time she bought the album. That was two weeks ago. The same song that has woken her up every morning since. It calms her. It is familiar. But then she remembers seven words that make her blood run cold: *I know what you do every day.* As the words enter her thoughts she cannot recollect why they fill her with dread. In her mind's eye she sees bricks and a yellow scarf. The images quickly disappear. Inhaling deeply under the covers, her eyes still closed, she suddenly realises what this lone sentence means. It sends a chill down her spine. It was the last email she read before… before what? She cannot remember anything after receiving it. That fateful message had frightened her like nothing before. But did she receive it at work or at home? Was Tina there? Maria is unsure. Her memory is clouded in a fog. She frowns. She would not have left work unattended. It must have been a bad dream. She wants to check her phone but her head feels heavy. She does not have the energy to move.

The song finishes and starts again. Maria has not set the song to play on repeat. A feeling of terror paralyses her. Her gut instinct tells her to stay where she is safe.

Scared to look out from under the duvet, Maria questions whether she is at home. She is certain that she is in her bed but an air of unfamiliarity surrounds her; the bed sheets feel foreign and the smell of her skin is different. The fear ebbs and flows in her mind. Her heart is beating furiously and there is a faint smell of aftershave. Is it on her body? Or has it just been sprayed? It's familiar. Maria knows the fragrance, but is unable to place it.

Her fear intensifies. *He* must be in the room with her, but what room? Whose room is she in? And how is *her* music playing? She can hear the beeping of the refuse van and she senses it is morning. Straining her ears, she cannot hear anything else. Afraid, Maria inches her hand down her body and is relieved that she is clothed. But on opening her eyes, she cannot see. The duvet is thick and has only allowed in a fraction of light. Her hand feels brushed cotton. After a moment's hesitation, she knows the feel of the clothes on her skin. They are *her* pyjamas: white with red hearts.

Closing her eyes, Maria contemplates her options. Her breathing has become difficult and her mouth is dry. A bitter taste lingers at the back of her throat. The duvet she was enjoying only moments ago is now suffocating her. Unable to hear the sound of anyone in the room, she considers moving. Maria has to get out from under the covers but she is afraid of what might be outside. There is silence now, just a faint clicking sound, and then a rustle as the compact disc pauses before starting again, playing the same song. She didn't hear the noise the first time but now she is confident that it is her music system; only her music system makes that noise. Then she can hear her own breathing again: shallow and loud.

With great care and holding her breath, Maria slowly pulls the duvet down below her chin. Opening her eyes, she sees that she is at home. She lets out a sigh of relief. Her vision is blurred but Maria instantly recognises her loft apartment. "A good investment," her father had said before her parents announced their move to Australia. She takes in the bare brick walls. A chill makes her body shiver. The bricks had been a selling point: "The Manhattan look," the estate agent had said.

She shifts slightly and pushes the duvet further away from her. Raising her head, she glances at the alarm. It flashes seven o'clock. Maria twists her legs off the bed. She examines her sore wrists but finds no visible marks.

Maria lifts her head. Her neck begins to ache. Her mind feels clouded and heavy. Has she been drugged? She stumbles as she rises from her bed. Steadying herself, she starts to look for anything out of place. Nothing. Her apartment is how she would have left it. A blast of cold air from the open skylight gives her goosebumps on the back of her arms and again a sliver of doubt crosses her mind.

Maria thinks back to her childhood. At eight, she was convinced that a monster lived in her bedroom cupboard; at twelve, after seeing a UFO land, she believed that her neighbour was an alien; and, at fourteen, she decided that her uncle was working for a secret intelligence organisation after she saw him stepping into a blacked-out van near her school's playing fields. Her family and friends had always called her a storyteller and a fibber. Now Maria couldn't help but wonder if she had just woken from a nightmare.

Maria brushes her thoughts aside. She immediately switches the stereo off and looks for her mobile phone—always within reach. It's not there. She frantically searches her room but cannot find it. Maria walks down stairs and opens her laptop. There are no emails of any significance on her machine. Maria notices that the bolt on her front door has not been pulled across, but that doesn't mean anything. Her friends would have said it was unlike Maria because the Maria they knew was cautious. She always checked that her straighteners were unplugged at least twice before leaving the house and she always made sure she had house keys. Her new friends didn't know that just over two years ago Maria nearly burned down her apartment with curling tongs and would often throw stones at her little sister's window to wake her up so she could let Maria back in. Not bolting the door had been a hangover from Maria's previous self, or so Leanne had said. Maria liked the idea that she hadn't completely changed and so she rarely pulled the bolt across.

Maria immediately double locks the front door and walks into the kitchen. The stainless steel units that she had fallen in love with now feel cold. Maria pads over to the thermostat. She begins to feel dizzy. Bumping into the wall, she has to stop and steady herself before she can turn the dial towards twenty. A man stands in her kitchen peering into her fridge. He is tall, much taller than her five foot four inches. His white t-shirt is stretched over his biceps. His jeans are faded.

"Who are you?" Maria tries to shout but her throat catches.

Silence.

Maria gasps, squeezing her eyes shut. But when she opens them the man is no longer there. Her hand rises to her throat. She cannot breathe. There is a pain in her chest, which she tries to rub away. *Breathe*, she tells herself. *Breathe.*

A hollow noise comes out of Maria's mouth, a vacant laugh or a cry for help. She is not sure. *Is this a joke?* The calendar on her kitchen work surface tells her it is September, represented by an image of a beach and a coconut tree lurching towards the ocean. Maria knows from spending far too much time in a travel agent's office that this picture has been taken in Raratonga. The Cook Islands. The dates have been pulled off. It reads Monday 28 September.

It can't be, Maria thinks. She locates her remote and turns on the television. It's an old set, no bigger than fourteen inches. It does not quite fit in with her modern apartment. She is thankful for the electronic television guide but not what it tells her. It *is* the 28th. Maria instantly remembers the beeping of the refuse van she had heard earlier. They always collect on a Monday. Maria's hands start to tremble. She has lost two days of her life. Lifting the telephone handset, she begins to dial Owen's number, but then she remembers that she can't. Not anymore. Anger quickly shows itself and Maria raises a clenched fist. She would not be comforted by his soft, gentle voice. She would have to face this alone. Maria lifts the receiver again. She wants to speak to her best friend. Leanne would have been with her on Friday evening, Maria is sure of it. But Maria's mind draws a blank. Without her mobile phone she does not recall her friend's number. Maria throws the phone at the wall. Collapsing on to her sofa, tears begin to fall. Tired and scared, Maria starts to cry. Rubbing her sore neck, she knows she has to call the police.

With distant eyes, Maria stares at the presenter on screen. "Maybe nothing happened," she says to convince herself. Trying to piece her memory back together, she thinks back to the days leading up to last Friday. She had met her friends from the book club at Marconi's. Inadvertently, she had drunk far too much. Her memory of that night was sketchy. She had spent much of the evening deep in conversation with Sunil. What were they talking about? Had she told him that she liked him? That he was the first person to give her butterflies in her stomach since Owen? Thursday was an ordinary day at work—not good, not bad. Her hangover had not been a help, but Friday… Friday was a blur.

Today is Monday. So much could happen in two days. Maria feels light headed. Her stomach churns. She knows she must head straight to the police before work. But what would they say? Work would be difficult, but perhaps Tina would know something. Maria was supposed to work on Saturday. Did she speak to Tina about not going in? Glancing over at the telephone, she notices that there is no blue light flashing. She does not have any messages. Perhaps, then, she had spoken to her manager? Or had someone deleted them? A sinking feeling comes over Maria. *Had nobody tried to contact her?* She remembers her mobile phone again and frantically starts looking for it. But then the doorbell rings and Maria's heart stops.

2

Maria hesitated outside the police station watching a young girl with tangled brown hair walk down the steps towards the street. The girl was wearing a dark brown coat and bright red skirt. Her eyes were puffy and red from crying. Black mascara stained her cheeks and her tights were ripped. A cloud of vapour left the girl's lips every time she took a breath. Maria knew that it was cold, but did not feel the temperature. Her body was numb. Maria looked around at last night's litter and derelict red brick buildings, lingering from Leicester's industrial age. Taking a deep breath, Maria climbed the stairs. She passed the young girl, careful not to look directly at her.

Entering the station, Maria approached the desk. Waiting for the receptionist's attention, she nervously looked around at the off-white walls. A poster of a teenager asking her if she was a victim chilled her. She had still not recovered from the fright the doorbell had given her just over an hour ago. It had only been the postman with a parcel from her parents, yet she had convinced herself it was the man from her earlier vision. She would be helpless up against his bulky frame. Maria had stood motionless staring at the door, beads of sweat rapidly forming on her brow. A post office *sorry-you-were-out* card fell through her letterbox and her muscles relaxed.

"I should have clocked off an hour ago," the receptionist said to a police officer, who shrugged and walked away. The lady behind the desk rolled her eyes, wearily, before asking Maria what she wanted.

For the first time that day, Maria heard her own voice. It was hoarse. Clearing her throat, she explained that she would like to see an officer to report an incident. To her relief, the receptionist didn't ask her anything further. Instead, she handed her a clipboard and pen. A blue form followed.

"Fill this out and bring it back to me. Someone will see you shortly after," the woman said.

Maria took a seat along with several other people. Most were scribbling on the same blue form. Looking around the room, she caught the eye of a man sitting in the corner. She immediately looked down, pretending to concentrate on her form. Maria was certain that his face was familiar. His eyes were on her. She could feel her body temperature rising as suspicion took hold.

Had this man followed her? She had turned around several times on her way to the station but had not noticed anyone in pursuit. The man was wearing a bright orange baseball cap and checkered shirt. Maria's heart started pounding. Did he know something? Seconds later, she looked up again. He was not there. The man was talking to the receptionist. Maria looked away. Her pulse quickened and her fingers started to tremble. Her pen fell to the floor. She was certain they were talking about her. Maria stole a look at the man as she bent down to pick up the biro. He was laughing with the receptionist as they headed out of the station doors, hand in hand. Maria sighed, feeling her paranoia lift.

Maria looked at the questions. She rubbed her eyes and tried to focus. She completed her name and date of birth but, when it asked the nature of the incident she wished to report, she drew a blank. What exactly was she going to say? That she had been kidnapped? As far as she was aware nobody had missed her, there had been no ransom demand and there was no physical evidence that anything had happened to her. Her mind immediately flicked back to her eight-year-old self. How quickly her parents had swept aside her fears about the cupboard monster. She had heard them talking that night. They had thought she was asleep. Laughing about her being a "fantasist." An incomprehensible word at the time but she had heard it many times since.

Maria shook away the memories. She was always told she had an overactive imagination but this was different. What had happened to her on the weekend was not part of a fantasy. *But what had happened? Had she been drinking with friends and blacked out?* It was an unlikely scenario. She had never blacked out before. And what about her sore wrists and the email she remembered receiving? Maria pushed a curl of brown hair behind her ear. Perhaps she should speak to Tina and Leanne first, she reasoned. Maria looked at her aching wrists free from any bruise, scratch or blemish. The drowsy feeling and bitter taste had disappeared with a shower and mouthwash. She had examined every inch of her body that morning and there were no visible marks. The old Maria crept further into her shell as doubt took hold of her. *Would the police even believe her?* She wasn't sure if she believed herself. Even more worrying was the thought that they would think Maria was the one with the problem. Maria glanced at her reflection in the glass opposite her. Did she look like someone who had been abducted? Maria hesitated as she took the blue slip of paper from the clipboard and shoved it into her bag. Then, quickly, she stood up and left.

*

Maria pushed through the shop door of her workplace instantly noticing that Tina was in a good mood. She was talking animatedly on the phone, although her expression quickly soured when she saw Maria.

Maria shuffled to her desk and took off her coat, hanging it on the hook behind her. Putting her handbag in the drawer, she found her mobile phone and let out a sigh of relief. But the phone was dead. Putting it on charge whilst she logged on to her computer, Maria now berated herself for leaving the police station so abruptly. Maria looked over at her colleague, wondering if she knew anything. Tina had deceptively kind eyes but an angular nose and thin lips gave her a somewhat sinister appearance; more in tune with her personality. *Should I ask her? Or will she expect me to explain why I wasn't here?* Maria didn't have time to debate this further; Tina's conversation about calla lilies and birds of paradise was coming to an end.

Tina checked her manicured nails before she replaced the receiver back on its stand. Maria tried to look busy. "How was it?" Tina asked. "Was it worth leaving the shop unattended?" Tina cocked her head to one side and looked directly at Maria.

Maria opened her mouth to speak, but the words would not form. How could she explain an absence she didn't understand herself? Her only option was to tell Tina. Maria's heart sank at having to confide in her manager; Tina had never asked Maria a single question about her life in the entire nine months that they had worked together.

"It was only the Lake District, not Lake Garda!" Tina gave a haughty laugh.

Maria took a sharp intake of breath. The Lake District? She wasn't quite sure what Tina was saying.

"Nice of your brother to organise it for you. I did think you were looking rather down in the dumps lately." Tina offered Maria a rare smile before pouting her lips. "It hasn't cheered you up much," she said, raising a perfectly arched eyebrow at her colleague.

A brother? The word jarred in Maria's head. She did not have a brother. Her heart began to beat a little faster. Maria could see Tina's painted red lips moving but she could not hear anything. Panic took hold of her. *The Lake District?* She had never been to the Lake District. Maria wrung her hands together. Tiny beads of sweat started to form on her brow. Why would anyone take her to the Lake District, and, if she had been there, how did she wake up back in her own bed? It didn't make sense. Why would someone want to abduct her? Maria had no known enemies. Over the last year or so she had lived a quiet life. Even if they had abducted her, it did not make sense that they would then return her to her own apartment. Surely her captor would not have dragged her through her building, unconscious, without someone raising an alarm. If her flashback had been accurate, the man who was standing in her kitchen had not been wearing a mask. How were her captors confident that she would not remember anything? Maria tried to make sense of the situation. Perhaps she had gone away to the Lake District? Perhaps she had known this man? Maria pinched herself to bring her back to reality. Of course she hadn't gone to the Lake District. She didn't even have any male friends she would contemplate going with. Maria closed her eyes, desperately suppressing her urge to be sick. She tried to remember a lake, a man, anything. But it was useless.

She remembered nothing. Maria tried to forget the feeling of sickness that was stirring inside her. She wanted to confide in someone, but she couldn't tell Tina. The only person she could think of telling was Alice. Maria immediately started to dial her number but then quickly disconnected. Her heart sank a little deeper.

"It was risky leaving the office like that," Tina said, in a threatening sort of tone.

"Well..." Maria tried. She knew where this was heading.

"Imagine if Tom had come by. You owe me..."

"But... I..." Maria started, unable to form a coherent sentence.

"I didn't mention it to Tom," Tina smirked.

Maria knew she would be paying for this for the rest of her time at Tommy Travel. If she was not Tina's dogsbody already, she certainly would be from here on in. The thought should have angered her, but it didn't. The man calling up pretending to be her brother did. Maria pressed her lips together. *Who would do this to me?* Maria tried mentally to compile a list of men that fit the description of the silhouette in her kitchen that morning. She kept drawing a blank. Who did she know who worked out regularly and looked like they were on protein shakes? Few people Maria knew took the gym seriously. The man in her hallucination had an air of confidence. He was familiar with her apartment. He knew where things were. Maria wanted to scream with anger at this man who had violated her. She felt dizzy and faint and needed fresh air. Tina was talking to her again but she could not hear what she was saying. Maria looked towards the shop door, desperate for a cool breeze on her skin.

"Luckily for you, Howard is very charming," Tina said, taking a carrot stick from a small plastic bag and waving it at Maria. "He explained your moods of late."

"I..." Maria tried again, walking over to the water cooler to pour herself a cup of cold water. *Howard.* She tried to place the name. She couldn't. Unsteady on her feet, she fell back into her chair as she heard the shop door open. Maria jumped and Tina shot her a wry look. But before Maria had time to justify herself, two girls in their late teens started walking towards Tina's desk. Anxiety gripped

Maria—the jangle of the shop door opening had stirred a memory. She closed her eyes, but it did not come. Tina placed her uneaten carrot stick back into the bag. Maria heard mumbling of round-the-world tickets and breathed a sigh of relief; the girls were going to take some time.

Scrolling through the emails she had received over the weekend, Maria looked for anything that appeared out of place. There was nothing suspicious. She looked for the strange emails she received on Friday and located them. Maria needed to know that they were there, that she hadn't made this whole thing up. Then, as the words appeared on her email, Maria was forced to relive the last few moments before she was taken.

3

The last day Maria could recall was Friday the 25th. It had been a quiet afternoon in the office. A boring day. Receiving a message had provided her with some much-needed light relief. The first bizarre email consisted of one line. It read:

Life is too short.

Playing with this single sentence in her mind, Maria scrolled through to the end of the message. It said nothing more. The statement intrigued Maria and she couldn't help but wonder who had sent it and why. It didn't look like spam. It was sent solely to her email address.

On an average day, Maria would receive twenty or thirty emails from the general public, wanting to know if April was a good time to visit Bali or if there were any cheap holidays to Greece. Well, that was her job; she was a travel agent's assistant. The email made Maria think about just how dismal her employment was. She had snorted at the job title when she saw the advert in the paper, and then again when she applied for the position. Now, she was actually doing the job she had been so dismissive of all those months ago. The recession was desperately affecting her career. But she considered herself lucky that she at least had work. Maria was being paid to sit around and mop up all the mistakes that her only colleague made.

Tina was the travel agent. She knew little about the job she was supposed to do, often referring her customers to Maria. Yes, it was dry in Bali in April, and Maria could tell, without looking at her computer, all the latest deals to Greece. There were always good deals to Greece. Maria knew the only reason she was employed as an assistant was the company's way of saving from a higher wage.

Come to think of it, where was Tina? *Last-minute wedding shopping*, Maria correctly assumed. Another extended lunch hour that Tina was taking. Maria never took liberties the way Tina did, but maybe she would start. She heard a noise in the kitchenette in the back room and went to take a look. Typical of Tina, she had left the window open and the cover of the camomile tea box was flapping in the wind, repeatedly hitting the fridge. Maria shut the window and put the kettle on. She poured the hot water over her tea bag. It had been left in her mug since earlier that morning when Tina had kindly offered to make her a hot drink but had been subsequently distracted. Reaching into the biscuit jar, Maria took out two chocolate digestives, put the lid back on, then opened it again to take another. She tried to shove thoughts of her current diet to the back of her mind. Maria knew the guilty feelings would creep up on her pretty soon after she had swallowed her last mouthful. For now, she would enjoy the five-minute chocolate fix. Nestled back at her desk, tea in hand, Maria Shroder did something that she wouldn't normally do. Boredom had her in its grasp.

Hitting the reply button, she took a sip of her camomile tea. It was a little bitter. As usual, she had left the tea bag in for too long. Maria scooped the bag from her mug and dropped it in the waste paper basket before returning her thoughts to that email. The content of that message was true. Life was too short for wasting her days away doing a job she didn't like. And if she thought about it, life was too short not to speak to Alice either. Maria was young – only twenty-two. She had her whole life ahead of her and she was wasting it. In less than the time it took her to swallow her first digestive, she had managed to convince herself the email was sent directly to her for a reason. Curiosity got the better of her.

Who are you? And how do you know what I do?

She typed her reply and hit the send button. Her eyes had begun to close. "Why is this job so boring?" she asked out loud, trying to wake herself up.

Maria was hoping for a witty and flirtatious answer, something that would keep her entertained for a couple of hours. Ten minutes passed. Nothing. A few clicks of the mouse and Maria realised the actual email address was generic. Maria rolled her eyes. There was nothing as foolish as responding to junk email. Giving up on her potential afternoon fun, she started playing solitaire on her computer. Then she saw the little yellow envelope icon flash at the bottom of her screen. She finished her mug of tea.

"Cheap thrills," Maria smirked, as she opened it.

I know what you do every day… Maria.

There it was, another single line, but this time it did not amuse her. A shiver ran down her spine and her stomach turned. Her right hand stuck to the mouse with perspiration. This was not the kind of entertainment Maria had in mind. She tried, unsuccessfully, to convince herself that this was a prank. It made no sense. She laughed out loud trying to dissipate her fears, all the while repeating to herself that this was someone familiar simply having a joke at her expense. There was something about this last remark that made her want to sit up and look behind her. Again the drowsy feeling returned but the urge to turn around was growing stronger. As she swivelled on her chair, she blacked out.

4

Just remembering those final minutes made Maria's hands shake and her breathing shallow. "Bricks," Maria said under her breath. She caught herself. "Bricks," she tried a little louder. For no reason she could think of, she wanted to say this word out loud. Maria mulled it over in her mind for a few moments but drew a blank. Now, back in the place where she was abducted, she realised that it had not been such a good idea to return to work. Maria frantically looked around her desk, shuffling her papers and opening her drawers. She avoided Tina's glare, certain that there had to be some clue around her desk as to what happened to her.

"Did the cleaners come over the weekend?" Maria asked.

Tina looked towards Maria and frowned, turning her attention back to her customers.

Maria found nothing. Staring at the emails from Friday she wondered what her next move would be. She had an email from a fake address, and a hoax call to her office but was it substantial enough to prove something had happened to her? A blind panic set in as Maria realised that she could be abducted again. She gripped the edge of her desk, pushing her nails into the soft pinewood. Maria didn't want to be alone but neither did she want to be in the office. Just looking at her computer made her feel ill. Before she could stop herself, she hit the delete button on the emails. But the minute she did that she regretted it.

Switching on her mobile phone, Maria saw seven missed calls, all from Leanne, two answerphone messages and a text from her parents. Dialling her pass code to retrieve her voicemail, she suppressed the urge to be sick. It was Leanne asking her to meet up on Friday night. She deleted the message and moved on to the next. The second message was Leanne again, but this time annoyed with Maria for not showing up.

Maria deleted this last message. She had missed over two days of her life and nobody noticed she was missing. She felt small and insignificant. Worse still, she felt the loneliness of life without Owen and Alice. *Howard* didn't call Leanne to explain, but Leanne knew everything about Maria. Brother or friend, Leanne would know if it was false.

Maria had not been anywhere for a weekend in ages, let alone the Lake District. No one before or after Owen had ever taken her away. She missed Owen. If only she had him to protect her now. It was what she loved most about Owen when they were together. He always made her feel safe; made her feel protected. But it was useless thinking of him now.

Maria sighed, toying with the idea of going back to the police. She glanced over at Tina who, for once, looked interested in what she was trying to sell. Tina was not often enthusiastic unless it was her wedding that she was talking about. Maria hoped for the sake of the two girls that it wasn't. She thought about telling Tina that she didn't have a brother but then thought against it. It was not as if Tina would care. Dialling Leanne's number, Maria pressed her mobile to her ear.

"Where have you been?" Leanne bellowed at her with her bubbly voice. "Did you not get my messages? Disastrous is all I can say about Friday night…"

"Oh," Maria said, angrily. Leanne's problem felt so insignificant.

"What's the matter?" Leanne asked. It wasn't often that Maria was so hostile.

Maria didn't know where to start. But Leanne was the closest thing she had to family. She trusted her like a sister and she needed to tell someone.

Leanne tried her best to be patient. Sensing that something was wrong, she hoped her instincts were not right. Tentatively she asked, "Did you meet up with Alice like we spoke about?" But her question was met with a silence; desperate for chatter, Leanne said clumsily, "You see, all it took was bumping into her again after all this time."

Hearing her sister's name being mentioned like that, out loud, struck a cord with Maria. She had forgotten about her run-in with

Alice a couple of weeks ago. They had met, after nearly two years of avoiding each other, by chance, in a new wine bar in Braunstone Gate. How amazing her sister had looked. Alice had always been slim but now she was verging on a size eight. A dark blue Bodycon dress hugged her in all the right places and a pair of skyscraper heels made her look four inches taller. Sun kissed, like she had been somewhere exotic, Alice had stood propped against the bar sipping on a flute of champagne.

Maria had assumed that her sister had taken up modelling again, but she didn't have the courage to ask her. Alice certainly looked like she had money from somewhere. But then she had always liked the nicer things in life and she had always managed to find boyfriends who gave her that lifestyle with the jewellery to match. Owen hadn't been one of those men. He hardly had the cash either, but then what did Maria know. People change, and, after all this time, how well could she say she really knew Owen? The Owen she knew would never have done what he did.

Seeing Alice that day had been too much for Maria. She was afraid Owen would turn up and her heart would break all over again, but more than that she realised how much she missed her sister. Alice always knew what to say and how to make her feel better. She had been the one person Maria could talk to about anything and they had been inseparable growing up, until it all went so terribly wrong.

If that email had been someone trying to tell her something about her relationship with Alice, then, yes, they were right, life was too short. That much was correct. If Maria wanted any normality with her sister, she knew she would have to put the Alice and Owen incident behind her. Even though it was Alice who had crossed the line, the emotional roller coaster Maria had been on for the last twenty-four months had started to slow down. Maybe it was time to reach out to Alice. But Maria quickly thought against it. The idea of letting her little sister back in her life was just too much for her to cope with. For now she would have to make do with her surrogate sister Leanne.

"Hello. Earth to Maria. Are you there?" Leanne shouted down the phone.

"No, I didn't meet Alice," Maria snapped. "But that's not what I need to talk to you about. I need to talk to you about where I've been," Maria said. She looked up at Tina who was drumming her fingers on the table and glaring at her, having finished with the two travellers. "I'm at work, but can you come round to mine after?"

"No probs, sweetie," Leanne said, chewing her lower lip. She had never heard fear like this in her friend's voice.

5

Penelope looked at the bathroom door. She could hear the shower beating on his body and she knew she had to tell him. Penelope closed her eyes. She had broken away from her domineering and over zealous Catholic parents just in time to realise that there was more to life than Sunday worship.

If Penelope thought about it, far away from the clutches of her family, the only person she could thank for meeting the man in her life was Ciara. The voluptuous five-foot-eight vixen had approached her in the supermarket, of all places. Wearing her signature sky-high black Louboutins and leopard print jacket, Ciara offered Penelope a chance to be someone else. Instinctively, Penelope had turned the job offer down, offended by Ciara's assumptions. But as Ciara placed her business card in Penelope's hands, Penelope found herself strangely drawn to the woman in front of her. Was it Ciara's effortless glamour or her confidence, attributes Penelope yearned for, that made her change her mind? She wasn't quite sure. But three months later Penelope was having the time of her life.

To Penelope, this new job was a challenge, a teenage rebellion that she had never experienced. On her first day Ciara had pulled her aside. "Get the men to buy you as many drinks as possible and don't let those go south!" she said, winking at Penelope and jabbing her right breast "It's the best and only advice you'll get here." And, of course, she had been right.

★

"He's new!" Sarah said one evening in Rustle, as she pointed towards a tall gentleman seated at the back of the bar.

"I've already seen him so I call first dibs!" cried another girl, applying her lipstick backstage midway through an outfit change to a pink satin thong and bra.

"No way! I saw him first!" Sarah said, peering through the stage curtains, her arms crossed against her bare chest and her eyes focused on the blond customer. "Look at his tanned skin and chiselled jaw. Shazeen, you don't even like men with blond hair. How old do you reckon he is? Mid-thirties?"

Penelope strained her neck trying to catch a glimpse of this customer who was making the other girls so excited. They were right, he was good looking. His eyes flicked around the girls on stage as he slowly sipped on his drink. Penelope turned away. She knew that he was out of her league. She walked over to the mirror and started to apply the red lipstick Ciara had bought her, then she ran a brush through her newly dyed blond hair and smiled. She couldn't believe how different she looked.

Later that evening, Penelope fiddled with her bra as she tentatively climbed up the stairs that led to the stage. She looked at the customers directly in the eye as she had been told to do. Shazeen had said it was a sure fire way to get a punter to buy a drink or, better yet, a lap dance. She stumbled and hoped that nobody noticed but there was some jeering at the back of the club. Penelope held her head up high and gyrated on stage just as she had practised, slowly removing her lace cover up, until her body was nearly bare and the song came to an end.

Her heart was racing and her legs trembling as she climbed back down off the stage and slipped a Lycra black dress on. Ciara had caught her by the wrist and had handed her a neat whiskey on a black tray. She pointed to the blond gentleman in the corner of the bar. "He's asked for you," Ciara said, barely audible over the music.

"But…" Penelope started, her hands shaking.

"No buts," Ciara said with a disapproving look. "He asked for you."

Penelope blushed.

"Be confident," her mentor whispered in Penelope's ear as she walked away. Penelope took the drink and placed it on the man's table. She unsuccessfully tried to cover her cleavage as she did so.

"Have a seat," he said, looking at her eyes instead of her breasts, unlike most other customers.

Penelope hesitated. Girls who worked at Rustle were not supposed to sit down with customers unless they were bought a drink.

"A drink?" the man called Jason asked, as if reading her mind. He knew the drill. Penelope smiled, nodded over to the waitress and sat down, noting Jason's watch and shoes. She was beginning to get the knack of assessing what customers would pay for based solely on their attire.

"Have what you like," Jason said confidently as Carry-Anne approached them.

"I'll have a vodka tonic," Penelope said, mustering up her confidence. The waitress winked at her and walked away.

"I'm new here," Penelope said, playing with a lock of her hair between her trembling fingers. It was part of her job description to start the conversation. Rule one: Make the customer feel comfortable.

"So am I," Jason said. He swallowed his neat whiskey. His eyes still focused on Penelope. "I'm from the States. I don't know many people here," he continued.

Penelope looked back at Jason. He was good looking but she didn't understand why he was taking such a keen interest in her. She wanted to keep him talking; she wanted to know everything about him. "Well, perhaps I can show you around sometime?" Penelope asked. She braced herself for rejection, but Jason didn't hesitate. He quickly took her up on her offer.

★

"Three dates in one week." Penelope could hear the girls gossiping in the corner of the dressing room. She had fretted for days, not knowing what to do or who to tell, scared that she would get in trouble. But Jason put an end to her worries when he stopped visiting the club. In the eyes of the owner, what Penelope did would have been a sackable offence. "Why buy milk if there's a cow at home?"

"Someone taking such an interest in one of the girls doesn't generally happen here. The others are jealous, but they'll get over it. There's a no-squeal policy here. Trust me, no one wants to get in the way of another girl's *Pretty Woman* moment," Ciara said, putting a cigarette between her painted lips. And she had been right, the other girls soon came around.

They had gone to a bar after the early shift that day and, after one too many Cosmopolitans, Ciara had nearly choked when Penelope confessed that she was still a virgin. Ciara had dragged Penelope to their local club and plied her with Sambuca and Midori until she found a suitable victim. Then she pulled Penelope's skirt a little higher and pointed her in his direction. "He's good looking and you're good looking. That's how these things work," Ciara said.

"No..." Penelope had started.

But Ciara cut Penelope off. "You will *stay* a virgin at this rate. And your first time with Jason will be a disaster! Think of this as a trial run. Now get on with it. It's always best to lose your virginity to a nobody. And this is one helluva good looking nobody." *It's about time that Penelope realised just how good looking she is*, thought Ciara. She needed to lose her virginity to improve her confidence; a beautiful girl with no confidence would never be stunning in Ciara's eyes.

Ciara winked at her new friend, taking Penelope's drink from her and pushing her in the direction of the unsuspecting man. Penelope, still adjusting to four-inch heels, tried to casually and confidently stroll over in his direction, her heart beating as fast as it could. She looked back at Ciara, who was mouthing something to her. Squinting her eyes, she tried to make out what her friend was saying but, as she walked backwards towards the bar, Penelope bumped straight into her target. Penelope caught sight of Ciara laughing, whilst at the same time apologising profusely. She felt a fool but it had broken the ice and they had hit it off, at least from what she could remember the following day.

Ciara had been right. After that one-night stand, she found a new confidence. There was no pressure that it would be her first time with Jason.

And with Jason, Penelope wanted it to be different. Penelope had slipped a multi-coloured sequin skirt over her newly tanned legs and stood looking at her reflection in the mirror. She had asked for a martini hoping it would give her some courage, but as they started talking she found their conversation was natural. It flowed so easily she didn't need the alcohol.

When Jason and Penelope arrived at her two-bedroom house in Stoneygate, she knew where things were going to lead. It was only her second time but, like Ciara had said, the first had just been a practice run. The way Jason touched her told Penelope that he was experienced and she was grateful that Ciara had pushed her in front of that stranger. Penelope trembled as she led Jason to her bedroom. He was someone who should have picked Sarah or Shazeen, not her.

As she lay in her bed that evening, she tried to remember what Ciara had told her. It had been easier when she hadn't known the person. It had been easier when she was drunk. As Jason lay on top of her, she could smell the alcohol on him. He was inebriated and for that she was glad. She knew that she could cover up her lack of experience this way. For all the good those three martinis had done her, she may as well have had water. Sobriety returned to her in a flash. Jason was gentle with her. Their lovemaking was intense and Penelope felt a surge of happiness as she had her first orgasm. It was nothing like her one-night stand. There was no drunken fumbling, no awkward moments. With Jason, Penelope felt a connection. Afterwards, she left Jason sleeping and padded over to the bathroom. She removed her makeup thinking of her conservative upbringing and smiled. She had found her sexuality and finally she felt like a woman.

6

Penelope rolled over on to her side pulling the white sheets up to cover herself, her hand instinctively resting on her belly. The sun poured through the gap between the curtains making her long blond hair glisten in the light.

She watched Jason dry himself as he stepped out of the bathroom. Penelope smiled at her boyfriend. He loved her. He had even joined her book club and attended most of the meetings with her. Something she had not expected of him, but had come as a lovely surprise. But Penelope, not used to things going so well in her life, was looking for a fault.

"Why doesn't he mind me stripping or lap dancing?" Penelope had asked Ciara one day.

"You should be glad about that, honey," Ciara said. "That is one modern man. Has he offered to pay your rent?"

"No," Penelope responded.

"Then he can't expect you to give up your job. Consider yourself lucky."

Penelope had taken Ciara's advice and tried to push the thought to the back of her mind but occasionally this question resurfaced.

"Do you not mind me continuing with my job at Rustle?" she asked, as Jason rubbed his blond hair with a towel. *I need to ask one more time before I tell him*, she said silently to herself.

"Nope," Jason responded.

Penelope persisted. "Shazeen's ex wanted her to give up. He said that he didn't like other men staring at her body."

Jason raised his eyebrows at his girlfriend.

"Well?" Penelope said, encouraging some kind of verbal response.

"I want you to have your freedom and your independence. I don't want to control what you do. Yeah, it makes me a bit jealous. But it's your choice," Jason said. Looking remorseful, he added, "I once had a girlfriend give up her job for me and it didn't work out."

"What job did you make her give up?"

"I didn't make her give it up," Jason said, narrowing his eyes. "I was earning enough for the both of us and she wanted to give up her job so she did." Jason walked back into the bathroom and rubbed pomade in his hair.

"Sometimes talking helps," Penelope shouted after him.

"When you are ready to give up Rustle, you'll know." Jason walked back to the bedroom and kissed her gently on her forehead. Penelope allowed him to end the conversation. She had her answer and she chose to accept it. Her inexperience with men worried her as much as her fear of happiness and she didn't want to lose Jason.

Penelope took a deep breath. How was she going to tell him? At first she had been horrified. Perhaps her parents had been right to be so over protective. Perhaps she was unable to make her own decisions. But then it dawned on her that her fear was not because she was so unhappy with the situation, but because of what her family would say when they found out. Realising this made her breathe a little easier.

Penelope knew that what she had become would never make her parents proud. She had gone from a good Catholic girl with a private education to a pregnant stripper in less than a year. Penelope sighed.

7

"So you didn't just pull a sickie at lunchtime today. You actually look terrible," Leanne said, trying to lighten the scene as she walked down the corridor towards Maria. As Leanne took a few steps closer she noticed a man in navy blue overalls changing the lock on Maria's front door. Maria looked unwell. Her face was drawn and pasty as if she had not seen the light of day. Dishevelled hair replaced a mass of brown curls and she was wearing a thick white dressing gown over her clothes.

"Not a break-in I hope," Leanne said, trying to dissipate her own anxiety and somewhat apologetic for having just told her best friend that she looked awful. She noticed the new chain fitted to her friend's door and she squeezed Maria's arm for reassurance. As Leanne stepped past the locksmith into the apartment Maria gave her friend a knowing look. One that said they would talk about it later.

"I got us some takeaway menus on my way. Pizza or Chinese?" Leanne continued towards the huge sofa. She plunged into her usual corner and stretched her small arms under the sofa to find her slippers. Locating them she smiled at Maria in a small triumph. Leanne noted Maria's troubled expression and sighed. She would stay over and make sure her friend was alright.

Maria couldn't choose between the two cuisines. She just didn't have an appetite so Leanne picked. She ordered what she thought Maria would want: Hawaiian. She herself hated the thought of fruit on pizza but it had never let her down in making Maria feel better. Ordering a Meat Feast for herself, Leanne's mouth began to water thinking of the pepperoni and ground beef topping. She thumbed through *White Oleander*, the latest book Maria was reading.

They had both joined the book club a few months ago although Leanne had never reached book two. She had barely got through book one: *A Room With A View. No wonder so many people had dropped out*, she thought. But Leanne had supposed that was how book clubs retained the more committed members like Maria, and quickly got rid of the flaky ones like her. Leanne had only joined because she felt she ought to read more. Books were not her thing; no sooner than she read something, she had forgotten the story. Television soap operas were more to her taste.

Maria walked over to her friend and slumped down on the sofa, still unsure of how to bring up the topic of her abduction. Leanne studied the flashing television screen in front of her. She had learnt over the past seventeen years of friendship with Maria, that the only way to get any information from Maria was to bite her tongue and keep silent. But patience was not Leanne's strong point.

Maria looked at the pizza menu on the coffee table. The thought of food repulsed her. She tried to focus on what she was going to say to Leanne, but something was lurking on the periphery of her mind. It slowly came into focus: a silhouette in the light of an open fridge and a hand with a leather strap tied around the wrist, holding something. Maria gagged.

"You say something?" Leanne asked, looking at her friend, desperate to find out what was going through Maria's mind.

"No," Maria said. The nausea churned her stomach. What had she just remembered? It wasn't just a vision she had seen. It was a feeling as well: fear. Had she been held captive in her own apartment?

"So the reason why I needed you here..." Maria started tentatively. Her right eyelid began to twitch. "...you mustn't tell a soul."

"Of course I wouldn't!" Leanne reassured her best friend.

"It's serious," Maria looked directly at Leanne. Leanne was not the best keeper of secrets. She had told everyone about their friend's pregnancy scare, back in college, after she had been sworn to silence. And her secret-keeping skills had not improved with time.

"I promise," Leanne said a bit louder this time as she bit her fingernails. Maria never had big secrets, not after Owen. "I promise," Leanne said again, crossing her legs.

"…It's about the weekend," Maria continued, staring blankly at the television. She recounted what she could remember from that Friday afternoon right through to Monday.

Leanne listened intently, trying to make sense of it. She scanned her friend's body with her eyes; there were no marks, none that she could see. She couldn't help but think of Maria when they were young: Maria who used to tell tales, Maria the dreamer. But then she caught a look in her friend's eyes, a look of sadness and confusion. Would Maria really make something like this up? No. Maria had changed since Owen. The dreamer had been replaced with someone who made realism a way of life.

"Well, you couldn't make it up!" Leanne said, trying to alleviate the tension, but as the words left her mouth she knew they were inappropriate.

Maria was silent.

"Can you forward me the emails?"

Maria bit her lip. "I deleted them."

"Serious?"

"Yes," Maria buried her head in her hands. "What was I thinking? I just couldn't bear to see them there."

"But from what you said they were your only evidence. Surely there must be a back up?"

Maria bit her lip. "Our machines are programmed to wipe our deleted files and emails every evening. Something about insufficient memory. The emails have gone."

Leanne eyed her friend with caution.

"You don't believe me," Maria cried.

"Yes, I believe you," Leanne said. She reached across and hugged her friend. Nothing had changed in Maria's life in the last few months, so why would Maria make something like this up? Leanne quickly shoved her reservations to the back of her mind. "Of course I believe you," she repeated. Leanne fell silent. She wasn't good in situations like this. Silently she wished that Alice was still around. Alice would have known what to do. Why did their sisterhood have to disappear like it had never happened?

"Have you been to the police?" Leanne asked, knowing the answer already.

"I tried, but then I got to thinking. What exactly would I say? 'Excuse me, Officer, but I was kidnapped for two days.' No ransom or anything, no bruises or scars, no evidence that I was taken. Nobody looked for me or noticed that I was missing," Maria sighed, her eyes moist.

"All I have is one phone call that was probably made from a phone box from someone pretending to be my... my brother." Maria's voice caught and she wrung her hands. "Leanne, look at it, there's nothing. No evidence whatsoever. They'll probably think I was drinking and passed out, that I don't know my dates. That's certainly what I would think," Maria said, frustrated by Leanne's question.

"But why would..." Leanne started, then stopped herself. She knew that questions would not make it any easier for Maria. The thought she had abandoned earlier promptly returned to her mind. Could Maria have wanted some attention after Alice and Owen had walked out on her so brutally? Leanne banished the thought from her mind. Maria wouldn't make up something like this.

A knock on the door made Maria jump. Leanne answered it, handing over a twenty-pound note in return for pizza. Whilst Leanne tucked in, Maria abstained. She could not face food. *Food*, Maria thought. The last meal she remembered was Friday lunch time, a tuna baguette. Whoever had taken her would have fed her, wouldn't they? And if they had, why couldn't she remember? Maria examined her arms again. There were no visible marks at all. Maria placed her hand on her stomach—she just wasn't hungry. Leanne looked at her friend and started to say something but quickly stopped.

"You must eat something, Maria, otherwise you'll make yourself sick."

Leanne's comment was met with silent resistance.

"You must have been drugged... you must have been... that obviously explains the memory lapse. Try the police again or doctors even. They can test you, see if there are any traces in your system. That would maybe start an investigation."

Maria did not reply but instead began to cry, falling back into the warmth of the sofa.

"I need to do things slowly," Maria said. "Please, let's think about it tomorrow. I just can't face going now. I would have to explain it all again. I don't think I could cope." Maria held a piece of pizza up to her mouth but, gagging, she quickly put it back down. "I hate Hawaiian," Maria said under her breath. Her own words shocked her because, up until now, it had been her favourite.

Fetching a soda from the kitchen Leanne passed it to her friend. "Here, this will make you feel better," Leanne said, urging Maria to drink it. Maria put the bottle to her lips, glad that she had discarded anything in her fridge that had not been sealed. If they did drug her before, they wouldn't again.

Later that evening Leanne padded over to the chest of drawers by the side of Maria's bed and found her yellow overnight bag. She pulled out her pyjamas. A small white and blue cardboard box fell next to her feet. Leanne didn't notice it until she had changed and was putting the yellow bag back in the drawer. She picked up the small box and examined it. The label with the patient's name had been ripped off but the box looked familiar. Too familiar.

Leanne closed her eyes momentarily, wondering what to do with this information about her closest friend. In that moment she made a decision. Placing the little box back into the drawer, she switched off the light and went back to the sitting room to join Maria.

8

The following Tuesday Maria was getting back into a routine, but things were not quite the same as they had been before her abduction. Just yesterday, waiting for the bus, she had clenched her fists when a young girl merely asked her for the time; and she had nearly jumped out of her skin when a man tapped her on her back to give her a flyer that had fallen out of her pocket. Maria knew it would take her a long while to get back to *normal*, whatever normal was supposed to be.

Will I ever be the person I was before the incident? Maria asked herself as she looked out of the arched window of her apartment at the overcast sky. Her life had taken a dramatic enough turn for the worse after Owen. Now it had taken another one and Maria was losing any recognition of the person she was.

Two years ago Maria was the kind of person who used to live on the edge. She would have laughed at the person she was today: afraid of her own shadow, afraid of the dark. It just didn't make any sense, but then nothing did anymore. If she could just remember those stolen hours, Maria knew that things would be different. The incessant questions that swam in her head hadn't stopped since that Monday: Why had they taken her? Who had taken her? Where had they held her and what did they do to her? These questions had become the reason for Maria's existence; they were with her when she woke up and when she went to sleep, and they were slowly driving her insane. Worse still was knowing that she had missed her chance to get the police involved; if she had only been to the doctors or to the police. The final question that stayed with her was the most crucial. Why didn't she? What was she so afraid of that she didn't want to go to the police? Maria remembered the look Leanne gave her when she said she had deleted the emails she received. It was doubt, pure and simple, and there was no way of denying what she saw in Leanne's eyes. Leanne had even confirmed her suspicions by suggesting that she see a psychiatrist.

Maria sighed, picking up a Rubik's Cube from the coffee table. Leanne was her best friend and knew Maria like nobody else. She had stood by her when Alice had deserted her and helped her through one of the toughest times in her life. Whilst they were growing up Leanne was the impatient and dizzy one, Alice the quiet and sensible one, and Maria the adventurist and daydreamer. They had been like sisters until Owen had changed things. If Leanne doubted Maria then perhaps she *had* made up the whole ordeal.

Maria twisted the Rubik's Cube. She had been trying to solve it since last Christmas. She had once seen a documentary about people who made up stories for attention. But when was the last time she elaborated on something? Or even stretched the truth? Her attention-seeking days had left her with her puppy fat. Maria was a sensible young woman with a fantastic degree *with honours*. She was elected a class representative in sixth form and was a university rep. And above all, Maria reasoned, there was some evidence: the call her so-called brother, Howard, had made to Tina.

Maria dropped the Rubik's Cube to the floor and rolled her shoulders, trying to loosen the tension in her neck. When had she lost confidence in herself? It was Alice who had always been the shy one. Outside grey clouds threatened rain. A roll of thunder in the distance made her shudder. Maria knew she had to get on with her life. Something more than just work, she needed comfort and her book group was the perfect place. Good friends and the escapism of printed words. Maria decided to leave her loft apartment before the rain. What she didn't realise was that the next book choice would provide no escapism at all.

9

Maria arrived at Du Jour at five thirty. Out of the thirty people that started meeting in a quiet corner of the café three months ago, there were only about twenty left. Maria was glad that Leanne had dropped out. Not only did Leanne hate reading, but when they were together they tended to cling to each other, like no one else existed, and because of this they never met anyone new.

The book club offered Maria more than literary intrigue. It introduced her to a new set of friends from which she could leave all the history behind and start afresh. Now this was just what Maria wanted: a place where no one knew about Alice and Owen, and, more importantly, where no one would know about her ordeal. At least here, surrounded by newly found friends, she could try to forget.

As Maria took her usual seat at Du Jour she was happy to see Penelope walk through the door. She remembered what Leanne had said about her after their first book club meeting: "She is almost too sweet. Too eager to please." Maria smiled remembering Leanne's jealousy. "I'd rather have a few good friends than a lot of flaky ones," Leanne had said. Maria had paid no heed to Leanne's comments. Instead she had built up quite a friendship with the girl from the City of Spires.

Maria smiled at Jason as he walked through the doors. A dozen female heads turned. When Maria had first met him she had a soft spot for him, like most of the other girls in the book club. She had learned from Penelope that Jason had recently arrived from San Diego on a postgraduate course. You wouldn't think by looking at Jason and Penelope that they were a couple. It was only after one too many drinks in Marconi's one evening that Penelope confessed she and Jason were together. Penelope had sworn Maria to secrecy because, as she put it, "Jason wanted it that way." But she provided little explanation as to why. Maria thought it was odd because they were grown adults. Surely they could date in the open, but she refrained from telling Penelope what she thought. Penelope was so loved up, and Maria wasn't going to be the one to take away her joy.

"Ollie, this is a book club, not a film club!" Maria whispered to Oliver as he sat down next to her, carefully balancing his cup of tea on its saucer and holding between his teeth a DVD of *White Oleander*.

"Don't be a snob, my dear Maria," Oliver said, placing his teacup on the coffee table before them, dropping the DVD on the sofa and tipping his black fedora at her. Maria grinned. There was no one she would rather be sitting next to today than Oliver. He had a sixth sense for her feelings and he always knew how to cheer her up. At nineteen, he was younger than her and still at university, desperate to get into theatre. Just as their conversation turned to clothes, Sunil, the last member of their little niche of friends, walked through the door, helping a young mother with her pram.

"Good weekend?" Oliver asked Sunil as he approached their group.

"Great." Sunil's response as usual was short and sweet. He smiled at Maria knowingly and then quickly looked away.

What? Maria wanted to ask. His look had made her feel anxious. Maria frowned but when Sunil offered her a drink she couldn't help but smile. She politely declined and he sat down.

"You don't come across guys like that these days, so chivalrous," Penelope whispered as she took a seat the other side of Maria.

Maria narrowed her eyes at her friend.

Penelope nudged Maria in the ribs and winked at her. "I remember the other Wednesday at Marconi's. You know I wasn't born yesterday."

Maria stared into her book hoping that Sunil would not notice her blush. Penelope could be a terrible tease when she wanted to be. Her heart still yearned for Owen but Penelope and Leanne had been persistent in telling Maria that she needed to start dating again.

Maria knew that she had spent most of that Wednesday evening deep in conversation with Sunil. They had talked for hours. About what she still wasn't quite sure thanks to the bottle of wine she had shared with Penelope. She knew that bits of the conversation had involved his family and an arranged marriage. Had they kissed? Maria was uncertain but she had an inkling that something had happened between them.

Sunil certainly wasn't acting as if they had shared something special. He made no effort to talk to her now. Had he not felt the connection between them that she had? Maria felt childish, like a teenager with a crush. She continued to look into her copy of *White Oleander*. Had Sunil regretted confiding in her? Or did he know something? Something about her abduction perhaps? Maria looked up at him and caught his eye. She quickly looked away.

"You okay?" Oliver asked.

"Just a little tired," Maria said.

"You have holdalls under your eyes, not handbags, love." He winked at her as he sipped his tea.

Maria shrugged. She loved Oliver but was in no mood to delve into the reasons why she was looking so washed out. Instead she rested her head on his shoulder.

"Deception, huh?" Jason said.

Maria looked up startled before she realised he was talking about the book.

"But saying that, it was very interesting…" Jason continued.

Penelope looked at Jason as if what he was saying was gospel.

"Where were you last week? You missed a great meal out," Oliver said to Maria, draining his cup.

"Family issues," Maria replied, hoping that would be enough to put him off.

"Well..." Oliver started but then he noticed her scrunched face. "You know if you ever need to chat…" he whispered as Lawrence, who ran the club, talked up his last book choice.

Maria stayed quiet during most of the discussion of Janet Fitch's *White Oleander*. She had finished reading the book mid-September. It was funny that she remembered more of the novel than she had of what happened to her that fateful weekend. There was an interesting debate going on between the group about betrayal but Maria found it difficult to concentrate on what Lawrence was saying, her mind continually going back in time to her blocked memory.

Maria had come to the club this evening hoping to find some solace, but after the pleasantries were over with her new friends, her mind had begun to drift. Somehow this normal monthly activity had made her ordeal seem even more real, and she found herself willing the two hours away. She was itching to get back to the security of her apartment, to a nice warm bath and bed. She didn't think she could face Marconi's after this.

"Now to disclose the book for our next meet!" Lawrence exclaimed with excess of enthusiasm. He eyed each member of the group individually.

Maria hoped the book choice would be lighthearted. She needed something to take her mind off things.

"Come on, Loz," Oliver said. "Just tell us. You're cutting into our drinking time." Oliver turned to Maria and whispered, "You are coming out after this, aren't you?"

Maria smiled. "Hmmm, why not," she said, not wanting to discuss it any further. She would go across the road to buy the next book and make her excuses then.

Lawrence continued, his vivid green eyes scanning the crowd, "A book that has been recommended. Yes, for once my arm has been twisted and I have taken on a recommendation. The book for October will be *The Sinner* by J Rupert." His eyes stopped on a lady in the front row with fine black hair. She blushed and Lawrence looked away before he continued. "It's a book that I have not yet read. So, readers, this will be a novelty for all of us. I think you will find it very interesting from what I have heard. Get your copy now, over the road." Lawrence said decisively as he waved a garish black and red book in his hand. The gathering from the book club filtered out of the coffee shop on to London Road into the dark evening.

Maria crossed the road to the university bookshop with the others and started scouring the shelves for the book.

Sunil picked up a copy and flipped it over. "Langford and Sons. They don't publish just anything. Their books are pretty good."

Sunil flicked the cover open and looked at the author biography. "Hey, didn't this guy die recently?"

"Who?" Oliver asked, picking up a copy and flicking to the About the Author page.

"This Rupert fellow. Suicide, wasn't it?" Sunil responded.

"It was. I read about it not so long ago. I can't remember how he did it, or why he did it, for that matter, but it certainly shot his book to fame. A story written by someone so terribly depressed… it should be an interesting read," Penelope said, then added sarcastically, "Maybe that's why Lawrence chose it."

"Maybe we shouldn't make such sweeping generalisations," Jason snapped, silencing Penelope.

Just as Jason opened his mouth to say something, Sunil interrupted: "Did he not say at the start of this club that in the first four months he wouldn't take any of our recommendations?"

"But it's not *our* recommendation, is it? Probably one of his friends'," Oliver said.

"Murder again. I'm sensing a theme with Lawrence's choices," Sunil said. "A girl blacks out and wakes up in her own bed not being able to remember a thing."

A shiver ran down Maria's spine. The blood drained from her face and her hands felt as cold as ice. This had to be some kind of sick joke. She pulled the book out of Sunil's hands.

"Hey," Sunil looked at her quizzically.

"She's not feeling so good," Oliver responded, putting his arm around his friend. She was shaking. "You okay, Maria? Why don't I drop you home?" Oliver said.

"Thanks Ollie," Maria said, walking with a copy of *The Sinner* towards the till. Her eyes fixated on the blurb of white letters on the black back cover. She would be grateful for the company. Maria hated being alone ever since the incident. Leanne had been brilliant, just being there without her having to ask. But how long could she rely on her best friend for? Leanne had her own life too. As they left the bookstore, a fine mist of rain made Maria shelter closer to Oliver.

"You need to take it easy," Oliver said, rubbing her shoulder. But Maria knew that she would not be able to take it easy. Not now she had *The Sinner* in her hands.

"You two not coming to Marconi's? You missed last week as well," Penelope said. She looked disheartened.

"Sorry Penelope," Maria said.

*

Oliver had insisted on walking Maria to her door and she was grateful, but she now felt obligated to invite him in. She was still on edge about having anyone other than Leanne in her apartment. *The Sinner* burned in her hands as she opened the door to her apartment. She was desperate yet anxious to read it.

"It's one hell of a storyline, don't you think?" Oliver interrupted Maria's thoughts as they walked through her front door.

"Yeah," Maria tried to sound uninterested, not wanting Oliver to know that this book had piqued her interest more than he could have imagined. "A weird storyline is to be expected from someone who was about to kill himself. I wonder how he did it?"

"Hanging, slitting your wrists, an overdose, jumping in front of a train. They're all little cries for help, you know," Oliver said.

Maria saw a flicker of sadness in Oliver's eyes and she held her breath. She had always assumed Oliver was so happy-go-lucky. He always had a smile on his face, he always knew how to make her laugh. She should have scratched beneath the surface a little. Maria reached out to him and squeezed his hand for reassurance but he quickly moved away.

"Amazing apartment," Oliver said, trying to change the subject. "Mind if I use your bathroom."

"Course not," Maria said, "over there." She pointed towards the blue door that Oliver was walking towards.

Oliver stayed for a cup of tea before he returned to Marconi's. He had marvelled at the architecture, at how a converted old textiles mill had made such a glorious loft apartment. "I am absolutely jealous that you live here. It's spectacular. The perfect *Come Dine With Me* kitchen. I couldn't have designed it better myself."

Maria looked at the stainless steel with fresh eyes. Ever since the incident she felt that she was a prisoner in her apartment, but today, for the first time in a week, it felt close to home again.

As soon as Oliver left, Maria religiously bolted her front door and checked all her windows were locked. Then, nestling herself on her sofa, she opened the book. As Maria started reading the first page of the novel, tears started to prick the back of her eyes. But as she continued to read a question began to loom over her. Just who had made this recommendation? Lawrence had never suggested a recommendation before. It was too much of a coincidence for this book to be introduced to the group so soon after her *incident*. Did someone in the book club know and was playing a game with her? Maria knew she would have to find out who suggested the book and then… well, she was not sure what she would do then, but at least she would have a lead. Her body tensed as it dawned on her that someone in the book club not only knew about her ordeal but was very much a part of it.

10

"Have you told her yet?" Oliver asked over the thud of the loud music.

Jason paused, taking a large sip of his neat whiskey and turning away from the tall brunette who had offered to buy him a drink. "No," came a barely audible reply. Jason shifted slightly away from Oliver. He looked into the distance, his eyes focused on a couple dancing intimately towards the back of Marconi's. The couple looked young and in love, making Jason think back to the life he left in San Diego.

The moment Jason had stood on British soil he knew he had made the right decision. Things at home had not been right for a while and he had needed time away to clear his mind and reassess what he really wanted. When the consultancy he was working for offered him a place on a Master's course in Business Administration in England, he had jumped at the chance.

Jason had told his family that his education was essential and that he had no choice in the matter. His boss said that if he couldn't do the Master's then he would lose his job. "In a recession!" they had remarked. "Yes," he had responded confidently, and they had no reason to doubt him. The family he loved sent him off with their blessings, but they did not realise just how desperate he was to get away.

Jason looked back towards Oliver who was drinking a vile looking red and orange concoction with a purple umbrella perched on the rim. "Who told you?" Jason asked sullenly.

"About you and Penny? Or your wife back home?" Oliver asked, tilting his head to one side.

"Both," Jason said, grimacing. Penelope had promised him she would keep their relationship under wraps for now. Why did all the girls want to confide in Oliver Sanderson? They obviously saw something in him that Jason couldn't.

"I just happened to be walking through Stoneygate when I saw you leaving Penny's house," Oliver confessed.

"I could have been there to see her housemate," Jason said. *So it wasn't Penelope who shared their secret.*

"You could have but you weren't. You and I both know that Penelope doesn't even have a housemate," Oliver paused. "You were there to see Penny. I asked her later that day and her smile pretty much gave it away."

Jason closed his eyes. Soon everyone on campus would be talking about them. "And Eleanor? How do you know about her?" Jason asked, rotating his whiskey glass in the palm of his hand.

"Eleanor, huh. Well let's just say a little birdie told me."

Jason rolled his eyes and took another sip of his drink to calm his nerves. Oliver wasn't the type to revel in someone else's misery, so why was he taunting him like this?

"Who else knows?" Jason asked sheepishly.

"Don't look at me like that. I haven't said a word. Penelope's a friend. I don't want her to get hurt." Oliver played with the umbrella in his drink. "You need to tell her soon."

"Don't threaten me. You don't know the full story. What it was like for me."

"How would you like it if Penelope had a husband tucked away somewhere in the background that you didn't know about?"

"Eleanor was everything I ever wanted," Jason explained, ordering another double whiskey. "She was independent, fiercely so. She was loving and caring."

Oliver raised an eyebrow.

Jason thanked the bartender for his drink and took a sip of the amber liquid. "We wanted to build a future together, Ellie and I. We had planned out our entire lives together." Jason thought about Eleanor's long brown hair, high cheekbones and slender waist. He pictured her in their living room, sitting on their mocha couch, watching the waves roll in on Ocean Beach.

Eleanor had made that house their home from the day they signed the deeds. Large ornamental shells that cost the earth had littered their living room. Swatches of fabrics arrived daily until she had picked out colour schemes that echoed their coastal retreat.

But Jason's relationship with Eleanor had soured just three years after they had stepped over the threshold and, as much as he tried to deny it, it was the long awaited arrival of their baby, Alfie, who had caused the rift. But he wasn't going to tell Oliver about his son; that was, if Oliver didn't already know. "Ellie started to change, Oliver. It was awful. Imagine waking up to someone you just don't recognise anymore."

Oliver sucked on his straw swallowing the syrupy liquid that was doing absolutely nothing for him. He nodded at Jason, encouraging him to continue. Jason's excuses were futile but tears had formed in his eyes and Oliver couldn't help feeling sorry for him. Jason didn't deserve someone to confide in but Oliver could hardly leave him alone. Not just yet.

"Eleanor lost her independence. You couldn't tell at first. It isn't something that happens overnight. It happened gradually. She had quit her job, you see, and so she relied on me for most things. She would wait for me to come home each day and nag me. She started to worry about little things, things she would have generally brushed over before. Just a drop of milk spilling on the sofa would send her into a mad panic. Before Al..." Jason stopped himself. "Before, red wine on our white carpets would never have fazed her."

The memory of milk on their sofa reminded Jason again of Alfie. Jason missed him. He missed their son more than anything. If only he could hold his little boy now. Jason had left Eleanor alone with a one-year-old and guilt was beginning to creep in. Jason knew that he should have been more understanding with Eleanor. After all, being a parent was new to them both. But Jason couldn't help but notice that his wife's whole world began to revolve around that child. He couldn't do anything right. It was his damn child as well! And she had snubbed his parents so badly. After Alfie was born she refused to let them stay longer than a weekend, saying that they were interfering with her parenting abilities. Jason worried that Alfie would grow up not knowing who his grandparents were. But all he had done was run away from the problem.

"Eleanor and I needed the space. That's why I came away. Oliver, I don't care about completing a Master's degree."

"And how does Penelope fit into all of this? You could have had your pick of girls on campus, slept around as much as you wanted... Why have a relationship with Penny? That's just not right." Oliver looked towards Jason but his focus was elsewhere. Oliver's eyes drifted in the direction of Jason's stare. Penelope had just walked in with another girl. They walked towards a smaller bar at the back of the club.

"When I left San Diego, Eleanor and I decided we needed a break. It was the only way. We're separated now," Jason said.

Oliver narrowed his eyes at Jason. "Separated or on a break? Those are two completely different things. If you're on a break, it doesn't give you the right to have a full-on relationship with someone else!"

"Separated," Jason lied. Eleanor didn't think they were separated and Jason hardly gave her any inclination to think that. They had spoken last week, and something in Eleanor's voice had changed. She sounded more confident, more in control. She had started back at work part time and was letting her retired mother babysit. Perhaps Eleanor was getting back to her old self. He imagined her holding Alfie while she spoke to him on the phone, his plastic toys in vibrant reds, greens and yellows, scattered around their living room.

But still Jason wasn't ready to go back. As usual, he had managed to complicate matters further. He had fallen in love with Penelope.

11

Jason thought back to his first meeting with his new love. He had taken himself to the university bar, hoping to meet some social postgraduates after realising that his flatmate had no interest in socialising.

He glanced around the tired looking bar. A group of girls wearing tiny mini skirts were knocking back shots of a bright red alcohol that smelled of mouthwash. They were teetering in their heels. One of them caught Jason's eye and, with a hand covering her lips, said something to the others. They all started giggling. Jason put them at eighteen: first years. He knew that freshers would be too easy a target. In fact, Jason knew he could easily bed most girls in that bar. But after being with Eleanor for so long, he had lost some of his confidence; there had only been a few occasions when he got to play away from home.

Jason gulped back his pint and headed out into the cool night air. He passed a van selling kebabs and the smell of the meat intoxicated him. Having not had dinner, he knew that he would have a raging hangover after a few more drinks if he didn't eat. The pint on his empty stomach had already hit him, so he didn't mind so much when he saw the dirty knife the kebab seller used to cut the meat of the doner. He ate his dinner from a polystyrene container with lashings of chilli sauce and mayonnaise as he walked towards the centre of Leicester. By the time he had finished, he was standing outside what could only be a strip bar.

He hesitated. It had been an old habit that he had vowed never to get drawn into again. But he remembered just how much he had enjoyed them, paying for the occasional private dance. He knew Eleanor would not approve. Of course not, what wife would? She had turned a blind eye to his indiscretions in the past, but she wouldn't anymore. There was no excuse. Jason started to walk on but stopped. He and Eleanor were on a break, he reasoned, and, more importantly, his wife would never find out. He popped a mint into his mouth and entered the club.

After that Thursday, Rustle had become a regular occurrence and, even though he knew his visits to the club had to stop, Jason didn't see any need for urgency. He was only in England for a year, after which he was determined to return to Eleanor. But one evening he saw Penelope in the dark recesses of the club. Standing half naked with four other girls around her, there was something about her that appealed to him. Penelope's blue eyes had an innocence to them, yet she was sexy and provocative, her body perfectly toned; there was no doubt about that. Four dates later and he found himself waking up next to her. Whilst she slept next to him, Jason realised what it was about her that first attracted him.

Penelope had the same features as Eleanor. He had never dated a stripper before, but now he knew what made Penelope stand out that day. That morning Jason had stayed for coffee and ate the scrambled eggs on toast she had made, even though he hated scrambled eggs. Penelope was Eleanor before Alfie. Jason had even found himself going to the book club Penelope had mentioned. He cursed himself for doing this; it was something Eleanor had always wanted him to do with her, and he had always made up some excuse as to why he couldn't. Now he was attending a book club with his wife's doppelgänger.

Jason knew what he was doing was wrong. He knew it was Eleanor who he loved, but there was something about Penelope that he just couldn't resist. A weekly habit had soon turned into something more, and when his visits to the club ended, he continued to spend time with Penelope. Initially he had excused his behaviour, passing it off as a fling before he returned home to his wife. But the more time he spent with Penelope, the more he became infatuated with her. Jason knew that if Eleanor ever found out, she would do everything in her power to keep Alfie away from him, and the thought of losing Alfie pained him, especially after all they had been through. Jason was stuck. He knew he had no choice but to return to his wife.

Jason had decided to come clean with Penelope, but he kept putting off telling her the truth about his life back home. When he finally plucked up the courage to do so, he realised that it was too late. He had fallen in love with her and the fear of losing her meant too much.

So Jason had kept his wife a secret, but he knew time was running out. Now that Oliver knew about Eleanor, there would be others around campus who would know his secret too. Jason couldn't keep this truth from Penelope for much longer. Swallowing the remnants of his whiskey, he decided he had to tell her. But he wasn't prepared for the secret Penelope was keeping.

12

Maria woke in the dark with a startle, certain that she had heard a noise: the slamming of a door. Her front door. And the wind chimes, she could definitely hear the faint ring of the thin aluminium flutes. Leanne had recently installed them for her at the entrance of her apartment so that Maria would always know when her front door opened. In a top floor apartment, Maria knew there was only one entry point. But those chimes were not helping—they were making her more on edge than ever. Every time the wind caught them she almost jumped out of her skin.

Maria's palms were moist and her heart was racing, her rapid, shallow breathing drowning out any other sounds she thought she could hear. She tried holding her breath but she could only hear the blood rush in her ears. She tried to slow her breathing; inhaling slowly through her nose and exhaling through her mouth, just like Leanne had taught her, to try and compose herself. *Bricks, Bricks, Bricks.* That word was taunting her, why? She spat out the word one last time hoping to get rid of it.

When her heartbeat had stabilised, she tiptoed downstairs and looked around. The front door was bolted from the inside. Maria realised there had been no noise. It was just a bad dream. She crept back to bed and switched on her reading light. Glancing at her watch, she let her shoulders drop with a sigh of relief. It was three thirty in the morning. Maria had remembered switching off the lights in the sitting room and heading upstairs to bed at around one o'clock with *The Sinner* clutched in her hand. She had been desperate to complete the novel and get to the bottom of the story's abduction, and perhaps her own. When her bedside alarm clock flashed two fifteen she had finished the last page. She remembered the dreary ending of *The Sinner* that bore no resemblance to her own life at all. Yes, the book had mirrored how she woke up that morning on the 28th of September, but that was all it had done. The other two hundred or so pages had not given her any clues as to what had happened to her. In fact, it had left her even more confused.

The Sinner, or the abductor, in the book had used Rohypnol to drug his victims and make them forget the trauma he had slowly put them through. The protagonist, Diana, did not remember a thing, until three days later, when her captor wrote to her. On receiving the letter, something in Diana's mind had clicked. She remembered being tied up. She remembered being raped. In fact Diana had remembered her abduction in detail. The conclusion was that The Sinner was psychotic; an easy out to a difficult plotline. The villain of the piece, repulsive to women, had secured a victim the only way he knew how. It was one of those books that had no sense to it. But as Lawrence had said, truth was often stranger than fiction.

J Rupert would not be up there on her list of favourite authors. She looked again at his author profile. Could she really see a familiarity in his eyes? Or was she just seeing things? He was from San Diego, a connection to Jason perhaps, or was that the imagination of a fantasist?

No matter how hard Maria tried to deny it, she knew that her abduction was just not a storyline. There had to be a reason why someone would do this to her—she just didn't know how to find out. She was certain that someone had planted *The Sinner* as the next read at the book club, most probably because they knew about what had happened to her. And by her reasoning, if they knew about her ordeal then they were most likely to be part of it. What were they trying to achieve by recommending the book? Was this all a game? It was like the emails all over again.

Failing to get any further sleep, Maria got out of bed and put her dressing gown on. She shuffled downstairs towards the pile of post that she had disregarded since that weekend. She went through the bills and the junk mail carefully looking for some thing out of place. Nothing. So at least the perpetrator was not a copycat. She shuddered thinking of Diana's suicide at the end of the book. Again, her thoughts wondered to J Rupert. *Did he have some dark secret that made him put an end to his life too?*

Maria stopped herself as the thought of Diana's rape entered her mind again. She was reading too much into it. This wasn't some fiction novel. This was her life. She should have listened to Leanne and seen a doctor or gone to the police. Why had she been so stubborn? It would be difficult for anyone to believe her now. Hindsight was such a clear and beautiful thing. Maria knew that if she was going to move on with her life she needed to put it behind her. She needed to let it go. She tried to think about the book club instead, about Penelope and Jason, and about the sadness she had seen in Oliver's eyes when he had walked her home. Maria put *The Sinner* in a kitchen drawer that she rarely opened and crept back upstairs. As she lay in her bed, under the duvet, she tried to block out a feeling at the back of her mind. It was the same feeling she had experienced when she woke up on the morning of the 28th. It was sheer terror. The sheer terror of knowing that she had been abducted, wondering if someone could get back into her apartment. And then, of course, there was that familiar fragrance.

13

Maria stood in the doorway of her ensuite, steam from the shower rising behind her, desperately trying to escape into her bedroom. She looked crestfallen. Leanne was busy studying the A3 chart she had compiled of what she could remember of the book club members and of what Maria had told her more recently. Leanne was desperate to play detective and help jog Maria's memory.

"I'm late," Maria said. A single tear ran down her cheek.

"For what?" Leanne asked without taking her eyes off the paper before her, completely unaware of Maria's dilemma. Studying her chart intently, Leanne was wondering who the most likely suspect from the book club could be. She had also compiled a list of questions and statements she wanted Maria to mention during their next meeting, the all-important meeting where they would be discussing *The Sinner*. Failing to receive a response from Maria, Leanne shifted her gaze to her friend, instantly noticing the dark circles under Maria's eyes and her gaunt appearance.

The weight that Maria had been trying to lose for years had suddenly disappeared, as if by magic. Leanne wanted nothing more than to protect her dearest friend. She sighed. Maria, who had once loved colour all around her, had changed her bedding to white, and had even replaced the purple and pink polka dot towels with plain white ones. The Maria she knew had truly disappeared. It pained Leanne to see her carefree friend so tired and weak, so afraid of her own shadow. Leanne knew that if she could just find out who did this, she could halve Maria's worries.

It took a moment to register before Leanne realised what Maria was getting at. It had been her first thought when Maria had mentioned the blackout, but she dared not mention it. Not when Maria was so delicate in those early days. Now, looking back on it, she knew she should have said something. Leanne was annoyed with herself. Trying to protect her friends usually did more harm than good.

"You didn't see a doctor like you promised me that time," Leanne said softly.

"I tried. But like when I was at the police station… I got cold feet." Maria pushed a brown curl behind her ear and looked towards her feet.

Leanne knew she should have dragged her friend to the doctor's kicking and screaming, but she didn't and there was nothing she could do about it now. Had Leanne been in the same position, she knew Maria would have forced her to see a doctor long before now. Why was Leanne never the good friend she wanted to be? How she wished Alice were around.

"I went to the surgery and I sat there amidst the crowd. Then I heard my name being called out on the tannoy and I just didn't respond," Maria said. "I sat glued to the seat and when a receptionist came round and asked me if I was Maria Shroder, I fled. I just stood up out of my seat and left without a single word. I just wasn't thinking straight. I was scared. You know, that they would think I was making it up or something," Maria said, fiddling with a lock of her hair.

"I should have come with you," Leanne said. "You should have told me." Leanne bit her lower lip and inhaled, trying to find her voice of calm. Why was Maria so worried that people would think she was making it all up? Surely she would want to do everything to help her situation, not make it worse, which was exactly what she was doing by being so stubborn. Was there something more to this incident than Maria was letting on? Again, Leanne wished for Alice. Alice knew Maria like the back of her hand; she would know what to do. Leanne took another deep breath, resting her chin on her hand. She would have to remain positive for her friend. "You've been stressed. That is such a contributing factor," Leanne said as she sprung up from the bed and put on her coat. "So how many days late are we talking?"

"About ten," came Maria's feeble reply. Her eyelids were drooping as if she couldn't carry on. "I just didn't think… I mean, with all that happened, missing days of my life. It kind of threw me." Maria looked at Leanne with fear in her eyes, "I didn't think of the date until now. Shit, shit, shit. This can't be happening. Oh God. The girl in the book, Diana, was raped. I didn't think." Maria steadied herself on the blue velvet loveseat at the edge of her bedroom. She and Alice used to sit in it for hours together when they were younger. When her parents announced their move, it was the only piece of furniture Maria had wanted.

Maria heard the front door slam and the tinkling of the wind chimes as Leanne left the flat. Maria sat down on the worn patch of the blue velvet fabric, hugging her knees to her chest whilst her tears stained her cheeks.

★

Twenty minutes later Leanne had found her friend just as she left her. Making herself comfortable outside Maria's bathroom door, she mentally crossed her fingers and prayed to the God who was generally so good to her during her hours of need. Leanne, for whom practicality was a rare occurrence, had been trying to work out a plan of action should the test prove positive. She had the picture on the pregnancy test box ingrained in her mind. Positive: Horizontal pink line. Negative: Vertical pink line.

Maria opened the door to the bathroom clutching the white stick. Placing it on the dresser, she sat back down on the blue velvet seat.

Leanne had perched herself at Maria's feet knowing it would be a very long three minutes. She bit her nails as she wondered what she would have done if she was carrying a rapist's baby. She juddered and shook the thought from her mind. She needed to stay calm for the sake of Maria, but inside her thoughts were running away with her.

Leanne reflected on her own life. Children seemed years away. She didn't even have a proper boyfriend. For Maria to have motherhood thrust upon her, in such a cruel way, seemed like an undeserving double punishment. She rested her head on the love seat, the one she never got a chance to sit on as a child because Maria and Alice were always on it. How she wished they were all ten again, without the heavy responsibilities that came with age.

"Okay, I think three minutes are up," Maria said, waking Leanne from her thoughts as she nervously stood up from her seat and padded over to the dresser. Her heart had still not grown used to the levels of adrenalin that were now running through her so frequently, making her feel sick to her stomach. She picked up the white stick, her fingers trembling, knowing that her fate was sealed in the result.

"It's negative, I think." She suspended her state of relief, unsure if she had read the pink lines correctly. She handed the test to Leanne who confirmed the result with a huge smile and a nod of her head. Maria's body relaxed and the tears began to stain her cheeks again.

Leanne wrapped her arms around her friend who started to cry uncontrollably for all the emotions that had coursed through her body over the last hour. Maria knew she had been naïve. Even after reading *The Sinner* she had not for a moment thought that she too could have been raped. Well, she had, but it had just been a fleeting thought. She had convinced herself she would have remembered something like that. The book had been useless; it had not unlocked any memories at all.

"You can't imagine what was going through my head, Lea," Maria said later that evening as she sunk into her bed.

"How stupid I've been. I didn't even think… I mean I didn't think about what *he* could have done to me… it would have been a *he*, wouldn't it?" Leanne, who had taken to sleeping in Maria's bed rather than in the spare room, handed her some tissues and Maria dabbed away her tears. "I should have gone to the police. Why can't I remember, damn it? *He* could have done anything to me and I just don't know."

Leanne didn't know how to put into words what she was about to say. But she had held her tongue last time and it had not done her friend any favours. She was the one that had to think straight now and point her friend in the right direction. She had to help Maria even if that meant forcing her to go to the doctor's at this late stage. "Look Maria, it may be an idea doing an STD test at the clinic, you know?

Just in case. You may not be pregnant but you… you know, you may just want to check to be safe."

Maria looked up at Leanne, disillusioned. It was something else that she had failed to think about.

Now that Leanne had the chance, she added, "And you should still go to the police. It isn't too late. I can take you myself."

Maria lay silent on the bed knowing that her friend was right. For a moment she toyed with the idea of how she would feel if she knew what had happened to her. Surely that would ease her mind; it was the not knowing that scared her so much. Maria was certain that once she knew exactly what had happened, she would be able to put it behind her. But then Diana had found out and what good had it done her? She had taken her own life. Maria allowed herself the luxury of delving in her inner most thoughts for just a second. Did she really want to know what had happened to her or was she afraid of the truth?

14

Maria switched off her laptop after scouring the Internet for the two words Alan had mentioned. Alan was a friend who had lived on the same floor as her in their university halls of residence. They had been close, a bit too close, in the first year. Now, after several failed attempts at a relationship, they were just friends. He was a good friend though; they had never lost that closeness, the closeness you get with just a small handful of people in your lifetime. Friends you can call in the middle of the night for no rhyme or reason just because you want someone to talk to. With Alan, even when they hadn't spoken in months, they always picked up from where they left off.

Alan was studying to be a doctor and was now out in Wellington, New Zealand with his girlfriend. Maria had always said that she would visit, especially now that her parents were in that part of the world. But with the path her life was taking, a trip out there seemed further away than she could imagine.

Maria had called Alan on the pretence that her friend had recently had a loss of memory after a night out. After persuading Alan that alcohol was not a cause, he finally suggested that the symptoms she was describing sounded like hysterical amnesia.

"You know, pet," he said, mixing his Newcastle accent with a New Zealand twang, "something traumatic could have happened. Must have happened. The brain blocks it out because it's just too painful to remember. The memory should return within what, say forty-eight hours. If alcohol or if Rohypnol was present..." He trailed off.

"What are the side effects of that?" Maria asked casually.

"With alcohol? You know how you have gaps in your memory after a particular boozy sesh? With Rohypnol, it's worse.

Think gastrointestinal problems, dizziness, confusion…" Alan replied. "Something your friend should see a doctor about."

No alcohol was involved, thought Maria, and, yes, they would have had to drug her surely to keep her quiet and sedated. "If drugs were used, what are the chances of her recovering her memory?" Maria asked.

"Limited really, but it depends what drug. Your friend should have blood tests done and see a doctor, not just take my advice. It could be a symptom for a neurological disorder."

"What if she experienced some kind of flashback, though?" Maria thought back to the silhouette of the man next to an open fridge and the leather band around his arm, ignoring Alan's comments about seeing a doctor.

"Flashbacks generally mean there's some kind of memory there. Maybe a fifty-fifty chance of recovering memory. If it is hysterical amnesia, her memory should return fairly quickly. If not, there may be permanent memory loss. It's rare for memories not to come back with this type of amnesia."

"So what happens now?" Maria quizzed Alan. "Because it's been over two weeks and she doesn't remember anything," she said anxiously.

"A shrink. The memory may be too painful for your friend to cope with the truth. Her brain doesn't want to deal with it, so, boom, it's blocked it out." There was a pause. "Maria…" Alan started, "if there was a problem, a serious problem…"

"I didn't know our brains were that complex," Maria intentionally interrupted.

Alan was silent.

Maria quickly changed the subject. She asked him questions about his new girlfriend and his new life before saying goodbye. As she disconnected, she wished for a split second that they were back together. He was always so strong and always looked after her, but that was a long time ago, before Owen.

In Maria's weak state, she struggled to think of Owen. She had loved him so deeply and intensely, and when he had moved on to her sister it was like part of her died. It was a clichéd thought but she had honestly felt that he had ripped her heart out and stood on it. In fact, it felt like he had jumped on her heart repeatedly. The break up had been made even more painful by the fact that she and Alice had been so close. They had spent their entire lives together and now Owen had ruined that. Their sisterly bond had been broken and their relationship would never be the same again. People had said to Maria afterwards that friends and sisters could have similar tastes, that they often fall in love with the same person. But it had never happened to Maria and Alice before.

The contents of that first fateful email Maria had received still remained with her. Life was too short and Maria knew that she had to forgive and forget. She was the elder sister and she had to be the stronger one. What she was now going through had finally made Maria realise that family was important, and Owen wasn't worth losing Alice over.

Maria found courage in a box of white wine, which she had taken to drinking since the incident. It had initially helped her to sleep and numbed the pain. Putting her glass on the coffee table, she picked up her mobile and started writing a text to her sister. After bumping into Alice at the wine bar, she thought her sister would have tried to make contact. They had, after all, exchanged numbers. Was Alice avoiding her because she was still with Owen? The thought of them together sent a shiver down Maria's spine. It had been over two years—perhaps they had broken up. Maria knew she would not take it well if her sister and Owen were still dating, but she would have to get over it.

"Maria," Leanne said, interrupting her trail of thought, looking over the balcony of the mezzanine level. Leanne could see Maria's face wet from tears in the blue glow from her mobile phone. Maria looked up at her friend, Leanne's brown bob of hair a mess, her pyjamas twisted around her body as if she had just woken up. Maria had completely forgotten that she had asked Leanne to stay over.

"Was Alan helpful?" Leanne asked.

"Yes. I suppose he was."

"Who are you texting at this time? You need to get some sleep, like now. Whatever you're doing, it can keep."

Maria snapped her phone shut. She placed her mobile phone on the table and headed upstairs without a word, too tired to argue with her only true friend. Her message to her sister would keep.

15

Maria walked rapidly out of the GUM clinic on Marley Street with her head down, hoping that no one she knew was passing by. As soon as she had turned the corner, she breathed a sigh of relief. She knew that waiting for the test results was going to be much more painful than waiting for a three-minute pregnancy test. With each passing day, despite a lack of any symptoms, Maria had managed to convince herself just a little bit more that she had some kind of infection antibiotics would not be able to cure.

Her mindset had told Maria that something was wrong and so she started going to the toilet more frequently and had duly stocked the fridge with cranberry juice. With each day that passed, she was torn between whether she imagined this whole ordeal or whether she actually knew that something bad had happened to her. Dream or reality. To choose the former would be easy. She could forget the whole incident, but the emails, the call from Howard to Tina and the gnawing feeling in the pit of her stomach could not be ignored.

Maria held back from confiding in Leanne about her persistent doubts. The last thing she wanted was her friend to doubt her as well. Leanne had been her rock and had agreed, without hesitation, that someone in the book club knew about Maria's abduction. They were both certain that *The Sinner* was no coincidence and, for Maria, this book was another piece of evidence to prove she wasn't making it up.

Maria stopped herself from thinking about *The Sinner*. It was a slippery slope into the depths of depression once Maria started thinking about Diana's fate. Maria's thoughts of the protagonist soon spiralled into thoughts of all the atrocities that she may have been subject to whilst she was out cold. And then the dreaded burden of her self-doubt began to quash her. Episodes like this usually ended up with Maria crying herself to sleep.

Today was going to be different. Maria made a short list of psychiatrists she had found online and circled the three she thought could help her recover her memory. Sitting with her back against the sofa, Maria pushed her hair behind her ears and silently rehearsed how she would explain to a psychiatrist what happened. Leanne studied her A3 chart again. The chart had progressed nicely over the last couple of days and most of the empty text boxes had now been filled with information on each of Leanne's suspects.

"I can't for a minute think it could be Jason or Penelope," Leanne said. "As you say, they're so hung up on one another—they wouldn't have time for you." Leanne pursed her lips. "Jason has no connections to you. He isn't even from round here. No motive." Leanne looked at Maria for reassurance but her friend's face was blank. "Penny, well, her sickly sweet nature is criminal but..." Leanne raised her eyebrows at Maria. "...I know she's your friend and all that, but she's the bunny boiler type and we all know that those are the types who would do something crazy for love..." Leanne said. "...but then again, *Tia Maria*, no motive. What's her background? Do you know?"

Maria smiled at the affectionate pet name Leanne had given her years ago. It took her back to happier times, but only for a second. A humiliating vision of her legs spread at the GUM clinic soon returned to her suppressing her second of happiness.

"She's from Oxford. Bookish. I like her," Maria said. "She hardly looks like she has the strength to move a body, though." Maria mustered up the energy to look through the familiar faces Leanne had downloaded from a social networking site and stuck to her chart. Maria pencilled in crosses next to Jason and Penelope's names.

"Hey, don't take her off our list!" Leanne said, rubbing out the cross. "If she is so bookish, maybe she read *The Sinner* before. Think about it. Penelope could have suggested it. She's so good looking, she could wrap any man around her finger if she wanted help with something—like moving a body..." Leanne furrowed her brow while she chewed on the end of her pencil. "I've seen the way Lawrence looks at Penelope. In fact, Jason is from San Diego, where J Rupert is from. And you said they have something going on." Leanne smiled at

Maria, happy with her deduction. "We can put a question mark near both their names," she said, pencilling in the marks.

"It's not really Penelope's genre, that kind of book. She's into the classics and the popular stuff. She doesn't really read dark books," Maria said, defending her friend and reinserting the cross. Maria would not let Leanne's petty jealousy mar her new friend's name.

"You would *want* to throw people off the tracks, wouldn't you?"

"It has to be calculated then," Maria said, with a look of realisation, as if someone had just told her that the earth was not round. Then, conceding to Leanne's point, she added, "Fine, leave her on!" Maria closed her eyes. "Stupid chart," she mumbled under her breath. Maria knew the chart wasn't going to get her anywhere, but she didn't want to hurt Leanne's feelings, nor did she want her friend to leave. Having company was now paramount to Maria's existence.

"So who does read that kind of genre?" Leanne said, scratching her head with the end of the gnawed pencil and emphasising the word genre, which was fairly new to her.

"Well, Ollie, sometimes. But like Penny, he prefers popular stuff. I can't see him being party to anything like that. He has his own issues."

"Go on," Leanne said, desperate for some gossip. She too was growing tired of playing Miss Marple. It wasn't as easy as she had first thought.

"It's private. He wouldn't want me talking about it," Maria said quietly. Oliver hadn't told her anything. It was all just an assumption. And she wouldn't do that to Oliver—spread rumours that were not necessarily true. Maria looked at the chart again and sighed. "This is useless. I can't believe I'm looking at my friends. It can't be any of them."

"*New* friends," Leanne said, clearing her throat. "*The Sinner* is too much of a coincidence. Maybe the person who did this got the idea from it. Maybe it's all one big practical joke."

"Some sick practical joke, Lea"

"What about Sunil? He's the last on my list," Leanne said.

"Sunil is a bit of a dark horse. Quiet. Moody sometimes. But to be honest, I can't really see a motive there either," Maria said. She hadn't told Leanne that she had spoken to him in depth just the Wednesday before her abduction.

"Don't rule him out just because you have a soft spot for him!" Leanne said, gathering her belongings. "In television detective shows it's always the one you least suspect," Leanne said as she stood up. It was time she returned to her own home. Maria was right, they were certainly no Morse and Lewis. Leanne knew it was no good pointing the finger at Sunil without a shred of evidence. Sunil was what Maria needed. He would be a good distraction for her friend right now. Leanne looked at her friend. She still had dark circles around her eyes. If only Maria wasn't in such a bad way, Leanne thought, then she could leave the house and meet Sunil for a drink or something.

Leanne wondered if she should encourage Maria to date Sunil. A smile formed on her lips. She was much better at doing things like that! "Look, find out who recommended the book first—let's take it from there," Leanne said decisively. She kissed Maria on the cheek and closed the front door behind her. As Leanne headed down the corridor, she heard the clank of three bolts being pulled secure as Maria counted: One, two, three.

★

Maria tore open her test results with trembling fingers and a knot in her stomach. As she read through them, a wave of relief calmed her nerves. She was in the clear. For the first time in weeks she felt elated, and quickly called Leanne to tell her the good news. After putting down the phone, Maria decided that today was her lucky day; a new day to get her life back on track. She immediately called Dr Timms.

Dr Timms was top on Maria's shortlist of psychiatrists. There were two reasons why Maria chose him. Firstly, his office was conveniently based in central Leicester. But secondly, and most importantly, he was renowned for his work on hysterical and dissociative amnesia. He was currently listed in the Yellow Pages as a general psychiatrist but hours of online research had given Maria the evidence she needed about the good doctor. She had read an article which clearly stated that he was part of a new emerging group of psychiatrists adopting an innovative therapy for patients with amnesia. The therapy had received several, positive critiques from professionals in the field.

In the article, *A Hypnosis to Remember*, Dr Timms was acknowledged as one of the founding members of a regressive therapy. Regressive Recollection Therapy, or RRT, as it was commonly referred to, involved five intense therapy sessions accompanied by meditation exercises at home. The idea was to explore a patient's current and past emotions and memories. This would identify core feelings, anxieties and trigger words. The resulting information would define a patient's reactions and feelings to certain people and situations.

Once the keywords and background information were identified the psychiatrist would take the patient right back to the moment they lost their memory through hypnotherapy. The information and trigger words would be presented during the hypnosis to unlock the trauma that had caused the memory loss in the first place.

Of course, along with the positive reviews for this ground breaking new therapy came harsh criticism. There were outcries from well-established psychiatrists that practiced in this field. Dr Totlle, for example, clearly stated that "Each patient is different, you can't just assume five sessions will cure everyone." Dr Lavav questioned, "How can you recall and put to bed serious, traumatic incidents in just six hours?" There were even suggestions that psychiatrists practicing RRT were creating false memories and encouraging confabulation during hypnosis through the power of suggestion.

The last article Maria saw on the Internet stated that some experts had called for a ban on practising RRT. One psychiatrist was almost sued by her patient for being forced, through hypnosis, to remember something that he just could not cope with. The patient was left with no real way to deal with what he learnt of his past and had become suicidal until he was placed within a support network.

RRT had gone underground since that particular article was written. Since then, there was hardly anything written on it, though there was no indication that it was no longer practised. As Dr Timms was based in Leicester, Maria could think of no reason as to why she couldn't give it a shot.

Maria needed to put an end to the cloud of doubt that kept circling her. Was her abduction a dream or was it reality? Maria was certain a professional would be able to see it clearly. She had made an appointment and nearly fainted when they told her the cost.

16

Sunil was glad that no one had seen him leave Marconi's so early in the evening. He had slipped out whilst Penelope and Oliver were deep in conversation. Oliver had been kind enough to take a chance on Sunil all those months ago and introduce him to the rest of the group, but Sunil had an uneasy feeling about his new friend. He couldn't help but notice that Oliver Sanderson had taken a keen interest in Maria lately. It worried him. Maria and Oliver were always huddled together and talking in hushed tones to one another at their monthly book club meetings. That closeness made it almost impossible for Sunil to get a chance to talk to Maria alone. Today Oliver was all over Penelope. For a split second Sunil questioned Oliver's obvious sexuality and wondered if it was all just for show. But that was ludicrous. Everyone knew that Oliver was gay.

Sunil put Oliver out of his mind. He had bigger problems to think about. Walking home under the streetlight, he counted the cracks in the pavement as he told himself that he was worrying about nothing. He had been certain last week that Maria had not remembered. He was certain, because if she had remembered she would have said something to him by now. He took a deep breath as he reassured himself of this fact. But Maria had barely spoken to him since that day. It was almost as if she was avoiding him. She had not said much to him at the last book club meet and she had failed to turn up for drinks tonight. Sunil mulled over the situation in his head, losing count of the pavement cracks. He knew that this was not just something you could pretend didn't happen. His stomach twisted as he thought about that day.

Pulling his coat around him, Sunil protected his body from the icy wind that disproved the warm November the weathermen had predicted. He felt his phone vibrate in his pocket, but he let it ring. The only person that would call him at this time would be Omar, and he was in no mood to speak to Omar today. It was his fault Sunil was in this mess in the first place.

Twenty minutes later Sunil let himself into his warm apartment the other side of Victoria Park. It was an old building, a house that had been converted into two apartments. The landlord had tried to modernise it by putting in wooden floors and a new kitchen, but it still smelled of damp, like an unloved antique store. He looked around at some of the cumbersome furniture. The end of the lease on the apartment was fast approaching and Sunil was looking to rent something a little more modern and closer to town. Walking through Victoria Park at night always worried him; it was where groups of boys in hoodies hung out, smoking spliffs and drinking cans of cheap lager. They were probably harmless but, nevertheless, they unnerved him.

The shop had been playing on his mind as well. Lorrie wanted the same week off as Jake and the manager didn't want to work Fridays. But the staffing issues and teething problems had an upside. They meant that Sunil got to stay in Leicester for at least another six months. It would provide him with more time to accomplish what he had set out to do. He flicked open the *Leicester Mercury* to the property pages and looked through the apartments to rent. A two bedroom spacious loft apartment caught his eye. Sunil recognised the King's View well. Smiling, he circled the property with his red marker pen. He would call the agent first thing tomorrow. He didn't need to see the place—he would be moving out.

17

Maria arrived outside Dr Timms office at ten past three. She had been lucky to get an appointment after a last-minute cancellation. At first Maria was hesitant when Dr Timms' secretary called her to bring forward her scheduled appointment. Maria had not mentally prepared herself as yet, safe in the knowledge that she would have at least a week before her meeting with the doctor. However, she was well aware that a week of waiting would be a period during which she would convince herself that therapy wasn't needed, even if they had taken her credit card details on making the reservation. Tina had allowed Maria to leave early from work that day. Maria saw it as a sign that she should attend this last minute appointment.

The door was a clinical-looking glossy royal blue set in a white frame. Maria scanned the intercom for Dr Timms and located it three names down. She buzzed through, looking directly at the little eye of the camera.

A tiny voice answered on the other side, followed by a buzzing sound that allowed Maria access into the building. She pushed through the heavy blue door and made her way up the stairs to Dr Timms office, making her arrival known to the small secretary who looked like she belonged to that tiny voice Maria heard only minutes before. Dr Timms' secretary, who had mouse-like features, was wearing a green blouse and cream cardigan as she typed away at her computer. Looking at Maria momentarily over the top rim of her glasses, she tilted her head, smiled, pointed to a wooden chair in the waiting room and then returned to her work. Maria noticed the dark wood panelling which dominated the room. A knot formed in her stomach. Did she really want to be assessed by a stranger with oppressive wooden decor?

When the door to Dr Timms office opened, Maria took a deep breath to steady her nerves. Her legs started to tremble as she knew they would. In a few moments, she would have to walk through that door. A short, tubby man with a receding hairline faced her. At first glance he didn't look like the sort of man that would visit a psychiatrist, but on closer inspection his eyes looked troubled. Maria assumed he had marital problems by the way he was playing with his wedding ring, which was far too tight for him. Dr Timms' secretary waited patiently for him to write a cheque. The short, tubby man made a further appointment for the following week. He scurried out of the waiting area and did not look at Maria.

"Dr Timms will see you now," the secretary said. Maria smiled, putting down the leaflet on depression, which she had been pretending to read. She entered the room with yet more oak wood panelling and a patterned carpet. Inevitably the flooring contradicted the modern front door. Gentle music was playing in the background, which had a calming effect. The room was homely, not clinical at all. Instantly Maria noticed that there was no sofa in the room and she felt somewhat cheated, but she knew that these feelings were just nerves. Not everything was how she imagined it to be. After all, this was her first visit to a psychiatrist. It was not an episode of *Frasier*.

Maria closed the door softly behind her. The initial consultation fee of seventy pounds had taken her into her overdraft but she hoped that it would be worth it. Hopefully the sessions would allow her to remember what had happened, and that was worth getting into debt for.

"Hello Maria, I'm Dr Timms," he said with a slight American accent, his plump hand reaching forward to shake hers. Maria smiled with relief, taking in his friendly appearance. She assumed he was in his fifties. He wore dark blue corduroy trousers with a pale blue shirt and he had a short white beard. Spectacles dangled loosely across his stomach. Maria couldn't help but think that he looked like Father Christmas. She was glad Dr Timms looked so gentle. If she was going to relive the incident, she felt that she would be comfortable doing so with him.

When Maria first sat down in the armchair, she was scared to bring up her self-diagnosis. She didn't want him to think that she was one of those know-it-alls as a result of a Google search. This had happened to her previously when she was sure she was dying of some rare cancer after looking up her symptoms online. She had explained all of this to her doctor, who soon quipped back that "Paranoia was a beautiful thing for the easily bored." A phrase, Maria was sure, her doctor had stolen from a recently televised Oscar Wilde movie. Maria's doctor had smirked at her, and it was the last time that she ever confessed to putting her symptoms in a self-diagnostic web application. She still couldn't pass on the opportunity to look up her symptoms online, but at least she had learnt not to share her findings with anyone in the medical profession.

Maria carefully explained to Dr Timms what had happened to her, careful to mention everything she could remember, but all he said was, "I see," which somewhat shocked her. Maria had mentally braced herself for a verbal tirade from the psychiatrist about contacting the police, but none of these questions came. "You have not been to a doctor, then, to see if you had any substances in your system?" was all Dr Timms asked. It was as if he could read her mind just by staring into her eyes with one of his bushy grey eyebrows raised.

"No... like I said, I didn't see a doctor soon after. You see, I was in shock," Maria said, averting her gaze to the patterned carpet.

"It's not just the residue of the drugs in your system that I'm worried about. Often amnesia of this kind can be a symptom for something else, epilepsy, for example, or a tumour, even a stroke. I wouldn't be doing my job properly if I didn't insist you get your blood and urine tested and have an MRI done."

"An MRI?" Maria's face fell. This wasn't what she wanted. She just wanted the Regressive Recollection Therapy. "Can't I just pay for the therapy like a private patient?"

"Well, yes, you can. But what if there is an underlying problem? Don't you want to know? Just to be sure? I could lose my license if I didn't insist that you go. I can refer you privately for an MRI."

"I don't have the money for that," Maria said.

"You could see your GP. They will be able to refer you."

Maria weighed up her options. "It could take some time," Maria said. "Suppose we start with the therapy and I see my doctor in the meantime to schedule the appointments. Would that work?"

Dr Timms pursed his lips. "You will see your doctor this week?"

"Yes," Maria said, hoping she would not be able to get an appointment. But she supposed the doctor was right. It would be better if she had all the tests done. Maria knew that she didn't have to say anything to her GP about the emails or the call from her fictitious brother. All she needed to say was that she had blacked out and was experiencing terrible headaches. She had seen it done on TV before and, in any case, her doctor was a pushover.

"So that's agreed," Dr Timms said, making some notes. "If there are no underlying medical issues then drugs may have had something to do with your memory loss. Benzodiazepines and anticholinergics are possibilities. After all, you say the last thing you remember was being at work. If it was an abduction, drugs could have been used. If they have, then it is unlikely that this therapy will work. Your memories will take a significantly longer time to resurface or, I have to warn you, may never return."

Maria was silent. She needed to mention the flashbacks, but the words would not form in her mouth.

"You think I can help you remember." It was a statement rather than a question. Not waiting for a reply, he continued. "Fugue amnesia, if that is what it is, is a very rare form of memory loss. It normally returns fairly soon, a couple of days later," he paused, reaching for the glass of cloudy lemonade on his desk. Taking a sip, he said, "If you were not drugged, your brain clearly does not wish to recall this event. The days that you talk about are the only period in time that you cannot remember." Dr Timms put his pen down and looked at Maria. After a moment's silence, he continued, "As you said when you arrived, you have sought me out because you have read an article online about my Regressive Recollection Therapy work with some of my patients. But it is not as simple as we have come to find out." He gave Maria a look she could not read. Was he angry with her? Couldn't he see he was her only hope?

Dr Timms' gaze turned sympathetic. "I am happy to help you talk through any of your problems," he said. Maria felt a warmth rising up from her chest. Did he too think she was making it up?

"I've had a flashback," she blurted out in her defence, a little louder than she had meant.

Dr Timms smiled at her gently. "Sometimes we make up memories when we do not remember. It's called confabulation. We find it difficult to have gaps in our memory, you see. If you are lucky, you will remember when you are more capable of coping. We must not drag it out of you kicking and screaming, so to speak. The truth sometimes—the things that we hide from ourselves—we do so for a reason."

Dr Timms agreed to treat her on the condition that she made an appointment for an MRI and provided him with the results within the first three sessions. Once that was settled, he asked Maria questions about her family. He wanted to know what memories sprang to mind when she thought of her upbringing. At first Maria was uncomfortable, finding the questions intrusive and irrelevant, even though she had read about Dr Timms' *modus operandi*. She answered him, looking back into her idyllic childhood. She remembered playing hide and seek in the garden with Alice and Leanne; going on Easter egg hunts, which Alice would always win; and her favourite memory of all: Alice plaiting Maria's hair on a Saturday afternoon. With these memories, Maria began to relax. She had nothing to hide. But, after she had answered his initial tirade of questions, a silence ensued.

Maria wanted to fill the void with words and so she did. She elaborated on her childhood. Told him stories of Alice, Leanne and herself. Since Owen, Maria had become withdrawn, so much so that the session with Dr Timms took her by surprise. She enjoyed talking about the person she was. The person she was before Owen. Not before long, Maria was closing the royal blue door behind her. To her dismay the empty feeling in the pit of her stomach returned as the door clicked shut. The truth was still far out of her grasp.

A cold sharp wind brushed passed Maria. It sent a short shiver down her spine as she stepped out onto the empty pavement. Something in the recess of her mind was reaching out to her. She squeezed her eyes tightly wanting to remember, trying to reach out to this glimmer of a memory. But too late, it had gone. She opened her eyes and started towards her apartment.

18

"So, ladies and gentlemen, what did you think? Didn't I say that some of you would be racing to get to the end?" Lawrence ran his hand through his thick dark hair before placing it back in his suit pocket. He looked directly at Maria with his green eyes. She caught his gaze and her heart froze. Quickly she altered her posture, opening herself to Oliver.

"Oliver Sanderson, tell me, what did you think of *The Sinner*? Was it a good read?" Lawrence asked. Maria suppressed her shock. She needed to stay alert.

"Well, I'm not sure the book was descriptive enough for me. I could picture the rooms vividly. Rupert perfectly described the dishevelled bed, the green hue of the record store beneath Diana's apartment, the sirens blaring outside and the prostitutes that stood on the street corners looking for some trade. From the description itself, I was transported to the scene. It was like I was there with Diana. I could even see what her attacker was wearing as if he were standing in front of me," Oliver paused for effect. "But to me it didn't contain, or should I say, portray the true emotion of the victim or the thoughts of her attacker. I didn't exactly feel what Diana went through, and I needed that for it to be a good book."

"It was very textbook," piped a voice from the back of the room, "an unsuccessful, lonely girl who was always trying to say the right thing to get some sort of recognition from her lecturer. It didn't really wash with me."

"Go on," Lawrence encouraged the voice.

"A psychopath on the loose, the author didn't have to think much. Rupert didn't have to create a real reason why the girls were taken. It was all excused by a mental deficiency. In my opinion, it's a cop out. Anything can be excused as psychosis; it should have had more depth to it."

Maria thought about her own attacker. Was it someone she knew? Just a madman on the loose? Or a stalker? Maria scanned the room but no eyes were on her.

"The author presumes that his reader is ignorant, so much so that he chooses not to provide a perpetrator with a motive to show that there's method to his madness," another voice said.

Jason opened his mouth to say something but stopped himself.

"Is it really possible?" Maria cleared her throat. "I don't think the plot is plausible. I mean, waking up in your own bed, nothing out of place, a convenient memory loss. A perfect crime, you could say." The words that Leanne had told Maria to say poured from her mouth. There was a moment's silence and Maria hoped that no one could tell that she was shaking with fear.

"Anything is possible," Lawrence said. "Clearly you were not a fan of the book." He tilted his head, looking at Maria inquisitively.

"I enjoyed the book," Penelope said, resting her arm on Jason's knee and looking over at her lover before turning back to Lawrence. "It was different to the other books we read and I think it could happen. There are psychotics out there and sometimes people don't have a motive. But if you read the book carefully, you'll notice that Rupert does not presume his reader ignorant. On the contrary, he allows us to explore the perpetrator's personal motives, albeit non-sensible reasons."

There was a pause in the discussion. Jason smiled at Penelope and she was grateful for his support. Since meeting Jason, she had come a long way. Her confidence within the book club was new. Stripping only gave her poise within the confines of Rustle, where she felt safe and in control. It was dark. The faces of her customers were obscure. In the bright lights of Café Du Jour, she normally felt exposed, but not today. Today she had Jason.

Penelope had still not told Jason her secret. There was something holding her back. Was it her old demons inspiring within her a fear of rejection? Feeling the warmth from Jason at her side, she began to gain confidence. Confidence to tell him what he had the right to know. Penelope returned Jason's smile with genuine affection.

Jason squeezed Penelope's knee, grateful for what she had said. He was smiling at her, but beneath his lips, his teeth were clenched. The choice of *The Sinner* was too much of a coincidence for his liking.

Lawrence clapped twice and looked at Penelope, a wry smile forming on his lips. "Yes, Penny," he said.

Penelope blushed, proud of the approval from the leader of the club.

"Well, I wanted to feel what was going through the victim and perp's minds, that would have made it a better book for me," Oliver said to Lawrence, removing his Fedora. Maria looked up and caught Jason's eye. He was staring through her, his face expressionless. There was something about his demeanour that told her he knew something. Jason looked away as Maria averted her gaze to the glass display of fresh crème patisseries in the corner of the café. When she looked back at him, he was sharing a joke with Penelope. Maria questioned her paranoia.

"Boo!" said Oliver, as he suddenly turned towards Maria.

Maria took a sharp intake of breath, looking at Oliver with wide, frightened eyes. She could hear Lawrence talking about *The Sinner* in the background.

"You okay?" Oliver asked, his brow furrowed, "You look like you've seen a ghost. It was only me!" he said, playfully punching her shoulder.

Maria flashed a fake smile at him. "I'm tired," she said, resting her head on his shoulder.

Oliver squeezed her arm for reassurance and kissed her on her head as Lawrence wrapped up the session.

"Well done," Lawrence continued. "You're all correct, of course. There is no right or wrong answer. But I like Penny's thinking..."

Maria stopped listening, not sure of what to make of the last hour. She had hoped it would have shed some light on her situation, but instead she was more in the dark than ever.

"It was okay. Not my cup of tea. To be honest, I didn't finish it," Sunil had responded nonchalantly when Maria had asked him his opinion. Maria had wanted to talk to him. She wanted to be close to him. But something held her back. Was it fear? Or was it because Sunil seemed so distant? Like he didn't care. Did he not feel a tingle every time he was close to her?

Maria's mind began to wonder about the new friends sitting around her. Why did Penelope jump in to defend the author? Was it to protect Jason, who looked so angered with the book choice? And why did Lawrence give her that chilling look at the beginning of the session. What did Lawrence mean when he said that some people must have been racing to finish the book? Maria couldn't help but think that one of her friends knew more than they were letting on.

★

As the book club drew to a close and the members dispersed, Maria felt her phone vibrate. She wondered how long Leanne was going to keep checking up on her like this. Maria flipped open her phone. The blue light reflected on her face as she glanced at the message. It was Alice. Instantly her stomach muscles started to tighten. Anxiety had her in its grasp as she read the words on the screen:

I'm glad you texted. Let's meet up Friday evening.
7.30 p.m. @ The Braunstone Bar
Alice XX

Maria cast her mind back to when she last sent Alice a message. She could not remember. Glued to the spot, the book club members walked out around her. Maria scrolled through her sent items; a message had been sent from her phone only yesterday. Maria took a deep breath as she scanned Du Jour—for what? She did not know. She thought back to what Dr Timms told her: "Think rationally when you feel like paranoia is taking over. Think of the most logical explanation." Maria took a couple of deep breaths to shake off her suspicions. Of course, she reasoned, she must have sent the message—she had remembered typing it, after all. Maria knew that all her typed messages were saved as drafts in her phone and that she must have hit the send button yesterday when she was sending a message to Penelope. Maria's heartbeat resumed its normal pace as she silently thanked Dr Timms for his rational tip. "It is natural," he had said, "to be jumpy after what has happened." Maria wanted to fall to the floor and cry for the person she had become as a result of her ordeal, but she knew that she had to be strong in front of her friends. She would have to wait until she was behind closed doors.

Content that she had sent the message to Alice herself, Maria headed over to Lawrence. He was sitting in the corner of the coffee shop scribbling furiously on a pad of paper.

"I was wondering if I could have a word…" Maria trailed off.

"Yes…" Lawrence said, pushing his hair back with his hand. He was mindful that the woman in front of him could have been one of those know-it-alls who was too scared to speak up in front of the group but still insisted on having her opinion heard. Whilst he usually had the time for people like that, today he certainly did not. A new idea for his manuscript had formed in his mind. He was rapidly trying to note it down, before it vanished.

"Maria. It's Maria." She noted his hesitation and quickly added, "I won't take up much of your time, really. It's just a quick question."

Lawrence pointed towards the seat next to him and sat back in his chair, taking a sip of his black coffee.

"I was curious as to who recommended *The Sinner*" she asked politely.

"Why do you want to know?" He looked directly at Maria without blinking.

Maria was taken aback. She did not expect him to be so direct. She weighed up her options. "I have been having some issues, you see. A friend had a similar thing happen and, well, I was wondering who recommended it," Maria said, trying to sound vague.

Lawrence gave her a quizzical look, "Wasn't it you who said that the plotline was non-sensicle?"

"Mmm…" Maria stammered, "I didn't believe my friend. I don't think the story added up. But after the debate today, I think I should give her the benefit of the doubt."

Lawrence gave her an inquisitive look. "Good friend, then?"

Maria looked at her shoes.

"Maria, look, whatever problems you or your friend have are your business, but I would certainly go straight to the police. You can't start pointing the finger at anyone who has read this novel. Yes, copycats exist, but what are the chances? I don't see what you'll gain by me telling you the connection. Who's your friend?"

"Oh, no one you know. And it happened years ago," she said, backtracking. Maria crossed her fingers in her pocket and looked dejected. She needed to know who recommended the book.

"The recommendation, if you need to know so badly..." he trailed off before adding, "Well, look here." Lawrence lifted some A4 sheets off the table and revealed a thickly bound, dark brown leather diary. Disdainfully, he opened it to last month's date.

Maria could see that someone had written across a page of notes in blue biro: "*The Sinner* by J Rupert." Lawrence snapped the book shut as Maria was absorbing the words, noting the handwriting.

"I make notes for my manuscript on diary dates. It's my method, I suppose. I didn't take kindly to this. But I have been extremely busy and last month was a tough one for me. Everyone around me knew that. I was struggling for a choice and quite frankly this came at the right time." Lawrence's tone was gentle but firm.

Maria took a deep breath. This was not the answer she was expecting. "I thought the person who recommended it to you also gave you a synopsis?" She conveyed her disappointment with a sigh.

Lawrence's voice softened. "Don't share this with the rest of the group, but I lied. Look, I love reading. I have recommended some books and I'm sure you would agree with that. It's just that I don't make much money from this club and, although books are my real passion, I've been snowed under lately, especially last month. This recommendation was a bit of a godsend, to tell you the truth. I will personally recommend the next one. That's a promise." He patted her arm.

"Oh, yeah, okay," Maria said, deflated. If Lawrence was telling the truth then *The Sinner* could have been recommended by anyone.

By anyone who knew she attended the group regularly. It was a dead end, but at least she had asked the question. She stood up and gave him an artificial smile.

"Can this stay between us? I don't want the other members…" Lawrence started, but Maria cut him off.

"Sure. Don't worry," she said genuinely. "Look, I don't suppose I could have that piece of paper…" Maria said, swallowing the disappointment rising in her throat. *Bricks, Bricks, Bricks.* The word returned to her. Maria closed her eyes. She could see flashes of a silk scarf as her hands were being tied, a silhouette in a kitchen, a hand with a leather band tied around it. Maria gasped. She could feel tiny beads of sweat forming on her back and forehead.

Lawrence eyed her suspiciously before ripping the note out of the brown leather book. "Sure, I don't need those notes anymore," he said, as he handed the torn page to her. "So what happened to your friend?" Lawrence asked.

"Huh?" Maria looked at Lawrence.

"Your friend who…"

"Oh, I'm not sure. I lost touch after a while. She never remembered what happened while I knew her."

"That's a shame!" Lawrence said as he turned back towards his notes, not quite believing the girl's story.

Maria shoved the piece of paper Lawrence had given her into her coat pocket. She then caught up with the rest of her friends who were waiting outside.

"What was that about?" Oliver asked as Maria stepped out on to the pavement, wrapping her red pashmina around her neck.

"Oh nothing, just a question about literature." Maria kept her eyes to the ground as they made their way towards Marconi's.

19

Oliver knocked back his garish cocktail. Only he and the bartender knew it didn't contain any alcohol. Sitting at the bar, he turned away from Jason. It had been nearly a month since Oliver had confronted him and nothing had changed since. Jason was lost in whiskey and showed no inkling in wanting to talk, so Oliver was left dwelling on his own life.

Oliver had realised he was gay just a few minutes before the rest of year eight realised it, and had subsequently endured their bullish taunts until he was eighteen. To avoid new phrases being coined about him, he vehemently denied his own sexuality. It did nothing to lessen the schoolboy jokes and the heckling from the boys in the year above. But Oliver thought that was his best strategy.

Puberty and his teenage hormones soon got the better of him and, at fourteen, he finally confronted his sexuality. It was only a kiss. Clichéd, it happened behind the bike sheds at school with a boy called Ray. Ray's parents were stuck in the sixties. They were all for free love and celebrated their only son's sexuality. Of course, he too got picked on, but he let it wash over him. It didn't seem to affect him at all and, because of this, the kids at school left him to his own devices. Oliver's parents certainly didn't know their son was gay and he didn't have the courage to tell them.

"I could tell a mile away you were like me," Ray had said to Oliver before kissing him directly on the lips. Oliver relaxed a little as Ray forced his tongue into his mouth. He was starting to enjoy the kiss until the boy with blue eyes and red cheeks pulled away and sniggered at him. "Langers would love to know about this," he said. Even now Oliver could remember the smirk plastered across Ray's face as he ran away laughing. Later Oliver had seen him behind the corner shop on the street that ran parallel from Oliver's home. Ray winked at him as Oliver walked home from school. As Ray leant against the red brick wall, lighting a cigarette, he caught Oliver staring at him and he smiled, a knowing smile that said it all. For the next year Oliver lived in fear that someone had seen them, or that Ray had decided to tell their peers, or worse still, tell the leader of the bullies, Langers. Oliver wouldn't have put it past him, but it seemed that Ray never did.

No sooner than school was behind him, Oliver started going to gay bars and finally began to understand himself. He loved college; it had given him his freedom, and now university had given him even more. One of Oliver's female friends at university agreed to sleep with him; he had wanted to be sure of his sexuality. And it was after this that Oliver had decided to tell his parents he was gay. In the back of his mind he was confident that they already knew. Since college, it was hard to miss his overexaggerated effeminate mannerisms, not to mention his increasing attention to fashion.

That evening, whilst having dinner with his parents, the words left his mouth. His knife and fork were poised over a leg of roast chicken and overcooked broccoli when he saw their crestfallen looks. Oliver couldn't remember what happened next. He knew he had tried his hardest to block it out since that day. What he did know was that he could never look at broccoli again. Now, whenever he was presented with the green, tree-like vegetable, it brought back the painful memory. He wanted to gag.

Oliver remembered fragments of that evening: there was some screaming and shouting. The words that stuck in his mind and hurt him the most were his father's: "You are no longer my son," he said, slamming the front door shut on Oliver. His mother wept as she sat huddled on the orange and brown carpet at the foot of the stairs. Mr Sanderson had given his son less than half an hour to pack his bags and leave.

The Sandersons had cut him out of the picture-perfect lifestyle they had spent their entire lives creating. And, with that, they had stopped his allowance. His mother, who Oliver suspected had known about his sexuality for a long time before that fateful dinner, called him occasionally, but they never mentioned that evening again.

Their conversations were laden with superfluous smalltalk about the weather, his media studies course and neighbours in the village.

Oliver had kept this painful part of his life a secret from his new friends. He had never told anyone about his parents' bigotism. He was simply too ashamed and hurt. He had moved a short distance from Great Bowden in Harborough to Leicester. He had built himself a new life and spent his time doing things he enjoyed doing. At the end of the day, Oliver had decided that it was *his* life and he had to live it *his* way. For the first couple of months he hoped and prayed every night that his parents would change their minds. Their disapproval haunted him like a ghost, following his every move, but they never did. It hadn't taken him long to realise that they never would.

When his parents cut him off financially, it had hurt him in the pocket as well, crippling his lifestyle and his addiction to shopping, one of only a handful of things that gave him five minutes of joy. But he was a survivor and, with this in mind, Oliver managed to avoid the black hole of depression that was drawing him in. He made sure he still kept on trend by spending most of his time on *eBay*. He had learned how to customise the most basic of high street fashion to suit his tastes.

Oliver had even started writing a column for a popular men's magazine, which paid some of his bills. The rest of his time, when he wasn't attending lectures, was spent looking for odd jobs that would earn him a bit of cash in hand. Oliver never let on about any of this to his new friends. He didn't want them to see him drinking water so he splashed out on mocktails. He knew deep down that his book club friends wouldn't care that he barely had two pennies to rub together, but every time he opened his mouth to tell Maria or Penelope, the words would just not come. After living most of his life behind a mask, being brought up thinking that appearances were everything, Oliver allowed the façade to continue.

Kerry, Oliver's first and last female conquest, had recently met up with him for lunch. She joined him at his table, and he was glad they were still such good friends. That day, sitting in front of him, she looked more like an all-American cheerleader who got straight A's than the punk rocker she had been when they had slept together. *That's university for you*, Oliver mused. *It allows you to express yourself any which way you fancy*. Oliver, who was considered a geek back home, now had the status of the campus fashionista and everyone wanted to be his friend. Oliver laughed, thinking of the hundreds of students arriving every year, shedding the skin of the past lives and being who they really wanted to be. Who they really were.

Kerry was now working in postgraduate admissions. She had been the one to tell him the news about Jason and Eleanor, and he had kept this information hidden for weeks before taunting Jason with it. But now he felt guilty that he had taunted his friend so badly. He knew he was no better than a school bully.

Looking at Jason's desperate state, Oliver wondered what he should do next. He had initially meant to scare him into going back to his family, to leave Penelope alone and unharmed. But that did not look likely with two semesters of his course left to run. And from the way Penelope looked at Jason, Oliver could tell that the damage had already been done. Oliver thought about the power he held in this situation. He had meddled in family affairs before and it had not come to any good. Oliver himself would not have liked it if someone else had told his parents about his sexuality before he did. So what gave him the right? Oliver weighed up his options, remembering his own torment at school as he fiddled with the cocktail umbrella in his empty glass. Oliver put his arm on Jason's back, wanting to apologise.

Jason turned towards him, his breath foul with alcohol. Oliver was about to say something comforting but something stopped him. Something held back his words. Oliver simply stood up and left.

20

Lawrence replaced the blue cap on his pen and set it on top of his manuscript. He was curious as to why Maria was so interested in his recent book selection. He hadn't wanted to give his secret away but Maria had pushed him, especially with that story of hers.

Lawrence didn't know why he had taken over the job of running the book club from Stuart in the first place. He had neither the time nor the inclination to really get involved, but it had served a purpose. Then a smile formed on his lips. Of course, now there was a reason for sticking around because now there was the Siren.

Rarely did Lawrence ever fall in love. In fact, before his encounter with the woman of his dreams, Lawrence would have said he had never experienced love. He had a phone full of numbers that girls had taken the liberty to store in his mobile, but never once did he feel a connection. This girl was different. The vision of beauty had sashayed over to him in something short, legs on show, but it wasn't just her looks that had attracted him to her. As he started talking to her, he realised just how much they had in common. Even though he never believed in love at first sight, he quickly changed his mind. She was elusive, like something out of Greek mythology, and for all he knew, dangerous for him as well. He nicknamed her the Siren.

The Siren disappeared from his life no sooner than she arrived. Fair enough—it had been a one-night stand fuelled by alcohol. But she had been the one to approach him. And she was the one who placed her hand flirtatiously on his thigh, whispering into his ear. He had taken her back to his apartment and she allowed him to undress her. As he undid the last button on her white silk chemise, it fell to the floor. He savoured each moment they shared together. To Lawrence, the whole experience was close to perfection. He had foolishly assumed that the feelings were mutual. But the Siren had thought differently. She had woken the next morning rather sheepishly and, after swallowing down a mug of coffee, she had left. The night was etched in Lawrence's mind and he continued to go back to the club in which he met her, hoping that he could speak with her again. He had no luck. Just as he was about to give up she had casually walked into Du Jour one Tuesday evening and signed up to his book club.

But at the book club, the Siren had time only for her friends. She didn't seem to give Lawrence a second glance or even remember her rendezvous with him. Never before had this happened to him. For once he was stunned into silence. Usually he was the one to turn away advances from women, and this made him want this object of affection even more. Each meeting, he vowed to speak to her before the finish, but she was always surrounded by people. Life got in the way and soon months had passed without an intimate word said between them. Lawrence knew he had missed his chance. As the Siren's friendship group closed in around her, Lawrence couldn't find a way in.

★

"What a day!" Jason said sinking into Penelope's sofa. He rolled his neck from side to side trying to loosen some of the tension in his shoulders.

"Did you get that piece of coursework in on time?" Penelope asked.

"Strategic Business Management? Glad to see the back of it."

"It's over now. I've hardly seen you the last couple of days," Penelope sulked. The hairs on the back of her arms stood on end as Jason brushed his hand passed her. She loved that she still felt that way about him.

"A two-thousand word essay in forty-eight hours is a bit time consuming, don't ya think?" Jason lied. He had finished his assignment weeks ago, but he had needed the last two days to figure out how he was going to tell Penelope about his wife. He was sure that if he didn't tell Penelope soon, Oliver certainly would. He had planned to tell her tonight.

"I guess," Penelope said, walking over to the sofa. She stopped behind him and, handing him a large glass of Merlot, started massaging his shoulders. "You are tense," she said, kneading away with both her hands on his left shoulder. "I need you to be all relaxed this evening. I've cooked."

"It smells like lamb." Jason turned his head towards her to kiss her on the cheek. He unclenched his fist realising just how stressed he was, and let out a deep sigh as sadness wormed its way inside him. Tonight he was going to break Penelope's heart.

"Not just any lamb. Lamb shanks. Your fave." Penelope smiled. She had left her lab early especially to prepare this meal.

"What's the occasion?"

"Just."

"I could get used to this." Jason flashed her a smile as he tried to ignore the picture of Eleanor that was forming in his mind. But the image of Eleanor was vivid. It was almost as if she was standing in their front room, wearing his white shirt, holding a roasting pan out for him to inspect. He remembered the smoke rising out of the charred piece of meat his wife had tried to cook. Eleanor had never been good in the kitchen, but she always tried and Jason had always pretended to love anything she attempted to make. They had ended up getting takeout that evening.

"What's the matter?" Penelope's voice brought Jason back to reality. "You look like you're in a world of your own."

Jason's smile quickly faded. He lifted himself from the sofa and reassuringly put his arms around Penelope. "I love you," he whispered. The words slipped out. He was not sure if he even meant them or if he had mistaken Penelope for Eleanor. The words took him by surprise. Of course he cared a great deal for Penelope, but did he love her? Even if he did, he knew he had to let Penelope go if he was going to return to his wife. And he would have to return to his wife. After all, they had history. They had a son together.

Jason wondered if there was a way to retract those three little words. He couldn't think of anything. How, now, could he now tell Penelope about Eleanor?

"I love you too," Penelope said, increasing her grip around Jason. She knew these three words were a sign, a sign that this was the right time to tell him. Penelope pulled away from Jason and looked up into his deep blue eyes. She ran her hand through his fine blond hair.

"I'm pregnant," she said, unable to hide her secret even for just one second longer. Penelope looked expectantly at Jason, but he was silent.

He looked into her eyes desperately searching for something that would tell him that she was joking.

Penelope squeezed his shoulders. "Say something!" she beamed at him. All Jason found in her eyes was love.

"Wow, I mean, wow. This is some news." Jason swallowed back his fear, trying to think of something positive to say. Confusion clouded his mind. "Mmm… in fact it's great news. How pregnant are you? I mean, how far along are you?" His breathing had quickened. Releasing Penelope, he let his body drop to the security of the sofa.

"Eight weeks. The doctor confirmed it."

Jason looked at Penny, disillusioned. "Oh!" was all he could manage. He couldn't help but wonder what was going through Penelope's mind.

"I know it's a shock. It's not like we were planning it." Penelope took Jason's hand and placed it on her belly. They both looked down towards their unborn child. Fear nestled itself within Jason. *Would she keep it?* Jason wondered. Of course she would. Penelope looked up at Jason as if all her dreams had come true. But then he saw apprehension creeping into her eyes.

"I haven't dared tell my parents yet. They would kill me," Penelope said, drawing him close to her, mistaking his fear for shock. "I am so happy, Jason. First I was scared, but now I know this is special." She looked at him for reassurance but he provided none. "This is going to be an amazing experience for us both," Penelope said out loud to calm her rapidly beating heart.

Jason looked at her, not knowing where to begin. "Look Penny, there are things we should talk about."

But Penelope placed a finger on his lips, scared of what he was about to say. She wanted the evening to be perfect. "Not now," she scolded gently. "We have tomorrow to talk. Of course, there are a lot of things to consider." She stroked his cheek and took his hand leading him to the table that she had set. "But tonight, let's celebrate."

21

"I feel sick."

"It's nerves, you'll be fine."

"I haven't seen her in so long. What if we have nothing to say to each other?"

"You'll have something to say," Leanne reassured Maria and stroked her hair.

"I wouldn't even have agreed to meet her if that terrible incident hadn't happened. When something life threatening happens, you realise how important family is."

Leanne knew more than anyone how Maria felt.

"But…"

"But what? It's been two years. Not that much time has passed between you. The damage is repairable. I promise. At least you have that second chance with your sister." Leanne walked over to the window and drew back the thick blue curtains, allowing the last of the evening light into the apartment. "I just know she wants you back in her life. Alice adored you."

"What if she's still with him? I won't know what to say then," Maria said.

"She's your little sister—blood is thicker than water. If they're still together, and I don't mean to sound harsh here, you'll just have to get over it." Leanne paused. "I mean, have you ever thought for just one second that maybe they're better suited?" Leanne closed one eye and winced as the words left her mouth. She waited to feel Maria's wrath. Nothing. She walked over to the window. Leanne had never liked Owen much. Yes, he had fawned all over Maria, but there were things about him that bugged her. With just one look, Owen could make Maria feel guilty when she didn't do what he wanted her to do. Maria would never have wanted to go to a car show when there was an offer of a girly spa day on the table. Maria's behaviour since she started dating Owen just didn't add up. On the one hand Leanne thought Owen was manipulative and controlling, but on the other hand he seemed so caring towards her friend. Leanne was undecided. After all, her taste in men was far from desirable. But there was something about him that she couldn't quite put her finger on. Leanne looked at her friend. Maria was standing in front of the mirror fiddling with her tan, mock-crocodile belt.

"Do I look fat in this?" Maria asked.

Leanne rolled her eyes. She walked over, adjusted her friend's belt and placed her hand on her shoulder. "I was looking through an old photo album the other day."

"Yeah?"

"You had that crazy leopard-print hair and you were wearing shoulder pads and neon, like an eighties reject. And I found pictures of our A-level ball. I completely forgot about your born-to-be-bad look. You were not worried about looking fat then!"

Maria blushed and shook her head. "That was then. I would never wear something like that now or do crazy things to my hair."

"No, you wouldn't," Leanne thought. She missed the old Maria, the Maria who stayed up late, stole alcohol from her parents' cupboard and dressed up like an extra from a music video. But that was Maria before Owen. Maria before the antidepressants.

Leanne sighed as she watched her friend apply blusher. One day she would get her old friend back and she was certain that Alice could help. "It was awful what Owen did. He's an absolute ass and deserves the worst. What they did *will* stay with you forever, but remember: Alice never knew. She still doesn't know. So it's not her fault."

★

Maria had been intentionally late. More than ever she had hated the dark evenings that November brought but she still didn't want to be the first to arrive. Wondering over to the bar, she had started to order a small glass of pinot grigio when she heard a familiar voice.

"Wait, Maria, I've got us a bottle."

A glass was never enough for Alice. Maria and Alice were almost complete opposites yet Owen had loved them both. No. He had never loved Maria. Owen would never have acted that way if he had loved her.

Maria turned to face her sister. Alice looked like she had lost even more weight since they had bumped into each other, before the incident. It didn't suit her one bit. Alice had lost her healthy glow. The dark circles under her sister's eyes were apparent no matter how much concealer she wore. Maria didn't say anything. They were strangers now.

Maria walked over to the table where Alice, just moments ago, was frantically waving at her. She sat down, taking in the bare brick walls that seemed to be taking over Leicester. A shiver ran down her spine. Maria straightened her back and looked towards the bottle of wine between them. She was scared to make eye contact. There was so much to say and she didn't really know where to begin. Maria opened her mouth to speak but was interrupted by a waiter who approached their table.

"Can I get you ladies anything?" He pulled out a chair from their table and swivelled it around. Lifting his leg over the seat, he sat down like a long lost friend. Pulling out a notepad and pen he awaited a response.

"No thanks," Alice offered with a frown. Maria could see her sister's annoyance. No matter how hard Alice tried to conceal her true feelings, her face always gave them away. But Maria was glad that the waiter had broken that awkward silence between them.

"Olives?" Maria asked, wanting to prolong his stay at their table.

"Certainly," the young waiter replied, but he did not hang around. He rose to his feet and shuffled the chair back into its original position. As he left the table, he winked at Alice. Maria eyed her sister. Even with Alice's gaunt look and obvious irritation, she was still the girl that men preferred. *When had Alice stepped out of Maria's shadow? And when had Maria stepped beneath hers?*

The quiet quickly returned to their table. "I've missed you," Alice broke the silence as she sipped the pale liquid in her glass.

Maria hesitated. She ran her finger along the condensation on her glass. She too missed Alice, especially after all that had happened. Tears began to prick the back of her eyes. She focused on a tiny scratch on her sisters wine glass and managed to blink them away. The waiter came over to where they were sitting and placed the olives down on the table. His scent was familiar. Maria closed her eyes. Something was lurking in her mind, a memory of what happened *that* weekend. *Had she been in this bar? Had the waiter been involved?* She tried to remember but the memory was buried too deep and she couldn't quite reach it.

"Are you okay?" Alice asked.

Maria's eyes were tightly shut. She opened her lids. The waiter had gone. "Sorry. I'm fine." Maria shrugged away any remnants of the memory, trying, with some difficulty, to concentrate on the present. She glanced over at the waiter. She didn't recognize him and he seemed completely uninterested in their table. Maria looked back at Alice's concerned look. Leanne was right. Alice didn't know what had happened when Owen had left her. Maria didn't have the right to be that angry with her. But Alice did go off with her boyfriend when the wounds were still raw. She had known how much Maria loved Owen. She must have known that Maria had wanted to spend the rest of her life with him, yet Alice had to have her way. What Alice wanted, Alice somehow always managed to get. *Could she forgive her for that?*

"I've missed you too," Maria said, still unsure if it was the right thing to say. But once she said it, Maria felt a strange sense of relief. Of course it had been the right thing to say and she had meant it. Just saying those words made Maria realise that she missed Alice more than she had thought. Maria reached her hand out across the table to finally feel the warmth of her sister's touch. They spoke at length about this and that, until an unsettling thought crept up on Maria. *Had Alice been the only one to blame in their divide?*

They had drifted apart that fateful year and if Maria was honest with herself she could not solely blame Alice for the distance between them. Maria had been the one to purposefully drive a wedge between them because she didn't want Alice to find out her secret. Although, on looking back, Maria was certain that Alice would have given her full support. Maria touched her brow. *Had she cut Alice out because she was ashamed?*

Maria knew that Alice was so much closer to their parents and she was certain that Alice would have told them her shame. Maria, although a little wild, was still the older, more sensible one. Alice looked up to her. It was never the other way around. But now Maria knew that, in trying to protect herself all those years ago, she had excluded her little sister from her life. So perhaps she had been the one to break the bond. Maria didn't want Alice to have the upper hand and yet now somehow she did.

Then, as the thought crossed Maria's mind, she noticed it. Sparkling under the spotlight above their table. It sat behind Alice's glass.

"I wanted to tell you sooner," Alice said, registering the direction of Maria's gaze and her look of utter horror.

"But..."

"The way things were between us. I couldn't. Not through a note or over the phone. It wouldn't have been right. I wanted to do it in person."

"So it's *him*?"

"Yes."

"Do you really hate me that much?" Maria asked.

"No. You can't think like that. How could you even ask me that?"

"How could *I* ask you that? You could have taken it off. My gosh, Alice, this is the first time we've arranged to meet in two years and I..." Maria trailed off, stuck for words. Her heart was racing and she could feel her head start to throb, but she did not want to cry in front of her sister. She quickly stood up and, taking a deep breath, started towards the door.

Alice too rose to her feet, with tears in her eyes. "You can't leave now. We need to talk," she said, grabbing her sister's arm with some strength.

"I'll be back; I just need some fresh air," Maria said, unable to think of anything else to say. She had no intention of returning.

Outside Maria was ready to get into a taxi back to her apartment. But with the rain beginning to fall, none of the black cabs had their lights on. Maria took shelter from the fat raindrops under the awning of the bar, turning her back towards the smokers who had gathered outside. She immediately took her phone out of her bag, dialled Leanne's number and quickly explained her predicament.

"Get back in there, Maria," Leanne scolded her friend, reminding her of the pact they had made when they were growing up: "Friends forever." *They said nothing would come between them.*

"I don't know if I can face her. I don't know if I can take it. How would you like it if your sister…"

"Don't!" Leanne screamed, remembering her sister's limp body lying in the bath. But it was too late, the words were already out.

"I'm sorry, Lea. I didn't mean…"

"Leave it, Maria." A cold silence followed. Leanne had been thinking of her sister quite a bit lately, given all that Maria was going through. She missed her. How could Maria be so insensitive? Leanne took a deep breath. She knew deep down that Maria had not meant what she had said. Alice and Maria had been so good to her when it happened. They had included her in their sisterhood and she never felt alone with them around. Now it was her turn to be there for them. Leanne had been the one who sent the message to Alice from Maria's phone. That had been the easy part. Now all she had to do was to get them to talk. She had promised Alice she would try. "Listen to me, Maria. If I had my sister back, I wouldn't let something like this keep us apart. You have to go back in there. Do you want another year of not talking to your sister? You don't want to lose her *this* way. You said it yourself earlier—your abduction made you realise." Leanne paused. "Remember, you need to hear her side of the story as well."

"What other side can there be?" Maria said, swallowing her shame. "He dumped me when I was at my lowest, a time when he should have been looking after me. Not throwing me to the side like a bit of rubbish. She knew I was hurting and just started dating him like I didn't matter."

"Fine, then, you know what? Walk away, get on a bus and go home. But this will bother you for the rest of your life." Leanne paused, knowing that her friend was about to make a huge mistake. She tried once more. "If you go back in there and hear what she has to say and still decide that you want to cut her out of your life, well, that's your decision. And it would be fair, because at least you would have taken the time to hear her out."

Silence ensued. Leanne wanted to say something more convincing but stopped herself.

"Okay, then. Half an hour, tops," Maria said.

Leanne breathed a sigh of relief before adding one last remark, "And Maria. If she doesn't know, maybe you should tell her."

22

"I need the money this week..." Sunil held his BlackBerry close to his ear. "You owe me." He looked up and saw Oliver standing in line, waiting to pay for his coffee. Sunil lowered his voice. "Yes... yes... Omar, haven't you done enough?" he said. "This was your fault. At least let me have the money... remember, you got out of this scot free. I get left with the fallout." Sunil paused as he glanced around the coffee shop, making sure that Oliver was not within earshot. Fiddling with his silver ring, he whispered into the phone, "No one is blackmailing you here. I need the money sooner rather than later so I can get out of this." Oliver was walking over to him. Pressing the red button on his phone, Sunil quickly placed it on the table as his friend threw a raspberry and oat bran muffin at him. Sunil caught it and pulled off a piece of the cake, popping it into his dry mouth. He swallowed it down with a gulp of tea.

"Money troubles?" Oliver asked. "You know, I know a guy who knows a guy."

"No!" Sunil said abruptly. He raised his eyebrows, wondering if Oliver had above average hearing abilities.

Sunil's niggle about Oliver returned. The girls certainly adored him and he was very thoughtful, but he seemed to revel in other people's misfortune. Oliver was always needling people for information they didn't really want to part with. As the niggle began to grow, a feeling of guilt began to creep up on Sunil. Who was he to criticise Oliver? It was Oliver who had been so kind to him when he had first stumbled into Sunil's music shop. Before Oliver had come along, Sunil had few socialising opportunities outside of work; but then again, maybe his life would have been less complicated.

Sunil caught a genuine look of concern in his friend's eyes and immediately scolded himself for being so easily irritated. He was the one with the problem, not Oliver. The shop and its slow progress had started to wear down on him, not to mention his other problems. He should have known better than to take it out on a friend.

"You know what families are like," Sunil added, taking a sip of tea. "Anyway, how have you been?" he asked Oliver, trying to steer the conversation in a different direction.

"Well, the parents have finally come around, and, more importantly, they've just given me a cheque to cover this semester's food, lodging and what I really needed: a clothing allowance!"

"You can offer to get Penny a drink, then," Sunil said.

Oliver looked up to see Penelope walking over to where they were sitting. He tipped his fedora at her and adjusted his snood.

"Hello!" Penelope said, beaming at her friends. "Leicester is so small!" she said. "I ran into Maria the other morning and now you two."

"Maria? I thought she worked most mornings?" Sunil questioned.

Penelope shrugged.

Sunil needed to talk to Maria and soon. "How is Maria?" he added casually.

"Good," Penelope bit her lip and looked at Sunil before adding, "A little distant, if I am honest."

"Distant?" Sunil asked with a curious look. "Why do you say that?"

"She passed it off as being tired, but I don't know. She doesn't seem herself. Maybe you should take her out sometime." Penelope winked at Sunil and then looked towards Oliver.

"What's this?" Oliver asked.

"Nothing!" Penelope said, laughing. "You're so nosey, Ollie. I'm just teasing."

Oliver looked at Sunil from the corner of his eye before turning his attention back to Penelope. He was about to say something but Penelope spoke first: "I'm meeting Jason in front of the market in about fifteen minutes." She looked at her watch. "But I really could do with a slice of fudge cake."

"Meeting Jason?" Sunil questioned. It was Sunil's turn to tease her now.

Oliver grunted.

"Well, we've decided to kind of let everyone know," Penelope said, blushing.

Oliver looked at her incredulously, his mouth gaping wide open.

Penelope hoped that she was doing the right thing. Jason was still reluctant to tell people about their relationship but, given their situation, she was going to be making more of the decisions. She couldn't see a valid reason why they should keep their relationship a secret. Jason was so vague as to why he didn't want people to know. These were her friends, Penelope reasoned, and she was carrying his child. They would all find out soon enough.

"Are you serious?" Oliver asked, his fists clenched in his pockets. Did Jason have no conscious at all? How much humiliation did he want Penelope to go through when the truth surfaced?

"Know what?" Sunil gave her his full attention now.

"Jason and I, well, we're kind of a couple now," Penelope said hesitantly, twisting a strand of blond hair in her fingers.

"I would never have guessed!" Sunil said with a touch of sarcasm.

Penelope smiled.

"Congratulations," Sunil said, raising his empty cup to her and shifting to his feet. "Let me get you that cake. Ollie, what did you want?"

"I'll get these," said Oliver reluctantly.

"Don't worry, you can get some next time," Sunil said, knowing that even with a cheque from his parents, Oliver would be struggling.

Oliver didn't push the matter; he just told Sunil what he wanted to drink.

Sunil returned with a tray of teas and a slice of chocolate fudge cake with a scoop of vanilla ice cream.

"So what are you and Jason getting up to today?"

"Oh, not much. Shopping, I guess," she said, leaving out the fact they had an appointment with her nurse in about an hour. Sunil shared a smile with Penelope. At least she had found happiness. Sunil felt empty inside. The three of them engaged in a brief conversation while Penelope ate her cake. Sunil's thoughts began to drift.

He started to think about his problem, which occupied most of his thoughts these days.

"Bye," Sunil heard himself say, as Penelope rose to her feet and headed for the door.

"Are you sure you are okay?" Oliver asked. "You seem a little spaced out."

"I guess. There's a lot going on with the business, you know, teething problems." Sunil pulled off the silver ring that his brother had given him and rubbed it between his first finger and thumb. How had he gotten himself into this mess?

"Business and me are worlds apart," Oliver said.

"I'm moving as well, which is more stressful than I thought."

"Not happy on Victoria Road?"

"I wanted to be close to the centre."

"Where are you moving? Do we get an invite for a house warming?"

Sunil was stupid to have mentioned the move to the biggest gossip he knew. "The loft apartments in the Cultural Quarter," he said.

"The ones with the swimming pool and gym? I think you've found a new best friend," Oliver grinned.

"No, the other ones. The King's View."

"Oh, I see. That's Maria's block," Oliver said with a frown.

"There isn't much else about. Leicester's a small town."

Oliver raised an eyebrow. "Leicester centre is inundated with converted apartments. I could name five this second."

"What are you getting at, Ollie?" Sunil asked. His patience was wearing thin.

"Nothing. Just saying, that's all. No need to be all defensive."

"I didn't even know Maria lived at King's View. But now I do, I'll make sure I look her up," Sunil said.

"I'm sure you will!" Oliver said, grinning.

Sunil smiled with relief. So that's what Oliver was getting at. Sunil took another sip of tea, avoiding Oliver's eyes.

23

"You just missed Si," Oliver said to Lawrence as he made his way over to the sofa.

"Si? Who's Si?" Lawrence asked.

"You know, Sunil, from the book club." Oliver noted Lawrence's disinterest and lack of recognition. "That guy I was telling you about," Oliver tried again, frustrated.

Lawrence frowned in a show of trying to remember.

"Oh, never mind," Oliver said.

"Speaking of the book club, that girl, what's her name? Marcia? Marni?"

"Maria, Lawrence. Get to know my friends, at least." Oliver rolled his eyes at his cousin.

"Yes. That's it. She stopped me the other day after our meeting and asked me who recommended *The Sinner*. She had some ludicrous story, it was very bizarre."

"Really?" Oliver asked as his interest piqued. "Well, she has been acting a little different lately. What did you say to her?" Oliver asked, with his eyes fixated on his second coffee of the day.

"The truth, Ollie, the truth. Some blighter writing all over my notes like that."

"*The Sinner*. Good choice, Lawrence. Very different to anything the group has read before. Much more innovative than Stuart last year," Oliver said, before asking what Maria's story was.

"Mmm, the characters could have done with a bit more depth to them," Lawrence said, ignoring Oliver's last question. He knew what his cousin could be like and there was something about Maria that told him she was vulnerable. He decided not to repeat what Maria had said.

"The farfetched story, Loz. What was it?"

"Something about a friend living in the same town as Diane at the time *The Sinner* was written."

"Huh? That doesn't make sense," Oliver said.

"See, I told you it was something stupid."

Oliver looked at his cousin. Was he lying to him?

Lawrence turned to face Oliver with his kind eyes and sincere smile.

Of course Lawrence wouldn't lie to him. He had no reason to. "Any ideas who recommended it?" Oliver tried.

"No."

"Well, it got your attention. It was almost like somebody knew you needed some inspiration." Oliver looked at Lawrence from the corner of his eye but his cousin's gaze was fixated elsewhere.

Lawrence opened his mouth to say something but hesitated. "It wasn't you was it, cuz? You're the only person with access to my notes."

"Don't be daft. Why would't I just tell you my recommendation? Anyway, it's not my kind of book. You know that." Oliver fiddled with his scarf, "And, excuse me, quite a few people have access to your manuscript. You're always leaving it lying around Du Jour."

Lawrence agreed. Oliver was right.

"I wouldn't be so covert as to scribble on your notes. I don't have any ulterior motives, whereas others might. In fact, I have a pretty good idea as to who it might have been."

"Really?" Lawrence said, opening a dog-eared copy of *Darlington House*.

"You could show a little interest…"

"What do you mean?"

"Jason."

Lawrence narrowed his eyes. "Book club Jason?"

Oliver looked at his cousin for a moment, gauging his reaction. It wasn't right to bring Jason into this. Instead he tried to change the subject. "So, back to Sunil. You'll never guess where he's moving…"

Lawrence sighed. "Is this the same Sunil publishing friend you have?" he asked.

"No. That's Sandesh and he's a television agent. He's not in publishing."

"I don't want to know, then."

"You're very bitter, you know. Someone will take your book on. Do you know how many famous authors have been rejected in the past?"

"Lots."

"Thousands. Then there are those who hit lucky when they've written utter drivel. It's a lottery, my dear Lawrence, a lottery."

"I had a response today. Or should I say another rejection. They said the plot was unrealistic, or something like that," Lawrence said, gesturing wildly with his hands. It was the same standard letter.

"Ah, so that explains the bitterness today."

"I just want a break."

"Don't we all. To take us away from this mundane life."

"What's so mundane about your life? You're a student. You have nothing to worry about."

"Worrying is like tragedy—it's universal. It affects us all no matter who you are or what you're doing."

"Encouraging, optimistic words."

"Maybe you should take a break from writing and trying to get published for a while. Have a breather. Focus on something else."

"Well, there's always..."

"Don't even say her name. I don't want to hear anything about the Siren today."

"I can't help it. I think about her all the time."

"As a friend, a good friend—family, in fact—let me tell you, again, that that ship has sailed."

"She's just so damn beautiful."

"Stop right there."

"Fine. I'll change the topic. How's Uncle Bob?"

"From one bad conversation to another. That's something I don't want to talk about. The situation is the same. Dad refuses to talk to me, Mum calls me when he is not around. What's so bad is that I feel I'm the factor pushing my parents apart."

"Not your fault. You can't help your dad's bigotism. You certainly can't be responsible for it."

"But if Mum lands up on my doorstep one day saying she's left him, I'll just top myself. I don't want to be responsible for that."

"How are you doing for money?" Lawrence asked with genuine concern. Oliver contemplated his answer, but he knew that he had relied too much on his cousin over the last couple of months—he already owed him hundreds. Lawrence himself was not very well off, holding down a couple of jobs and working so hard on his manuscript at the same time.

"I'm good, actually. In fact, Mum just sent me a cheque," Oliver told Lawrence the same lie that he told Sunil just an hour ago.

"You didn't mention that. All this talk of divorce, you were getting me worried. If he's sending you money then your old man must be coming round."

"I'm said Mum sent me the cheque. I doubt Dad knows anything about it," Oliver said, shifting in his seat.

"I bet he's coming round. I don't think your mum would send you a cheque behind your dad's back," Lawrence said optimistically, ruffling Oliver's hair again.

Oliver smiled at his cousin, whose eyes were filled with sadness. He didn't know which of Lawrence's worries was bearing down on him more: his unrequited love or his unsuccessful novel. Oliver was tempted to tell him his news, but he didn't want to give him any false hope. He had done that before. But this time Oliver was confident that something good would happen for his cousin. He could feel it in his bones.

24

Maria walked back into the bar. Alice was tapping away on her phone with her manicured nails. As soon as she saw her sister, she put the shiny black mobile back into her bag.

"You came back. I thought that you might have…" Alice trailed off. Maria walked steadily on her kitten heels, her eyes towards the ground.

"I know," Maria said quietly. "I thought about it."

Maria didn't know where to start, but Alice was brave enough to broach the topic first. "I met Owen when you two were going out. It must have been about four or five months into your relationship. Remember? We had arranged to meet for lunch at the canteen on campus."

"I remember. You were just starting at university and meeting Owen was one of the first things you wanted to do because I had talked about him incessantly that summer." Maria smiled, remembering her own excitement that day. She was so glad that Owen was going to meet her sister. Up until then there had been no secrets between them, and Maria wanted Alice's approval in some small way.

Alice had been excited too. She was happy about her sister's new relationship even though it meant that they spent less time together. Alice hoped that she too would meet the man of her dreams at university. She just never expected it to be the same man.

"We met for lunch right after I queued all morning to register with the university GP," Alice said, running her hand through her black hair. "Gosh, I spent that first week queuing rather than doing anything else." The sisters laughed together and for a split second it was like old times—Maria and Alice sharing all their thoughts and feelings with one another.

"Did you fancy him the first time you met him?" Maria asked, her nostalgia replaced with suspicion. Maria braced herself for the answer she didn't want to hear. Had Alice fallen for him then? Had *she* been the one to pursue *him*? Maria had always thought it was the other way round, but perhaps that was what she had wanted to believe.

"Well..." Alice started hesitantly, "I won't deny it, I felt a spark between us. Like there was just something there." Alice noticed the pain in Maria's eyes. "I didn't do anything. Don't think that for a second. Of course I didn't. I thought that maybe it was like a crush. You know? A crush on your older sister's boyfriend. That kind of thing. The thought left my mind no sooner than it had arrived. I promise."

"And?" Maria pressed her sister for more, as she crossed her arms and lay back against the chair. Why after all this time did it hurt so much? The betrayal and the humiliation. It had been eating away at her soul for the past two years. Perhaps she should have asked Alice about it before.

"That was it for some time." Alice played with the stem of her glass. "We were all so busy after that: you were wrapped up in Owen and your second year, I was a fresher so I had a million events and house parties to go to. I never thought about that spark. Well, not until..." Alice paused. "In fact, I never saw him again until..." She took another sip of her wine. Her mouth was dry. She wondered if Maria would actually listen to her version of events. Would the sister she adored put herself in her shoes and imagine how difficult it had been for her? Maria had certainly made her pay the price. They had almost lost one another—until now. Alice sighed, hoping that after the pain evaporated they would be on the road to being friends again. Maria's absence in her life had left a void Alice just could not fill. Alice had few true friends.

"We met again after that first meeting. Another three months must have passed. It was winter. You were talking about having Owen home for Christmas and getting him to meet Mum and Dad, remember?"

"Yes." Maria did remember. She remembered it very well. Owen was going to drive down from Market Harborough and stay with her family for the full Christmas break. But it never happened. His father had suffered a heart attack and was hospitalised the same day.

Owen had driven down on Boxing Day to give her a Christmas gift. It was a beautiful gold necklace with a pearl pendant. It symbolised the new Maria, someone who had swapped her platforms for courts. Maria believed that Owen had refined her in some way or another, and she liked that.

The necklace was the one thing Owen had given Maria that she still had. She never wore it. It sat in its velvet pouch under the pile of t-shirts that she never went near. One drunken night in a so-called "cleansing" ritual, she had burned all traces of Owen. But she had kept the necklace. It was too valuable to just burn. Remembering it now made Maria want to touch it again, feel the fine chain between her fingers. It was the one tangible bit of evidence she had to prove that Owen had loved her once.

Alice continued, pushing her poker straight hair behind her ear. "I was at Sarah's that morning and I was meeting a friend in town later that day. I didn't see him when he came to our house. I remember him leaving, though. I was waiting a few meters down the road just outside Sarah's for the bus." Alice looked at Maria wondering if she knew.

Maria's face was blank, the colour drained from her face. Her palms were damp and she felt nauseous. Her heart was beating fast, uncontrollably so.

Alice paused again. She wanted to reach out and touch her sister but she was afraid to. Instead she continued with her story. "As he was driving back, he passed me standing at the bus stop. I wasn't sure if he had seen me or even recognized me. I was so shy back then. I was freezing despite my thick coat, and then, strangely, he stopped a few meters away. I went over to speak to him."

"The man I wanted to spend the rest of my life with," Maria mumbled under her breath. Alice noticed her sister's expression change. She expected anger but all she saw was sadness.

"I asked him if he was okay or lost. He said he was fine, and he offered me a lift into town. He said he could drop me so I didn't have to stand shivering in the cold."

"The perfect gentleman," Maria said sarcastically.

"When I got into his car that day, the pull I had towards him all those months ago returned. Trust me, I didn't want to feel it again. I never wanted to have feelings like that for my sister's boyfriend. I know how much he meant to you," Alice's eyes pleaded with her sister. "I'm not that kind of person."

"Maybe you *weren't* that kind of person." Maria narrowed her eyes at her sister.

"Let me explain."

Maria shrugged.

"There was something that day. I could sense that Owen could feel it too. When I was getting out of the car, there was a silence between us, like we were both thinking the same thing."

"Oh, telepathy now. Please, let me in on what you were both thinking," Maria said.

Alice took a deep breath, she too had suffered, but she was determined to tell her side of the story. "We could tell there was a chemistry between us. We wanted to be with each other, but we both loved you too much to do anything about it."

"Wow, that's like something straight out of a movie. Love at first sight, was it?"

"Don't be like that."

"So why didn't he break up with me, then?" Maria asked, but she knew the answer. She knew it very well. It was all beginning to slot into place.

25

After Owen had given Maria that beautiful necklace on Boxing Day, they had silently made love in her room. Her parents were only downstairs but their need for each other had been too great. Afterwards, when they had dressed, they held each other at the end of the bed not wanting their meeting to end.

Owen had been upset, of course he had been. They didn't know what would happen to his father, who was in a coma. The prognosis was not good. But Owen had needed to get away and so had left his mother and brother at home in Harborough and made it to Leicester to see Maria. Owen had wanted to give Maria the necklace he had bought for her, months ago now, and he needed to release his desire for her. He wanted to feel the warmth of her skin, her brown hair between his fingers and her soft lips pressed on his. When he saw Maria, the numb feeling in his heart, the result of his father's heart attack, seemed to fade.

Maria had told him then, when she knew their love for each other could not be any stronger. She thought her news would lighten the mood. How naïve she had been to think that.

But when she took Owen's hand in hers and placed it on her stomach and uttered those life-changing words, she had expected more.

Owen responded in silence. A polite smile formed on his lips. At the time Maria had thought that he was overwhelmed, but later that evening, when he had left, she knew it was fear. Of course it had been—fear of their unborn child and knowing that he was too young to take on such a responsibility. But it was accompanied by an even greater fear. It was the way in which Maria looked at him, the way she had placed her hand on her belly that told him with no doubt that Maria wanted to keep the baby.

He had made his excuses, saying that he had to get back to his mother. As Maria closed the front door after Owen, she knew she should have refrained from telling him, especially when he had so much going on. It was too much for Owen to take on board that day, and she should have known that.

Before the holidays were up, his father passed away and Maria did not mention the pregnancy again. His father's death was a terrible loss to Owen, and his family had so much to deal with that she didn't want to burden him even more. Maria didn't expect Owen to return to university that week, but he did. Apparently his brother and mother had the situation all under control. But their relationship was not the same.

Maria knew why Owen had waited so long before he finally broke off their relationship and got together with Alice.

"How far along are you?" he had asked on their second night back at university.

"Seven weeks," Maria responded. "That evening after the house party on Friar Street…"

"Oh, I see," he said coolly.

"I guess we need to talk about it," Maria said. In the stark reality of her dorm room, Maria knew that if she had this baby it would break their relationship for good, and she was not sure if she wanted to risk that.

"I love you, Maria, but I'm not ready for this," Owen blurted out. "With all that's happened, I just don't think I could be a father." He walked over to her and held her in his arms. She could smell the citrus on his skin from the aftershave she had bought him.

"I didn't want a child either. I don't know, when I found out it felt good. I wasn't filled with dread. To me that was a sign. A good sign."

"Have you told your parents?" Owen asked.

"Not yet," Maria said sheepishly. She knew what her father's reaction would be. The thought of telling her parents made her feel ashamed and embarrassed. She would only tell them with Owen at her side.

He held her even tighter now, realising that there was a glimmer of hope for him. "What do you want to do? Are you ready to be a mother? It's a huge sacrifice."

Maria snuggled in closer to him and sighed. She had wanted it. Of course she had. When she saw those pink lines on that pregnancy test, she had smiled. She knew one day she would marry Owen and she knew together they would make good parents. But not wanting to lose Owen, she said, "You're right. I guess I was kind of thinking way too far ahead." While Maria's heart sank, she felt Owen's tension dissipate as he exhaled and pulled her closer towards him.

"You and me, we're going to make great parents, I just know it. Especially you, you'll be a fantastic mother. Just not now. We aren't ready."

There was an uncomfortable silence between them and somewhere in Maria's heart she knew that it was the beginning of the end. The thought made her feel weak inside. "What would I do without you?" she said out loud, but she wasn't quite sure for whose benefit. "These last couple of weeks have been treacherous for me," Maria confessed. "I thought it might be over between us. Don't ever, ever say that because I think I just might die. You hear? Promise me that we'll be together forever."

Owen pulled away from her and looked into her eyes. As requested, he promised that they would always be together.

*

"We met again afterwards. We spent time together in the aftermath of Owen's father's death. He needed someone," Alice interrupted Maria's thoughts.

"And I wasn't good enough," Maria said tartly.

"He said he couldn't talk to you about it. I swear to you, Maria, in all those meetings we had that January, we didn't even kiss. We wanted to, but we didn't because of you."

"Oh, lucky me." Maria's tone was bitter. She couldn't believe that Alice was being so frank with her. The truth hurt. She never realised that Owen was seeing Alice during that time, *that awful time*. But what Alice was saying was true. At the time Owen had said hardly anything about his recently deceased father, which Maria had thought was odd, but she knew that people handled grief in all sorts of ways and she didn't want to push it with him. After all, she had a problem of her own.

She looked at Alice's pained face and, despite her hatred for Owen, in that moment, she couldn't help but feel sorry for her sister. Laying out everything in the open like this was brave. Leanne was right. Maria would have to tell Alice about the baby.

Alice continued. "We started spending a lot of time together, and then one day he came over to our halls and he was exhausted and depressed. The evening had started off innocently. I opened a bottle of wine and one thing led to another. From that day on we spent most of our time together. We fell in love. Deeply."

Alice looked away from Maria, ashamed at what she was confessing to her. She was hurting her sister. "I know that it was wrong. I couldn't face you. I started distancing myself from you." Alice looked up at Maria and refilled her empty glass. She signalled to the waiter to bring another bottle. The wine was having little effect on either of them. Alice knew she would need more wine to get through her story.

Maria wrung her hands together. "I was distancing myself from you because I wanted to cut you off. I was the one driving a wedge between us," Maria whispered to her sister through tears. Alice's confession had initially filled her with rage but suddenly Maria felt calm.

"Why?" Alice asked, her eyebrows furrowed. "Why would you want to keep us apart?"

"I don't know," Maria lied. She was not ready to tell her story yet. The waiter brought over another bottle of wine in a black cooler filled with ice. Maria took in his strong perfume. It was familiar but she couldn't place it. The sisters were silent as he removed the empty bottle and retreated back behind the bar.

"That's how it started, Maria, that evening in February. It spiralled after that, it became something we couldn't control."

"In February?" Maria questioned her sister. "Do you know what date?"

"No, I don't. Sometime mid-February." Alice knew the date well. Owen hadn't been around on Valentine's Day but had made it up to her just three days later. He called it their very own Valentine's Day and had even proposed last February on the same date.

Maria looked at Alice expectantly. "Think," she said.

"I want to say the seventeenth but I can't be sure," Alice said eventually. She wanted her sister's suffering to stop but she knew this was just the beginning.

"The seventeenth? Why does that date stick out?" Maria asked again for confirmation.

"I don't know Maria, I just think it's that date." Alice looked away from her sister.

Maria knew that date well. It had been etched in her mind—it was the day after. Owen had left her saying that he needed to visit his mother, who was beginning to unravel after her husband's death. He had used that excuse quite a bit since returning to university and Maria had believed him. Who wouldn't? His mother had just lost her soul mate, someone she thought she would spend the rest of her life with. *How could he?*

26

Maria left Alice in the bar and excused herself to the toilet where she threw up most of the wine she had drunk. The 16th of February—the date jarred with her because, at the time, she had marked it in her diary in red. She had not spoken to Alice in days and she could not face speaking to her mother. The only person that she could cry with was Owen. She could not fault him then; he had been there every step of the way. They had wept together for the child they would never have, but they knew that they had made the right decision. Owen had convinced Maria of that.

"Are you sure this is what you want?" the woman in the white coat had asked on their first visit to the clinic. A doctor accompanied the nurse while they gently questioned her about her reasons for wanting to end this new life inside her.

"How would having this baby change your life?" the male doctor had asked. Maria had stuttered at first. She wasn't sure if she wanted to go through with the abortion. Owen had gently squeezed her fingers between his. Maria knew the answer. She had rehearsed it with Owen before their appointment because she knew she had to come up with a good answer so the clinic would perform the procedure. It worked. The doctor and nurse believed that having the baby would not be good for her own well-being or that of the baby's.

Maria had missed the nine-week window in which she could have taken the abortion pill. Now she was left with the only other alternative, vacuum aspiration. It made the whole process sound like some kind of beauty therapy, not an intrusive procedure that left you hollow and heartbroken. The doctor had explained the process to Maria but his words had been lost on her. She was unable to absorb what was being said.

Reaching the clinic at noon, Maria was early for her twelve thirty appointment. Everything was a monotonous blue and white, and the halls reeked with the smell of disinfectant. The room was full of women. Only a few men stood around accompanying their lovers, trying to disappear into the walls.

"Maria? Maria Shroder?" she heard her name being called out by a lady with red hair. That was all she could remember about her.

"Wait here," Maria had commanded Owen as she released his hand and walked towards the nurse. He didn't protest, which made her heart spiral towards the bottom of her soul.

She had entered the small room and changed into a hospital robe behind an equally small curtain. Maria was made to place her legs apart on to the metal stirrups as they had instructed and given a clear liquid through a drip to relax her. She didn't know what it was, and at this point she no longer cared. How vulgar and dirty she felt positioned like this with her legs spread out. A female doctor hovered at the foot of her bed. The smell of disinfectant was starting to make Maria feel nauseous. She was worried that it would suffocate her. She suppressed the urge to be sick. Shifting on the bed Maria, wondered if it was too late to call Owen in. Just to hold her one more time before they took away their baby's life.

Minutes later they were inside her. The nurse and the doctor were peering into her vagina. She could hear a mechanical noise. It scared her. Hot tears rolled down her cheeks and then the pain came, despite the anaesthesia. It was excruciating. Rarely had she suffered with period pains like Alice had done, but this pain was severe, like a laceration in her womb. Maria thought she was going to pass out. She lay there, her eyes screwed shut and her jaw clenched with pain. It felt as if hours had passed but the doctors told her it had only been fifteen minutes. She was told to rest and was wheeled into another room. A nurse placed a plate of biscuits and juice by the side of her bed and told her she would have to stay there for at least two hours. Maria didn't feel like she could move in two days, let alone two hours.

Owen came to her then, and held her hand. They were both silent. Maria felt her emotions bubbling up within her. Part of her was relieved; she would not have to be responsible for a child when she could barely look after herself. She could finish her degree and would not have to feel the shame of telling her parents and sister. She had barely spoken to Alice since Christmas and now the guilt for cutting her sister out like that was surfacing. Maria had been certain that Alice, who was closer to her parents than she was, would let slip about the baby. Maria was relieved that she would no longer have to lie to and avoid her sister. But with this feeling came one of devastation. She had destroyed their creation. Their baby. Maria pushed away her hair, which, damp with sweat, was clinging to her forehead. What if she could never have children again? What if this was her only chance to be a mother? Maria squeezed her eyes shut, trying to block out the emptiness inside her. Confusion engulfed her. She knew she needed to rest.

The following week had disappeared in a blur of cramps and blood. Maria barely remembered the seventeenth. The doctor had warned her that her hormones would be all over the place and she had been right. She had been crying incessantly for most of the day. Owen said he had to see his mother, who had started to fall into depression after her husband's death. Maybe Maria should have seen it then, but she hadn't. Two weeks after her last checkup, the emptiness was still there inside her. She realised she needed Owen more than ever before.

Time had been a great healer and, two months later, Maria realised that her life would have been different with a child in tow. For the first time since the abortion, she started to feel good about the decision she had made. But when she stepped into The Black Spoon on Earle Street that evening for a much needed night out with the girls, she saw Owen and Alice together and she felt her heart break all over again.

★

Maria splashed her face with cold water and reapplied her lipstick. Would Alice notice her puffy eyes? Would she know that she had been sick? Maria glanced at her watch. How long had she left her sister alone? She put her bag on her shoulder and headed back into the bar.

"That's how it happened, Maria. That's the truth." Alice looked at her sister for forgiveness. "I am so sorry. I never set out to hurt you. I wouldn't, because I love you. Please forgive me," Alice pleaded with her, for the second time that night.

"Alice, it's just so… the way I found out."

"I never meant for that to happen. We had gone for dinner, fed up of being cooped up in my room. We were deciding, that day, how to break it to you."

"Break it to me. How often did you talk about how you were going to *break it to me*?" Maria said. She gulped her wine back, hoping it would ease some of the tension but the wine was no different to water—it was not making a jot of difference. "Because you didn't *break it to me*. I saw you together, remember?"

"I remember."

"So tell me, Alice, why did Owen not finish with me sooner? You know, when you first got together over a month before I saw you two together? If it was one of those things, love at first sight, surely he would have wanted to end things with me as soon as possible," Maria pressed her sister. She wanted to know if Alice knew what she and Owen had been through.

"He said things were complicated between you. That you may not have taken it well, that you may have done something… you know, something stupid. Owen said that you were making plans for your future together. Dreams." Alice looked towards the table avoiding Maria's eyes. "I should have come to you. But by then our conversations were frivolous. You barely answered my calls."

"Dreams of a future together? I always was a fantasist, wasn't I?" Maria said, narrowing her eyes at Alice.

Alice was silent.

Would she have harmed herself? Maria couldn't answer that. She was fragile for the first month after the abortion. Had Owen been trying to dupe her sister or just protect her secret? Maria wasn't quite sure.

Now Maria was silent and Leanne's words from earlier returned to her. If Alice didn't know, then she had to tell her. Alice needed to know who she had agreed to marry. Owen had trampled on Maria's heart, but she wasn't going to let him hurt her sister.

The time had finally arrived. Maria looked at her sister. "Alice," she said, "there's something you need to know…"

27

Jason had spent the last few days in a state of confusion. Penelope's news had rocked him to the core and now he was certain he could not tell her about Eleanor. But he knew there had to be a way out of his situation.

"Abortion is murder," Penelope had said when Jason skirted around the issue of whether they were going to keep the baby.

"I'm just saying that a friend did it. I didn't say that we should. I would never condone something like that," Jason had said coyly. Jason had mixed feelings about abortion, especially after what he and Eleanor had been through with Alfie. But he couldn't deny that it would get him out of an extremely sticky situation.

"I don't believe in much of what the Catholic Church has to say, but I don't believe in taking a life," Penelope had reiterated.

Everything changed for Jason when he found out about the pregnancy. The information was like a persistent black cloud that just wouldn't disappear. It had blurred the way in which he saw Penelope. She wasn't just a girl that he had a fling with anymore. No, she was something else. But Jason couldn't help his feelings. Some days he loved her and other days he wanted to run back to his family in Ocean Beach—the comfort of reality where he belonged. But as the days passed, his doubts about Penelope began to grow and he knew that he would be unable to deny them for much longer.

Jason knew that his decision would change more than one person's life forever. As he gathered his thoughts, he saw Penelope walking towards him. Her blue and white skirt swayed from side to side and her hair was tied back. Pregnancy had changed her. In the last couple of weeks she had taken on a new maturity as if preparing herself for motherhood. It suited her.

"Hey, you." Jason couldn't help but smile.

"Hey," Penelope said, nuzzling her face in his neck. "You smell good."

Jason put his hand around her waist as they strolled towards the shopping centre. As they walked past a baby store, Jason felt her tugging at his arm.

"Let's take a look," Penelope said, beaming at him with eyes he couldn't resist. He sighed and followed her in.

"What if someone sees us?" Jason was hesitant as they walked through the doorway. The more they talked baby, the more real it became and his impending decision weighed heavier.

"No one will, and if they do, well then, quite simply we're shopping for my cousin's new born."

Jason wondered if Penelope had a cousin with a newborn or if lying came naturally to her. Penelope was busy playing with an assortment of blue and pink baby grows.

"I know it's early days but do you think it's a boy or a girl?" she asked.

"A boy," Jason said decisively.

"You seem very sure of that."

"I come from a family of all boys. It's in the genes. It will definitely be a boy," Jason said. He couldn't help but think of Alfie.

"Well, our family is littered with girls. It's going to be a little girl." Penelope held up a white broderie anglaise pinafore and showed it to Jason. He quickly held up some tiny blue denim dungarees in strong opposition.

Jason laughed. "A boy or a girl, it doesn't really matter, does it?"

"No, it doesn't."

"There will be so much to buy," Jason hesitated. "And you'll have to give up your part-time job." Jason had wanted Penelope to stop working there for some time now but had refrained from telling her this. After what happened with Eleanor, he wanted Penelope to have her own independence. He needed her to make her own decisions. But now things had changed.

"I still want to earn some extra cash. We'll need it. I was thinking that maybe I could do a short course in hair and makeup and start my own little mobile business." A male customer in the shop walked passed Penelope and stared at her longer than a stranger would have. Penelope swiftly turned the other way. She was tired of customers from Rustle eying her up when she wasn't working. She was sure they would think differently if their wives were about.

"I don't want you overworked. This is my responsibility as well," Jason said, forcing the words from his mouth. *Is it really my responsibility?* "You'll have to take it easy. Oh, and folic acid—I hope you're taking that!"

"I know," Penelope said, twisting her hair around her fingers and raising her eyebrows at him. "You know more than me!"

Jason shrugged, studying a yellow bib.

"We haven't yet discussed where we're going to live. I've never even been to America," Penelope said tentatively. Which country they were going to live in had been on Penelope's mind since she found out she was pregnant. She just didn't know how to broach it with Jason. He spoke so little of his life back home.

"The weather can't be beaten in San Diego," Jason said, "and the house..." Jason stopped himself. He couldn't talk about the house without picturing Eleanor and Alfie.

"There's more to moving to another country than the weather. The weather here's not so bad," Penelope said.

"We should discuss it," Jason said reluctantly. *Why am I playing along like this*?

"I don't expect you to give up your job or your life back home, but now that we're going to be a family, we're both going to have to make compromises."

"You're right. You could find work there easily." The words slipped out from Jason's mouth without meaning.

"I'll think about it." Penelope looked down at a white babygrow and smiled, relieved that he was considering their future. "Perhaps we can live there for a year or so first and then decide."

"You have it all figured out, don't you?" Jason pulled her towards him, smelling the sweet scent of the almond oil she occasionally dabbed behind her ears. *He did love her, didn't he?*

"I do." Penelope bit her lip and suddenly looked uncertain.

"What's the matter?"

"I haven't told my parents yet," Penelope said, picking up a tiny white babygrow. It looked so small. Penelope placed the garment back on the rack and headed towards the exit.

"You want to talk about it?" Jason asked, walking behind her. She reminded him so much of Eleanor now; the same look of sorrow in her eyes when she was upset.

Penelope rarely spoke about her parents. They had taught her from an early age that sex before marriage would mean she would go straight to hell; that a child out of wedlock would just be a beacon for her sin—visible to all.

"I guess I have to tell them sometime. I can't bring myself to do it just yet."

"They may just surprise you."

"Perhaps we should get married." Penelope braved to say out loud what she had been thinking for some time now.

"I don't want us to get married just because of the baby," Jason said. "It isn't a great way to start a relationship."

"Why not?" she asked, casually playing with her hair.

"I ask you to marry me and you say yes. You're happy for about five minutes, then you have a lightbulb moment somewhere in between changing diapers, wondering if the only reason I asked you to marry me was because of the little one. You start to believe that I don't love you and you start resenting me. It builds a rift between us and, boom, the relationship's over."

"You seem to know a lot about this," Penelope sulked, finally unable to control her true emotions. A ring on her finger would have solved a lot of heartache.

"*When* I ask you to marry me, it will be for the right reasons," Jason said, wrapping his arm around her. Penelope softened in his arms.

"Okay!" she conceded, even though Penelope didn't see his way at all. "Have you ever been afraid to tell someone close to you a truth that you know is going to hurt them? That you know is going to make them ashamed of you?" Penelope looked into Jason's eyes before adding, "It's so difficult."

Jason sat next to her on the shopping centre bench and took her hand in his. He wanted to make Penelope feel better. He wanted to make it easier for her because he knew how it felt. A proposal would make it easier for Penelope. Jason assessed the situation. Like him, Penelope was a hypocrite; she did not believe in abortion because of her Catholic upbringing but she was happy to strip for strangers in a seedy nightclub.

The lies were growing at a steady pace. Jason was beginning to believe in something he knew to be false. *And why?* To escape the life he had back home. A life that was almost perfect. All because he was too afraid to face up to Eleanor and deal with the situation they were in. Instead he had deserted his responsibilities and found solace in someone almost identical to the person he married. Jason's thoughts were of Penelope's unborn child and once more about how his decision would affect them all. He tucked a strand of blond hair, which had come loose from Penelope's ponytail, behind her ear.

"The lies have to stop here," he whispered under his breath.

28

Dr Timms looked at the letter Maria had just passed him. "I am glad you had the MRI," he said, smiling at Maria. "Your bloods are fine and so was the MRI, but I suppose they told you that already."

Maria sighed. The MRI had been an uncomfortable experience. Never before had she felt so claustrophobic. She was glad when it was over and her doctor had called her back into the surgery to tell her that she was medically fine.

"If you have another blackout, come in immediately. Don't wait so long," her doctor said. Despite the excess of questions her GP had asked about her alcohol consumption, Maria couldn't help but wonder if her doctor thought she was making it all up. She was glad she hadn't given her doctor any clues about a possible abduction.

Dr Timms looked at Maria and smiled before returning his gaze to his notepad.

Maria bit her lower lip and stared at the patterned carpet beneath her feet. It was clear that she was medically sound but Maria had hoped that, after four sessions, she would have made some progress. Her memory had not improved one iota. Yes, she had the occasional flashback, making her sweat with fear and dread, but that was about it.

"I can sense your frustration, Maria," Dr Timms said, breaking the tension that was slowly building.

"You know, Doctor…"

"Please, call me Graham."

"Graham, I had a sneak peek at what hysterical amnesia is, you know, online, and generally from what I've read…" Maria hesitated, unsure of what his reaction would be. "Patients who have suffered this type of amnesia generally get their memory back after forty-eight hours." Maria sighed and closed her eyes.

"We discussed this, Maria, at your first session. Remember?" Dr Timms took a sip of the cloudy lemonade on his desk. "Don't lose faith, Maria.

When you're ready, your memory will return. Regressive Recollection Therapy is not something that will bring your memory back overnight. You need to work at it as well. Have you done like I asked? Have you visited the places you have had a pull towards? Think about what we discussed in your last session: your upbringing, how you always thought you had to be the strong one between you and your sister."

"I don't see how thinking about my childhood is going to solve my memory loss. Something that has happened to me now!" Maria raised her voice.

"RRT concentrates on events in your past that have shaped who you are as a person today. The memories from that weekend are ones your mind has chosen to block out. The core of RRT is the belief that memory loss occurs in this fashion because of specific emotional-trigger events, events that create feelings and anxieties that cause your brain to shut down. Once you discover what these strong emotions are, then, as the therapy works, it should unlock what has caused this repression in your memory."

"So I must continue with the exercise?"

"Of course. Visit the places you mentioned to me last time: the park where you used to play with your mother and sister, the school yard where you spent the majority of your younger years, playing hopscotch at break times. Write down what you feel when you're at these places. Even if you feel that this element of RRT is not working, the information you provide will give me some insights for your hypnotherapy session."

Maria's eyes moved around the room.

"The hypnotherapy will come in good time."

Maria lifted her head and looked at Dr Timms, silently questioning whether he was just trying to make a quick buck from her or if he was genuinely trying to help. As far as Maria was concerned, the homework element was pointless. She couldn't help but think of *The Sinner*, the psychopath. No amount of digging into Diana's past would have foreseen that a psychopath, who was in no way related to her, would have abducted her. "It's just been so long now, and I don't find the meditation working. Perhaps hypnosis would..."

Dr Timms interrupted her. "A hypnosis, which you are not ready for. In this instance, I just don't think the time is now. Maybe in another few sessions." He looked at the desperation in Maria's eyes and attempted to console her. "Maria, let me tell you something. Localised dissociative amnesia is rare, but it has happened for a reason. You don't just wake up one morning and forget the last few days of your life. Something in your brain is blocking these memories because you could not cope with what happened during that time. Your stress levels have exceeded your coping capabilities."

"But I don't remember a thing. Look, here, at the diary you told me to keep of any memories or flashbacks that I might have. Maybe drugs were involved." Maria thumbed through the blank pages of the book backwards showing them to Dr Timms. All he could see was the word "Bricks" written on a couple of pages; the word that had been plaguing his patient since the abduction. Maria stopped at the beginning where she had made a few notes on her flashbacks.

"So why are you here, then?" he asked Maria gently, like a parent.

"Because…" Maria was hesitant. She sighed. "I didn't go see a doctor after the incident, I didn't go to the police like I should have. This was my only option." She repeated the same information she told him at her first session.

"You didn't go to the police, you didn't see a doctor. You came to a psychiatrist, one that specialises in Regressive Recollection Therapy," Dr Timms said matter of factly.

Maria frowned at his words. She wanted to ask him what he was trying to imply but she refrained. She closed her eyes and sighed deeply.

"You mentioned to me last time that, as a child, you were told you had a vivid imagination," Dr Timms said, glancing at his watch.

"Yes," Maria said, almost under her breath. She gritted her teeth, wishing she had never mentioned it in the first place. Why had she mentioned it?

"Let's take that statement for one moment."

"Dr Timms, I don't see the point…" Maria trailed off as she saw a knowing smile spread across the doctor's face.

"Maria, you must have mentioned it to me for a reason."

"Because I wasn't sure," Maria said. Her voiced piqued.

"You were not sure of what?" Dr Timms said in a calming voice, nodding his head as he spoke.

"If I had dreamed it all up. I mean, suppose I had?" Maria said, playing with her fingernails.

"So you came to see me to find out if you were making the whole thing up or telling the truth. There is something stopping you from trusting yourself. Yet your mindset and the way you think is very logical. But it is often the most logical of people who have nervous breakdowns." Dr Timms took another sip of his lemonade. "I believe, at the back of your mind, you know the truth."

Do you believe me or don't you? Maria said to herself, frowning. But why didn't she believe herself?

"You are very uncertain of yourself," Dr Timms said. "Why don't we talk about that flashback you had in the bar again?"

"We've been through all of this. I didn't remember much," Maria said, noticeably irked.

Dr Timms was persistent. He was used to patients like Maria, patients who were not confident enough to delve deep into their memories. "Let's try again, Maria. There was something in that flashback so there must have been a trigger present to set you off. Close your eyes and remember the scene." The doctor looked at Maria, who had done as he had asked. "Lean back and relax, breathe out deeply, be calm. Now, I want you to describe to me every last detail about your surroundings. The people, the smells, what you were talking about and so on. Are you comfortable?"

"Yes," came a feeble reply.

"Okay, now begin. Remember, it does not matter how insignificant the detail is, I want to hear it all. I want you to remember."

Maria cast her mind back a couple of days. She and Penelope had gone back to the same bar she had previously been to with Alice, where she had had an inkling of a memory. Maria wanted to return with a friend, without reliving the moment when she had laid bare her deepest and darkest secret to Alice.

29

That day, as Maria entered the bar with Penelope, she took a deep breath and glanced around, taking in the bare brick walls. In the light of day with her friend by her side, she couldn't believe that she had finally confessed to Alice about the abortion. Alice had, of course, been stunned into silence. Maria could see guilt beginning to consume her sister, but her own burden had lifted. Alice had not known, of course she hadn't. Alice had confessed to having started her relationship with Owen soon after Maria found out that she was pregnant. A sense of relief had flooded Maria as she finally realised that she wasn't the only one who had distanced herself from their relationship. Alice had done it too.

But after the sense of relief had settled, dread started to creep in again; it niggled Maria that Owen had failed to tell Alice about the abortion of his child. Surely, she reasoned, if he loved her sister the way Alice had described then he would have shared all his deepest and darkest secrets with her. Surely, what they had done had some effect on his life. Barely a week went by when Maria didn't think of their unborn child. But maybe Owen just wasn't like that. Maybe Alice was a fresh start for him and he had left his past in the past.

A smile touched Maria's lips. Would her sister stay with someone who had hidden such a big part of his life from her? Maria had noticed how Alice's mood had shifted when she had told her about the abortion.

*

"Maria? Are you okay?" Dr Timms broke Maria's train of thought.

"I'm fine Dr Timms," she said. She wasn't ready to share this with Dr Timms as yet. No, she was seeking out his therapy for a different reason, not for her complicated relationship with her sister.

Maria tried to relax, hoping that Dr Timms would not be able to penetrate her thoughts. He always seemed to know what she was thinking.

"Do not prevent yourself from remembering," Dr Timms said flippantly. Maria was not sure if she had heard correctly. He quickly added, "Please start then, when you are ready."

"Okay. So I was in a bar with a friend."

"Just a friend?"

Maria hesitated. "Yes, Penelope from my book group," she said finally.

"Continue."

Maria briefly opened her eyes to see Dr Timms furiously scribbling something down. Maria closed her eyes again.

Dr Timms looked at Maria for a second, her eyelids flickering. He smiled before asking her again to continue.

"So the waiter came over and took our order. I had a glass of white wine and Penelope had an orange juice." Maria stopped for a second remembering the scene. "He took our order and, as he was leaving, I had a flashback, I guess. But it wasn't for a long time, it was for, like, maybe a couple of seconds."

"And what did you see in this flashback?"

"It was strange, you know maybe it was déjà vu." Maria opened her eyes and looked at Dr Timms with realisation. "You know, Dr Timms, when I was in the bar the day before with my sister, a similar thing happened to me. I had just sat down with my sister and I could feel an image wanting to surface. Do you think it could have been a memory from one of those missing days?"

"It could well have been," Dr Timms said, his face expressionless, "or it could have been a memory you shared with your sister when you were young. Sisters can be close. Were you two close growing up?"

Maria bristled. "Yes, we were, we were very close. But you know how life is."

"Tell me."

"You know, boys and things got in the way, and we grew apart." Maria rolled her head back along the back of the chair.

"What was the main reason that you think made you grow apart?"

"University."

"I thought you were both at Leicester University?"

"We were, but we had different friends. We were on different courses and a year apart. We were too busy having fun to remember each other," Maria lied, with ease. "Silly, but it happened. That's why we met the other evening. To try and get back to where we were before university."

"Do you think your memory lapse had precipitated the meeting? Sometimes when something uncertain happens to us, we seek out family. We realise life is too short to bear grudges."

Maria was silent. Dr Timms' words echoed that email she had received. Was the doctor trying to link the two together or was it coincidence. "Yes," she said eventually, "that definitely had something to do with it. But on the other hand, we had bumped into each other shortly before the incident and I guess meeting Alice randomly was the basis for our get-together the other day."

"And do you think you have now got back to where you were with her from *before* you both went to university?"

"Yes, I suppose we did. We caught up on what went on with both of us during that time, especially the last two years when we really didn't talk much. And I think we'll be okay," Maria said with a genuine smile.

Dr Timms made a note before going back to their original topic of conversation. "So this memory you had when you were with Penelope. Describe it to me, in as much detail as possible."

"Dr Timms, it was only seconds, like I said. There was not much detail to it."

"Never mind, close your eyes, tell me what you saw. Take your time."

"I saw a wall and a hand… a hand of a man and I thought I heard something but it could have been the noise from the bar." *Bricks, Bricks, Bricks*. The word taunted her again. Maria gasped. "A brick wall," she said with terror in her eyes.

"The wall was familiar?"

"It's the wall in my apartment," Maria said with sudden realisation.

Dr Timms made a note. "You are certain of this?"

"Yes," Maria said, nausea welling up inside her. "It was my bloody apartment." She clenched her fist. "How dare they. Why my own apartment?"

"Before you saw this hand, did you hear anything specific? Smell anything?"

Maria tried to remember, pushing away her fear. It made her feel sick to think that she was held in her own apartment. She tried to recall if she heard or smelled anything in her flashback or when she was in the bar with Penelope. Maria was silent for a moment. Then she said, "The waiter's aftershave… it was strong but not familiar. I remember now because Penny commented later when he brought our drinks. The perfume had lingered in the air."

"And in your memory what was this man's hand doing?"

"It was in front of me, say a meter away, but it was the back of a hand, not the front so it must have been going away from me rather than towards me. And there was a yellow scarf on the floor near his feet. I don't know where. I remember a yellow scarf."

"Any distinguishing marks on this hand?"

"No, it was white… fine brown hairs on the arm… I think."

"Do you think this hand belonged to the silhouette you saw in the kitchen?"

"I don't know."

"And when you saw this hand, the yellow scarf, the feet, how did you feel?"

"Scared, but because I remembered something, maybe. Not because of who the hand belonged to. I don't know. I was confused," Maria paused. "The perfume. The aftershave. Perhaps it was the same one I smelled when I woke up on September 28th. I didn't know it at the time but now I remember." Maria frowned.

"This is progress, but don't be angry with your confusion. It is only natural." Dr Timms made a few more notes before asking, "Anything particular about this fragrance?"

Maria thought hard about the smell. It evoked something deep inside her. Something that frightened her. When she opened her eyes, she realised her t-shirt was damp with sweat.

30

"Of course she doesn't suspect anything, Shirty," said the man who had pretended to be Maria's brother, *Howard*.

"Are you absolutely sure? Now I think about it, it was a stupid idea," his accomplice replied. He hated being called Shirty. It reminded him of his past.

"I'm sure. Why are you so nervous all of a sudden?"

"It was something you said yesterday."

"What did I say? I was in a rush." He toyed with his ring before picking up his mobile and fiddling with it.

"You told me what Kitty said."

"What did I say Kitty said?" Howard rolled his eyes. He should have picked someone more competent. But at the time he didn't have many options.

"That on that last day, when Kitty arrived and told us that we had to let Maria go…"

"Don't bloody stop there."

"You said that Kitty reckoned Maria was in her senses."

"We knew that was a risk. She was in and out of consciousness all weekend. The bittersweet tincture worked better than expected. We got her back to her apartment, and from then all she saw was her own home.

"And two men and…"

"Yes, two men. And there is no way in hell she could recognise us." He halted the conversation with his cold stare.

"Why bittersweet?"

"The bittersweet berry contains solanine. Mix it correctly with skullcap and valerian and you have a strong sedative." He produced a small vial of an orange tincture from his jacket pocket. "A few drops can be easily concealed in a cup of camomile tea. Makes the victim blackout for a couple of hours."

Shirty shot him a quizzical look. "I thought we were just going to use your mother's benzodiazepine, her insomniac medication?"

Howard smiled. "It's good to try new things. Bittersweet is easier than benzo. No one I know has used it before. I had the benzo with me in case the tincture didn't work, but I wanted to test the bittersweet properties. I used the medication after that, once we were back in the flat. It's a good job my mother is on such friendly terms with her GP" Howard winked at his companion before continuing. "That trellis outside my house, the one with the orange berries? That's a bittersweet vine. A friend of a friend knows quite a bit about plants. In fact, he made the tincture. He came over a couple of months ago and pointed out the benefits. You could call it fate!" He smirked, pocketing the small vial with a look that said he would have further uses for it. He was a dangerous man, this narcissist with a God complex.

Shirty looked around the minimalist room. To an outsider, the room would look uncared for, a room that no one had bothered to decorate. But friends of Howard knew different. The room was exactly the way he liked it—clean crisp lines, unblemished white and smooth polished surfaces. Howard was agitated with the questioning, but he was too deep now and he was worried that Maria would remember. He wanted reassurance. "I know we kept our faces hidden… those masks were a good idea. But remember, we had taken them off that last day. Don't you remember how hot it was up there in her apartment?"

"We were pretty confident she wouldn't wake."

"Yes, we were out of her line of sight, but her blindfold had fallen off and Kitty wasn't masked… and our voices. We didn't think to mask our voices."

"But she doesn't remember it! You've tested it yourself with the damn book. It freaked her out but she does not remember. Believe me." Howard tried to keep his calm. His voice softened. "And you got what you wanted from this whole ordeal, right?"

"I suppose."

"You suppose!"

"I just feel so bad about it."

"After the event? You don't change, do you? You were always like this." Howard threw his partner a Machiavellian smile. "We're like gods, you and I, controlling the way things happen. It's that simple. Like puppets on a string. Maria needed this. Trust me, I know what's best for her."

Shirty buried his head in his hands as he realised what a huge mistake he had made by getting involved. Was his paltry benefit worth it?

"But, Howard, if she was in her senses, she might remember. It may come back to her slowly."

Howard narrowed his eyes and shot his partner a look of irritation; he should have picked a better name. "She won't. Trust me. *The Sinner* didn't jog her memory. You said yourself that if you could pull that off, we would be in the clear. The solanine and benzodiazepine won't let us down," Howard said, desperate to put an end to the conversation. He couldn't afford any second thoughts now. They were so close.

"We don't know if it was enough to keep whatever she saw in those few days suppressed. It's not a guarantee. We should never have done this. Memories may surface later."

"I did it to make Kitty happy. There was a good enough reason. And what harm really came to Maria? She lost a few days, that's all." Howard smirked, "The girl's a dreamer, a fantasist. Even if she wakes up tomorrow and realises what we have done, it's too late. It has been over a month now. What evidence does she have?"

"You're colder than I thought."

Howard raised his eyebrows at his partner. "The money. Have the funds cleared?"

"Yes. But there's something else."

"What?"

"The other *thing* you promised."

"You're relentless. And you say you have a conscience." Howard smiled, pouring himself a whiskey from the bottle on his desk.

"It was part of the deal. It's important to me, more important than the money, and it won't cost you a thing. Not a jot."

"Okay, okay, like I said before, I'll get it looked at and put in a good word. There's not much I can do after that. It's a business after all."

"Surely you can do more. In fact, I know you can do more. You're the owner, and look what I did for you! I could have been arrested. I still could."

"You were paid suitably for it. The money you received was more than adequate."

"Have you tried knocking someone out, someone you know, and then dragging them halfway across town to their apartment without being spotted? It's not as easy as it looks in the movies." Shirty looked at the man before him, the boy who used to taunt him as a child. Yes, he should have ignored Howard's pleas for help, but the prize had been too great to walk away from.

"Are you forgetting that I was there, waiting patiently for you in the car? I drove you straight to the apartment building. There was hardly any *dragging* involved."

"I had to take her up in the lift. That was a huge risk."

"Please. It was the service lift straight from the car park and I knew no one would be using it that day. I did my research."

"It's something I'll never forget." Shirty narrowed his eyes at his friend.

"You're persistent, I'll give you that. I suppose it's one redeeming facet of your character. I'll see what I can do."

31

"I'm going after the semester ends for the Christmas holidays. I've already booked my time off work and Jason says the weather in San Diego at that time of year is just fine." Penelope beamed at Sunil.

"Lucky you!" Sunil said.

Penelope had debated whether or not to tell Sunil her news. She didn't want to jinx her tiny bump, remembering the three months the doctor told her about. She had told Maria but had not broached the subject with her parents as yet. She tried to think about something else. "What are you up to these days?" she casually enquired.

Sunil hesitated. "It's been difficult setting up the new shop."

"Is that all?" Penelope asked.

Had Maria said anything to Penelope, Sunil wondered. "I suppose my mind has been preoccupied. There are two things in this world that cause me no end of grief: family and love."

"Family, they drive you insane having all these high expectations! Am I right?"

"Exactly so. I feel so pressured." Sunil said, "My brother, Omar…"

"Well, don't feel that way. Let's make a pact. We are who we are and family will just have to get over it." Penelope smiled at Sunil. She offered him her hand, feeling her own apprehension at having to tell her parents her baby news. "Let's shake on it."

Sunil took her hand and agreed that they had the right to be their own person, but it was for her benefit more than his. Sunil knew that if he didn't make a decision soon, his fate would be sealed. "And what about love?" he asked.

"Love is beautiful," Penelope said, unable to refrain from blushing.

"Ah, Jason. If you loved Jason and he didn't love you back, how would you feel then?"

"That's an awful thought," Penelope said. Just the thought of it brought tears to her eyes. She blinked them back, blaming her unpredictable hormones. "I believe in true love. If two people are meant to be together, they will find each other and they will both be in love with one another."

Sunil laughed. "That's what fairy tales are made of. Reality is not quite like that. Love can be beautiful, but love can also be cruel," Sunil said

"Cruel?"

"Unrequited love is cruel."

"Ah, unrequited love, something very close to my heart," Lawrence said from behind them.

"Lawrence," Penelope said, "you know Sunil?"

Lawrence looked at Penelope for a second longer than he should. A shiver ran down her spine. She quickly looked away as Lawrence shifted his eyes towards Sunil.

"Hi," Lawrence said, offering his hand, "I don't think we've met before. But you're in the book club, right? Oliver mentioned you."

"I am," Sunil replied, shaking Lawrence's hand. "I'm the quiet one at the back, which is why you probably don't recognise me."

"But you sit with us lot, Si, and we're quite outstanding," Penelope said.

"You're noticeable," Lawrence said, smiling. "I hope I'm not interrupting?"

"We were discussing unrequited love," Sunil said. "Something you are familiar with?"

"It's not worth talking about," Lawrence said.

"If Lawrence won't say, then tell us, Si. Who do you love who doesn't love you?" Penelope asked, turning away from Lawrence.

"If your love is not returned, it's rather humiliating to talk about."

"Unreturned love is not humiliating. It's real and humbling. Half the books in the world would not have been written if it weren't for unrequited love," Lawrence said.

"It's not what fairy tales are made of, though, is it?" Penelope enquired sarcastically. "And we all want a fairy tale, don't we?"

"Lawrence, you probably don't know, but Penny has found true love and that's why she believes in this myth."

Lawrence raised his eyebrows and took a sip of his coffee before turning to look at Penelope.

Penelope fiddled with an imaginary mark on her jeans.

"Is this true, Penny?"

"I've met someone," she said guardedly.

Lawrence tilted his head and looked at Penelope.

"I have to be heading off," Sunil interrupted, seeing this interlude as his chance to leave. Sunil had to make a decision and soon. But there were things he needed to do before he could decide.

"I'll come with you," Penelope said, and quickly jumped to her feet. She touched Lawrence's hand to say goodbye and felt her fingers tingle. She quickly pulled her hand back. "Sorry Lawrence," she said, glancing at her watch. "I just remembered I'm meeting an old friend in half an hour."

32

"I think you're right Leanne, she's definitely on antidepressants. Her behaviour patterns seem to follow what I've read about the drug: mood swings, loss of appetite… it's all there."

There was a pause on the other end of the line before Alice continued. "I feel bad but I think she's on them because of Owen." More silence ensued but Alice was quick to fill it. "Thank you for sending that message from Maria's phone. I really owe you."

"No problem," Leanne said through clenched teeth. Of course Maria was on antidepressants. She had found them in her apartment. Leanne bit her lip. The guilt was starting to eat at her. She should never have involved Alice.

"I was a terrible sister," Alice said. "I should never have done what I did. I live with the guilt of it every day."

"You're still with Owen, though," Leanne said confidently. She felt used. Back in September, Leanne saw no reason not to tell Alice about Maria's incident. After all, they had been so close growing up. Leanne had thought that Alice would help, but instead Alice just wanted to have her cake and eat it.

"I can't imagine my life without him. Do you understand? I love him," Alice said. "Even after Maria told me their secret." She paused. "I discussed it with Owen and I understand why he kept the abortion from me. He was protecting Maria. He didn't think it was right if he had been the one to tell me. He's a good person."

Leanne frowned. "But I thought you and Maria were resolving the whole Owen situation," Leanne said, sighing. She had told Alice too much now to retreat.

"We *are* resolving it," Alice said. "Maria asked me to have a think about it and I have. Believe me, I have done a lot of thinking over the last few days." She paused, noticing Leanne's unusual silence. "I appreciate you coming to me with this," Alice said gently, trying to keep Leanne on her side. "Together we can help her. Two heads are definitely better than one. Rest assured, by our sisterhood promise, I won't mention it to her."

Leanne was silent. The sisterhood between Maria, Alice and herself had long since died when Alice ran off with Owen. Leanne silently scolded herself for not remembering the pain Alice caused Maria when she picked up the phone to call her. *I'm a bad friend*, Leanne said to herself.

"I've been thinking about the whole abduction you mentioned," Alice said.

"What about it?" Leanne asked cautiously.

Alice raised an eyebrow on the other end of the line. "You don't think she made it up, do you? I mean, I'm not saying Maria is that kind of person, not for one moment. But it's something to consider."

"Why would she do that?" Leanne pressed, even though she herself had been thinking the same thing.

"Well, because… just because. She's alone right now and sometimes we just want some… *attention*," Alice whispered this last word. "In Maria's eyes, her situation needs to change—maybe it was the excuse she needed to reconnect with me and Owen again."

Leanne started chewing her fingernails before she confessed, "I've thought about this." Leanne looked around her room to make sure no one was listening, even though she lived alone. She couldn't be angry with Alice for saying exactly what was going through her mind. Maria was a daydreamer and she had definitely suffered from Owen and Alice's relationship. Maria had cut both her sister and ex-lover out and found herself alone. Leanne knew that Maria wanted Alice back in her life—she just didn't know how to get back there. But Leanne couldn't see her best friend stooping so low. And she couldn't betray Maria like this. "She may have had some deeper issues," Leanne said, "but to make something like this up. No, I just don't think so."

"Mmmm, I guess it's not like Maria, but it was worth mentioning. And another thing, didn't you think it was an odd thing to do? To delete the emails she received, I mean. Surely that was her only physical evidence?" Alice pointed out. "But then maybe I'm just trying to find a rational explanation for it. You did say she avoided the police and the doctors, didn't you?"

"I did, but…"

"We'll make sure Maria gets better," Alice said, interrupting Leanne. "You're a good friend. Just if you could help me on this one last thing…"

Leanne listened. "Okay, I'll do it," she said reluctantly. She was desperate for the conversation to come to an end. She pressed her ear to the receiver. Alice and Owen deserved each other, she thought, as she agreed. "Just put it out of your mind that Maria made the whole thing up. I just know Maria wouldn't pull a stunt like that," Leanne concluded confidently. But as she replaced the receiver back in its cradle, a sliver of doubt once again crossed her mind.

33

"How's Scott?" Maria asked.

Leanne rolled her eyes.

"Don't want to talk about it?"

"Another woman."

"Oh," Maria said sympathetically, putting a comforting hand on her friend's shoulder. Maria wasn't surprised. Leanne had a habit of dating men who treated her badly.

"I know, pathetic. I'll add him to my list of men to avoid." Leanne smiled but Maria could tell it was a brave cover-up.

"Well…"

"Let's change the topic," Leanne said, blinking back her tears and cutting her friend short. She drew Maria in for a hug as she stepped over the threshold of Maria's apartment. "I feel like I haven't seen you in months," Leanne said.

Maria laughed. "When we aren't on the phone to each other, it's because you're here!"

"I know," Leanne said, still holding on to her friend. "It's just…" Leanne stopped herself short.

"It's just?" Maria encouraged, as she released herself from Leanne's grip and resumed her position on the sofa.

Leanne slumped down next to her, wrinkling her nose. "I've not spoken to you about what happened with Alice and your last session with Dr Timms." Leanne had heard Alice's side of events but she wanted to verify if what Alice said was true.

"It's going nowhere," Maria replied, looking around to see if she could provoke another memory. It was no use.

"Dr Timms or Alice?"

Maria was silent.

"You know I worry about you." Leanne walked over to the kitchen and put the kettle on. She took out the chipped blue mug with pink flowers on it. It didn't match anything in the flat but Maria loved it.

"You mentioned the flashback you had when you and Penny were out and went over it again?" she tried.

"I suppose we did get somewhere. I could remember my flat."

"Your flat?"

"I must have been held here."

Leanne sighed. She couldn't imagine what Maria must have been going through. She shook her head, annoyed that she couldn't do anything to make her friend feel better.

"And a smell."

"A smell?"

"An aftershave. I went back to the bar and sought out the waiter that served us that day. The smell was probably what provoked my near-flashback when I was with Alice, and then again with Penelope."

Leanne gave her friend a wry smile. "That bar never has good wines, but it has decent eye candy."

"He must have thought I was mad. When he finally emerged from the back room and I asked him what aftershave he wore, he looked at me like I was a stalker."

"Did you explain?"

"I said that I really liked the smell and wanted to buy it for my boyfriend."

"He thinks you fancy him."

"Probably. More importantly, I went to the store found the aftershave and drowned a card in it. I sniffed it like an addict. I really did… and nothing."

"Nothing?"

"Nothing. So I bought a bottle of this fragrance. It's called *Forever.* The smell was so familiar in my flashback but I can't pinpoint why I know it."

Leanne took the bottle in her hand and removed the lid, smelling its contents. To Leanne, it smelled like any other ordinary male aftershave. "On to dilemma number two: how did it go with Alice?" Leanne asked.

"I need wine for that conversation."

"That bad?" Leanne asked, genuinely surprised. It was not how Alice had described her meeting with Maria at all. "Do you want to share an Indian takeaway and a bottle of white?" Leanne asked.

Maria nodded as she rested her head against the sofa. She closed her eyes and pulled her blue towelling dressing gown around her. Things between her and Alice had, in fact, improved. The guilt she carried for so long for not telling her sister about the abortion was finally lifted. Maria was almost on the brink of forgiving her sister for running off with Owen. After all, Alice didn't know that Maria had been to hell and back while she had been sneaking off with Owen.

"It went well with Alice," Maria said, as Leanne decided on a Korma over a Rogan Josh. "After my initial outburst, I went back in there. You were right, I owed it to myself. She's engaged to him now."

"To Owen?" Leanne feigned surprise.

"He hadn't told her about us, about the abortion."

"You did?"

"I felt so much better when I told her. Naturally Alice was stunned. Didn't say anything." Maria stared out of the skylight. "You know, if I were to marry someone, I think I would want to share that experience with them. I would want to share everything with them."

"Men are different," Leanne said, remembering Alice's words: *He's a good person.* "To them, the past is the past. Look at what I've had to endure with some of the men I've dated."

"But this isn't the past. They had been dating since that February. Can you believe the day after my…" Maria's eyes filled with tears. She focused her gaze back on the dark night outside her skylight. "I told her I wanted her back in my life. It will take me a while to get over what they've done, but I will get over it. I can't continue without my sister. I just feel that, since the abortion, everything changed for me and it has been one disaster after another."

Maria grabbed a tissue from a box on top of the coffee table. She walked towards one of the large arched windows in her sitting room. Looking over at the Performing Arts Centre, Maria could see couples holding hands as they disappeared through the doors of the theatre. She felt a stab of jealousy. She wanted to be carefree again; more importantly, she wanted to feel love. She sat on the large sky-blue cushion under the window while Leanne ordered their dinner.

Maria's appetite started to stir. *Bricks.* That word again formed on her lips. "Bricks," she whispered, as if unable to control her vocal cords.

"Sorry, did you say something?" Leanne gave her friend a curious look as she put the receiver down.

"Nothing," Maria said.

"You know, it would probably make you feel better if Alice knew about your abduction, Maria," Leanne said tentatively.

"I know," Maria said as she played with her fingernails.

"Alice isn't a bad person," Leanne said, desperate to have the old Maria back, the one who drove to the beach on a winter's day just because she wanted to. Leanne's lips trembled. This was Alice's final request. Leanne had to get Maria to confide in her sister. Alice had vowed to help if she did.

Leanne held the bottle of *Forever* to her nose again. "Cedar wood!" she exclaimed as she inhaled the fragrance once again.

"What?"

"One of the ingredients in *Forever*, I recognise it. It's the main undertone in this scent. The aftershave your captor wore had a similar ingredient to this one. He must have. All you have to do is narrow it down."

"So it could be cedar wood, citrus, bergamot or sandalwood. The list could be endless."

"No. definitely not sandalwood," Leanne said decisively.

"Big help. Leanne." Maria said, defeated.

"Hey, hey, missy, we'll get to the bottom of this. It's a start. Smell it everyday, you never know. And let's put perfumes on my list of the book club members. Your next task is to find out who wears what fragrance. Where's the chart? I can start filling in some more details."

"Okay," Maria said reluctantly, even though she knew she had thrown out Leanne's list of suspects days ago. "Later."

34

Penelope dimmed the lights and checked the oven. She wanted the evening to be perfect. Looking at her watch, she had just enough time to get ready.

Penelope quickly walked over to the spare room, which had rather deliberately become her dressing room. She slipped on her favourite black dress, which fitted, but only just. Her bump was getting bigger everyday now. She applied blusher to the apples of her cheeks, a neutral eye shadow and a thin stroke of black eyeliner. She moisturised her manicured nails and, as she stood in front of the full-length mirror, she sprayed her favourite perfume on her bare neck and wrists. Running her hands through her hair to untangle the day, she wandered back to the kitchen barefoot. She stopped to look into the large, silver framed mirror in the hall, checking her appearance one more time.

It was seven thirty and Jason would be arriving any minute now. Peering into the oven one last time, Penelope checked the colouring of the white meringue peaks on the baked Alaska. Then she uncovered the raw meat, wrapped in butcher's paper. Picking the fillets of beef with her red nails, she gently rolled each steak in the crushed peppercorns she had prepared earlier that afternoon. Methodically, Penelope turned the frying pan up to temperature and added to it a drop of olive oil.

Wrapping her "Kiss the Cook" apron around her waist, Penelope began to plunge the masher into the steaming potatoes that had just boiled. She added the usual ingredients: milk, butter and parsley, careful not to chip her nails. As the frying pan came to the right temperature, she carefully placed the steaks in the pan and momentarily enjoyed the sound of the raw meat sizzle. Her meal was almost ready but Jason had not yet arrived. She checked her watch again; he was never late. It was now 7.45 p.m. She told herself not to be so impatient—perhaps she should have waited before she cooked the meat.

Removing her apron, Penelope garnished the two plates she had laid out with salad. Topping the parsley mash with the perfectly cooked steak, Penelope took the plates to the set table. Jason would walk through her door any second now, *but where were the candles?* Frantically, Penelope searched through the kitchen drawers for the tea lights; she knew they were hiding somewhere. Locating them under a mound of takeaway menus, she lit them and placed them on the table. She stood back and looked at the table with a critical eye. *Perfect.* Now she was ready to tell Jason that she had made up her mind. She had decided to return to San Diego with him after he completed his Master's.

Her uncertainty on whether to move with him or stay in England had vanished after the dreadful day she had spent with her parents. Penelope remembered the look in her mother's eyes as single tear fell onto the tablecloth.

35

Max and Julia Leigh had driven up to Leicester and, having had to wait in traffic for the best part of an hour, were not in the best of moods. But the Leighs, as usual, hid their exasperations and put on happy faces to greet their only child, Penelope. She had taken them to the Italian café on the high street and, as she suspected, they had both ordered spaghetti carbonara. As they delved into their food, regaling tales about their neighbour's cat and how the church recently had its lead stolen, Penelope realised just how glad she was that she had finally broken free from their bland existence. Memories of church on Sunday with her white socks pulled up to her knees jumped to the forefront of her mind. She played with the idea of telling them that she was a part-time stripper now. They would probably choke to death. No, not today. Today she had more important news to tell them; news that would probably give them a heart attack.

"You look different," Julia had said between mouthfuls of pasta.

Penelope smiled at her mother as she played with her tortellini. Her appetite was fading, thinking about how she was going to broach her baby bump.

"She's put a bit of weight on," Max said to his wife as if Penelope didn't exist. "It suits you, Pen. You look healthy," he said, nodding at his daughter seated in front of him. Penelope wriggled in her seat as her appetite quickly disappeared.

"The hair colour is certainly different. And makeup. I don't think you wore this much makeup back at home," her mother added, examining Penelope's face.

Their daughter smiled politely. Despite her mother's sour expression, Penelope had deliberately toned down her makeup for today, knowing that her parents would disapprove. If they had seen her usual painted face, they would have thought she was a true slut.

Penelope took in her parents' neutral clothes: her mother in a grey cardigan and khaki chinos, her father in his favourite brown corduroys. They had not changed one bit. But these two people sitting opposite her were her parents. Despite her loathing of their uninspiring lives and lacklustre attitude, they had brought her up. And that she had to respect.

These were the people who still had her year-three pottery attempts on the kitchen shelves and who had kept her first baby shoes. They had been her personal taxi service until she had learned to drive, her removal company when she had moved to Leicester. No matter how hard Penelope tried to convince herself that she was better off away from their grasp, she could not deny the fact that they loved her. And, although she never said it, she loved them. Perhaps she could just class them as overprotective. Growing up, she had a ten o'clock curfew when everyone else was allowed out until midnight. Penelope was one of the few in her year who had to call first before she walked home from a friend's house, but she realised she couldn't hate them for this. After all, her parents' hearts were in the right places. Now she was about to break those hearts and fill them with utter disappointment.

"Dessert, coffee?" their waiter asked as he cleared their plates. "You no like the pasta?" the waiter asked Penelope in a thick Italian accent.

"I'm not all that hungry." Penelope smiled and lifted up her plate towards him. She no longer wanted to look at the tortellini smothered in a thick cheese sauce. The waiter frowned at Penelope. "I know you from somewhere," he said, examining her features.

"No," Penelope said. "I don't…"

"Ya, for sure, I know you. I just don't know…"

"I have a familiar face."

"Ha, ha." The waiter laughed before turning to her parents. "This face is no familiar, huh?"

Max and Julia smiled politely at the waiter. Penelope knew who he was. He often sat in the corner of Rustle with a whiskey sour. She had seen the waiter deep in conversation with Cassy, one of the new girls, on several occasions. Penelope liked Cassy—she too had been a church choirgirl.

"No dessert, thanks," her father responded, trying to hurry the waiter along. "Julia?" he asked, placing his hand on his wife's knee.

Penelope smiled. After thirty-five years of marriage, her parents were still so loving with one another. She imagined that she and Jason would share those feelings too.

"Oh, no cake for me, must think of these." Julia's cheeks turned pink as she let out a squeaky laugh, pointing with both her hands at her hips.

"Just a double espresso for me, then. I don't want to fall asleep on the drive home after that meal. Anything for you, Pen?"

"No thanks, Dad," Penelope said, looking towards the red chequered vinyl tablecloth, desperately hoping that the waiter would disappear quietly back behind the bar. The waiter took the order and left their table. As Penelope looked up, she glanced in his direction, just in time to see him turn and wink at her knowingly. Penelope blushed and returned her gaze to her parents.

"Well, it was nice you calling us up like this, Pen. You have a lovely flat," her father said, even though Penelope had overheard him whisper to her mother that it was small and pokey.

"So what about your social life, dear?" her mother enquired. "We haven't met any of your friends."

Penelope rolled her eyes. She knew the question her mother wanted to ask but Penelope didn't want to make it easy for her. She waited.

"Any boys we should know about?" Julia asked the question in the same manner that she had done when Penelope had been fourteen. But back then, she would have been sent to her room if she was seeing someone. They had spent her entire life making sure that she didn't have a boyfriend and now they wanted her to have one. A good Catholic one.

Penelope knew she had to answer her mother and she had left it right till the end of the meal to tell them. She could have told them when they arrived at her apartment that morning or as they walked around the Highcross, perusing various shop windows. And then, of course, she had the opportunity to tell them during their late afternoon lunch. No, she had waited till their coffee had arrived and Penelope knew that it was now or never. She toyed with the idea of waiting till they were safely back home so that she could break the news to them over the phone, but Jason had been right. This was something she had to do in person. Perhaps she should have taken him up on his offer to accompany her that day. He had been so supportive, but she had refused, afraid that her parents may scare him off for good.

"Well, Penny?" her father asked, his brows knitted together making deep crevices in his forehead.

"Yes, well…" Penelope cleared her throat. "I am seeing someone, actually." Under the table Penelope wrung her hands together.

"Well, who, dear? Don't tell us half a story," her mother chirped as her eyes darted from her daughter to her husband. She let out a nervous giggle. "Is he from the church? Is he Catholic?"

"His name is Jason, we've been seeing each other for some time now. You would really like him. He *is* Christian," Penelope said nervously.

"But not Catholic." Max shot Julia a look. "That's okay, I suppose," he said, looking at his wife again for reassurance. They exchanged a knowing look that said they would discuss it later. "Well, when can we meet him? Is it serious?" her father asked, swallowing the last sip of his espresso.

"Soon, very soon. You see, what I wanted to tell you is…" Penelope looked at both her parents before she continued, with trepidation, averting her gaze once again to the tablecloth. "What I wanted to tell you is that we… well, Jason and I… we're expecting a baby. I'm pregnant." There, she had said it, and as the words left her mouth Penelope felt an enormous sense of relief. But seconds later, along with nausea, another feeling started to creep in. Fear. She looked at her parents—her mother was as white as a sheet.

"W-w-w-what? I don't think I quite heard that," her father said, shaking his head in disbelief. Her mother was motionless, her mouth ajar.

Penelope coughed. "I'm pregnant," she said, louder and with more conviction.

"You are *what*, Penelope Leigh?" her father said, as the blood rushed to his face. It was as if he was insistent that he could not hear this crushing news.

"Oh, Max, stop," Penelope heard her mother say. Julia held on to her husband's arm, trying to steady his anger. Penelope took a deep breath. She wanted them to leave—she had never seen her father like this before. *Let them mull it over on the drive back to Oxfordshire*, she thought. Then perhaps she and Jason could go down to Thame and see them.

"Julia, did you hear what she has just told us?" her father asked incredulously, not removing his gaze from his daughter.

"Yes, dear. I did." Julia's words were barely audible. Penelope poured her mother some water from the jug on the table with a trembling hand. A tear rolled down her mother's cheek, which made Penelope burn with shame.

"Mum, are you okay?" Penelope asked, fiddling with the silver cross pendant around her neck.

"I'm fine…" her mother managed.

Penelope's father interrupted. "How could you? How could you do this to us? To yourself? Have we taught you nothing? You have sinned and now look what has happened."

"Dad, I…" Penelope tried. Her face was red and puffy. She fought back the tears pricking the backs of her eyes.

"I take it *it* was consensual?" Max asked, slamming his fist down on the red chequered tablecloth.

Penelope flinched. "Of course." Penelope could see the shame and anger in her father's eyes.

"You *are* keeping the baby?" came a feeble question from her mother.

"Of course, of course I am. I could never, never…"

"Good, I'm glad," her mother said, before turning towards Max. "I think it is time we left. There is nothing more here to discuss."

"That's it?" Penelope exclaimed, surprising herself with her confidence. She had expected a bad reaction, but this? Did she really deserve this? Not one word of support. How could they call themselves Christian? Their words were hurtful. Their reaction made her love for Jason seem like something she should be ashamed of. And suddenly she knew that they were wrong to make her feel like this. They had made her feel ashamed of her own feelings and actions her entire life. This time Penelope was ready to fight her corner. "That's it? You don't want to discuss this further? You can't shove it under a rug and hope it will disappear, like everything else that doesn't go your way. This is going to be your grandchild. Don't you even want to know when I'm due? How far along I am?"

"The less said the better. We don't condone your behaviour, you, you…" Max stopped himself before he could say it, but Penelope could feel the disgust he felt for her right at that moment. "You *are* going to marry this man?" Max demanded.

"I am," Penelope lied, her confidence dissipating. Of course she had thought about marriage. In fact, it was the first thing she *had* thought of. All her life she had wanted to get married, to have a fairytale wedding. She herself had wanted marriage before children. It just hadn't worked out like that. Finally she had met her prince but he didn't want a big white wedding… or a wedding at all, she had come to discover.

"We're going to set a date soon," Penelope continued.

"Soon! Well, nice of you to tell us like this."

"I never thought you had a selfish bone in your body," her mother said. "But you do, Penelope Jane, you do. You have changed so much since you left home. Look at you, prostituting yourself like this." Her mother took a breath. "How dare you wear that cross!" she hissed.

Penelope let go of the pendant she was holding onto for strength, and suddenly felt her right cheek smart; her hand immediately rose to touch where it stung. It took her a moment to register that her mother had hit her. Instantly she looked at her father, who had his arm protectively around his wife.

Hot, salty tears had started streaming down Penelope's face, which was now numb with shock. She looked around the little Italian café and saw several faces suddenly avert their staring eyes. She picked up her bag from the back of her chair and walked out.

36

Penelope shook away the painful memory as she turned her head to look at the clock in the sitting room. It was 8.15 p.m. She looked down at the plates staring up at her. The salad had wilted and the peppercorn sauce on the steak had formed a skin. She started to panic, not knowing Jason's whereabouts. Immediately she dialled his mobile number, but all she got was his answerphone. She tried to calm herself by taking deep breaths as she listened to his voice before leaving a short message. "Jason, it's me. Call me when you get this. I'm worried about you." Penelope paused, "I've got some news for you, good news," she added, hoping if he was in some kind of trouble and did hear her message, it would give him some hope.

Penelope hung up. Drumming her fingers on the table, she didn't know who to call. Walking over to the sitting room, she switched on the local news. *Had there been an accident?* She slipped on a pair of shoes to leave the house but then realised that wasn't the best idea. It had not been long at all and she was being paranoid. Penelope removed her heels and started to pace the length of the sitting room. It had only been forty-five minutes.

But Penelope could tell that something was not right. She could feel it in her gut. Rarely was Jason not on time. He always called, even if he was going to be five minutes late. She walked slowly back to the guest bedroom to take her makeup off. Pregnancy had made her cosmetics feel heavy and her pores clogged. She remembered that she had left her toner by her bed. Walking back into her bedroom, she instantly noticed the envelope on her pillow. Why hadn't she come into her bedroom sooner? "Penny" it said on the envelope in Jason's childlike scrawl. Her heart stopped.

Lifting the envelope to her face, Penelope could smell his aftershave—it was distinctively Jason. She turned it over in her hands, looking at the seal. Her fingers were trembling. Her hand automatically went to their unborn child. Taking a deep breath, she ran a blood red fingernail under the seam.

37

"I have news, good news, Loz… What the fuck happened in here? You look an utter mess. You sick?" Oliver asked, as he peered over his cousin's shoulder into the doorway of his apartment.

"Flu. I'm going to have to cancel this evening." Lawrence blew his nose into a tissue before adding, "She won't bloody return my calls."

"Ah, so you've bitten the bullet and actually called her!"

"Well, once…" Lawrence hesitated.

"You're never going to get the girl that way, are you?" Oliver shook his head and put his hands up in the air to stop his cousin saying anything further. "I don't want to talk about this. You could have pretty much any girl in that book club and you choose the most unattainable." Oliver grabbed Lawrence's chin and pushed his face in the direction of the large mirror above the fireplace. "Look at that chiselled jaw…"

"Stop it," Lawrence said, forcing his cousin's hand away.

"Fine. Topic change. I have good news."

Lawrence shrugged his shoulders.

Oliver thought about sharing the gossip he had about the Siren, but he didn't want to get Lawrence's hopes up and he didn't want it to sully his real news. "I have just been on the phone with *thee* Mr Drake."

"Drake being?"

"You can't be serious." Oliver raised his eyebrows and shook his head at his cousin's ignorance.

Lawrence held a tissue up to his red nose with a look of bewilderment.

"Nicholas Drake is quite possibly the best in the business."

"Not Nicholas Drake?" Lawrence asked incredulously.

"He is one of the three top dogs in the publishing industry in England. Remember I told you about that small publishing house that was brave enough to take on *The Sinner*? Well, they were the tiny outfit gobbled up by Langford and Sons. Remember we spoke about it the other day?"

Lawrence's eyes widened. "You never told me anything about this."

Oliver rested his hand on his chin. "Oh yes, you're right. I didn't."

"Well, go on then."

"J Rupert, author of *The Sinner*, managed to get his book published by Langford and Sons, which has also led me to find out who exactly scribbled the book recommendation on your manuscript notes."

"You're speaking in riddles now. How are the two even remotely connected?"

"J Rupert is none other than our Jason's uncle."

"Who's *our* Jason?"

"Jason, from the book club. The tall blond one that looks like he has stepped out of a magazine. He must have been the one to make the recommendation." Oliver paused. "Makes sense, now, doesn't it?" he said, as saw the look of realisation in Lawrence's face.

"Ughhh, I dislike him even more now. Wait, how do you know? He never mentioned it. In fact, he was very quiet about the book."

Oliver shrugged. "Maybe he didn't want to give it away. I couldn't say it at the meeting. I wouldn't betray a friend like that," Oliver said, shaking his head from side to side.

Lawrence ruffled his cousin's hair. "So, Mr know-it-all-with-a-conscience, why would Jason recommend *The Sinner*?"

"Isn't it obvious?"

"No, it isn't, as it happens."

"His literary uncle's book only became a bestseller once he died, once he had topped himself."

"Fact?"

"Yes, well. The book was taken on by a small publishing house in England, which is a strange thing to do. I mean, American novelists rarely broach English publishing houses. It's just not the way the industry works. Anyway, they took it on and it sold quite a few copies. When he died, it exploded—had a cult following in the

States. Rumour has it that J Rupert, the J of which stands for Jason, was a lonesome old chap with no one in the world but his sister and her husband and their son. J Rupert died leaving Jason all the rights and royalties for his novel."

"Really? Gosh, you think he would have said."

"Well, you would have known he had scribbled all over your manuscript notes then, wouldn't you?"

"That's no biggie, when you consider what insight he could have provided to the group. Maybe I'll ask him to do a little talk next month."

"You'll do no such thing, Lawrence! I've told you this in confidence. He's hardly going to do a talk if he didn't even mention it to anyone in the first place."

"Well, how do you know about it then?"

"The internet is a wonderful thing."

"That and campus life. You students seem to know all there is to know about each other," Lawrence said. "You know, I still don't get why he would recommend it though."

Oliver rolled his eyes. "The royalties. Plus, I think it's a nod of recognition to his uncle. I mean his uncle spent his whole life trying to get famous from it and then it only happens in death. Why shouldn't Jason push as many people to read the book as possible? It was what his uncle would have wanted. And he can earn some spare cash at the same time."

"Yes, but how much can he get, say fifty pence a book, if that. That's what? A tenner from the club."

"You'll never be good at selling books, Lawrence. It may just be a tenner but word-of-mouth promotion is not to be taken lightly." As the words left Oliver's mouth, he couldn't help but think of Lawrences's own manuscript, which had received at least twenty-four rejections to date.

"Anyway, back to my original point," Oliver started. "Langford and Sons was a small editing company based in Market Harborough. Real small; I'm talking two editors and a couple of freelancers. Well, Mrs Langford and her two sons took over the business when her husband died. Apparently they were more business minded than Langford Senior." Oliver paused, taking a moment to look at his cousin. He had hoped for a bit of drama but the sudden break from the story only irritated Lawrence.

"Go on," Lawrence said, impatiently.

"Mrs Langford ended up buying out a publishing house with her late husband's life insurance money. She merged the two businesses together and, Bob's your uncle, she turned a failing business into a most lucrative one. But it was her son, the junior Mr Langford, who got the business going. He snapped up Nicholas Drake from Hesters, making him an offer that wasn't that competitive in terms of finance, but the location was the hook. You see, Drake's mother was not well at the time, still isn't from what I gather, and he thought it best if he moved his family back to Leicestershire to be close to his mum—wait for it—who happens to live in Market Harborough. Langford Junior knew all this before he even approached him. I can tell you, that Langford Junior is a shrewd businessman."

"Interesting story," Lawrence said, trying to sieve out Oliver's overdramatisation.

"So, Lawrence, here comes the news you've been waiting for your entire life. Something that will make you forget the Siren. Yours truly has spoken to Mr Drake and he wants to see your synopsis *and* the first fifty pages of your novel."

Lawrence let out a laugh. "You've got to be kidding."

"Not a word of a lie."

"How on earth did he agree to speak to you?"

"An old school… acquaintance is pretty high up in the firm."

"And you just thought you would give him a call now, after all my years of suffering."

"I bumped into him. Did him a favour. He's just repaying it."

Lawrence glanced sideways at his cousin, still not sure if Oliver was just teasing.

"I have my ways, Loz." Oliver shot Lawrence a coy smile and tapped his finger against the side of his nose.

"You certainly do." Lawrence ruffled Oliver's hair again.

"It doesn't stop there, Loz. I haven't forgotten all those times you bailed me out since Dad… you know…" Oliver looked at the ground, before adding, "…cut me off and all that." He looked back up at Lawrence and grinned at him before delivering his pièce de résistance. "If you ask me, it's pretty much a tick box exercise. I think you have it in the bag; I am quite confident of that."

Lawrence looked at his cousin with his mouth ajar, an apprehensive smile beginning to spread across his face. Did he want to get into the publishing industry through the back door?

"The meeting is in two weeks. You'll need to send off your initial chapters before that." Oliver paused for a moment before adding, "You know Loz, this is your break. The break you have been waiting for and you deserve it."

Lawrence stood up from the sofa, leaving a large hollow where his body had been. "I think I'm going to keep that book club meet tonight. All of a sudden I'm feeling much better."

*

Sunil hovered in the lobby of the apartment building. He knew Maria would be down soon. The sliding doors of the elevator and the electronic ping signalled her arrival, and so he quickly busied himself with one of the magazines that had been neatly arranged on the glass coffee table.

"Hey!" Sunil heard a familiar voice behind him. He swivelled on his right foot and came face to face with Maria.

Instinctively, Maria took a step back. There had been a distance between the two of them since her abduction and this worried her. She wanted to reach out and touch his hand but she refrained. What was she so afraid of?

There was something holding Maria back. It bothered her that she still couldn't remember much of the night at Marconi's the Wednesday before her abduction. Had her drink been spiked then? She had more than her fair share of alcohol, but her hangover on Thursday hadn't been anything unusual.

Maria remembered fragments of that Wednesday night. She had spent most of the evening talking to Sunil. Slivers of their conversation had come back to her—something about an arranged marriage, the stress he was under. But there was something else. Her body was contradicting what her mind was saying. Her hands tingled and her stomach fluttered whenever she was around him. But she was still wary that she couldn't remember what was said between them that night. Sunil must have felt it too because he had actively avoided her since that Wednesday. Was she being paranoid to think then that he had something to do with her abduction? Maria didn't think so. The obvious thing was to ask Sunil but, again, something stopped her. Was her subconscious trying to tell her something? Maria took a deep breath.

"What are you doing here?" she asked, her tone of voice hostile.

"I was just on my way to Du Jour and I was a bit early, so I was flicking through a magazine when this article caught my eye," Sunil said, wondering if his excuse sounded plausible.

"What's it about?" Maria asked as she rose to her tiptoes and tried to peer into the magazine.

He hesitated, quickly casting his eye towards the page. "The reproductive cycle of… rats," he responded sheepishly as he caught a glimpse of fear in Maria's eyes. He instinctively took a closer look at her but the fear had disappeared. Had he imagined it?

Maria shook her head and scrunched her face. "No, I mean how come you're in this building?" she asked with a serious expression. Maria's emotions began to stir and her hands started to tremble, the colour slowly draining from her face.

"Are you okay? You look faint. Here, sit down." Sunil led her over to the faded blue sofa behind the glass coffee table. Maria was silent. Something wasn't right. Sunil had his hand on her shoulder. Was Sunil her captor? *No, it couldn't be.* Maria didn't want to run away. She wanted to fall into his arms. She wanted him to protect her.

"I moved here a couple of weeks ago. My landlord wanted to move back into the place I was renting on Victoria Road," Sunil said. "I wanted to be closer to town and this came up. It was in budget and available immediately, so here I am. You didn't think I was stalking you or something, did you?" Sunil tilted his head and looked at Maria as she looked away.

"No," Maria said after a long silence. "It's just… I've been a bit jumpy lately," she confessed. Maria took a few long, deep breaths, slowly digesting what Sunil had just told her. *Was he lying? Bricks, Bricks, Bricks*—a vision of a brick wall came to her mind. Then she remembered Marconi's, Sunil's breath laced with rum on her skin, their lips almost touching.

"Maria?" Sunil broke her concentration.

Maria took a sharp intake of breath, waking her from her trance. Her mouth was dry and colour began to flood her cheeks. Had they kissed? Is that what she had been trying to remember? The desire to be protected and wrapped in his masculinity drew her in towards him.

Sunil immediately rose to his feet. "I think you need some fresh air. Some water?"

"No. No water. I have some here." Maria produced a water bottle from her satchel and took a large swig. *Was it a just a daydream? Was it true? Had something happened between us?* Then she remembered the aftershave. As Sunil walked back over, Maria leaned into him a little closer and discreetly inhaled. No, it certainly wasn't *Forever*.

Paranoia circled her. Sunil sat back beside Maria and squeezed her shoulder reassuringly as she put her face in her hands. "I wish I didn't feel like this all the time."

"Anxious? Is that how you feel?"

"I suppose, like something bad is going to happen to me," Maria said, knowing that she was treading on thin ice. How much could she afford to tell him? The weight of her abduction was weighing her down. Maria desperately wanted Leanne or Alice to be with her, but it was no use. They were not always going to be at her side to protect her.

"Why would you think something like that? *The Sinner* didn't get to you, I hope?" Sunil smiled at Maria, taking her hand in his.

Her fingers began to tingle. "What did you mean by that?" Maria snapped, pulling her hand away from his.

"Nothing, nothing." He raised his hands towards his head, exposing his palms to her.

Maria calmed again and smiled, finally realising the funny side. "*The Sinner* didn't get to me." All of a sudden she felt foolish. She was doing her best to push him away.

Maria looked at Sunil. If he didn't have any ulterior motives, then she could use a friend in the building. She could hardly expect Leanne to keep staying over. But how would she know? How would she know if she could trust him?

"Alice again?" Sunil asked. "Is that causing you stress?"

Maria's eyes widened as she looked at him. Her eyelid twitched as it did when she was nervous. Only Leanne knew about Alice.

Sunil noticed the hesitation in her eyes. "You told me that day," he said. "The day we got completely drunk at Marconi's. Back in, I don't know, September." He pretended he was unsure of the date even though it was imprinted in his mind.

Maria looked at the floor while she tried to remember. No, she could not remember telling Sunil. "Not Alice. Things are better with Alice. It's the only good thing that's come from all of this."

"All of what?" Sunil asked.

"Nothing, ignore me," Maria said, rising from the sofa and massaging her neck with her hand. "I'm having one of those days."

Sunil noticed Maria's fragility and apprehension. Maybe she didn't know? It had turned out much worse than he had expected. He contemplated telling her but then stopped himself.

Maria looked at her watch. "We'll be late for Lawrence."

"*Darlington House*."

Sunil held the door open for Maria. There was a slight chill in the air as they walked down the street towards Du Jour. "I must admit it took me awhile to get into the book," Maria said, "but it was much better than *The Sinner*."

38

"I think Sarah wanted him to betray her, so that she had an excuse to hurt him. Physically hurt him," said a woman in a purple beret sitting by the newspaper rack. For a brief moment the other members of the book club were silent before the murmurs of chatter started to break the quiet.

"I don't think that was the case," said a man in a leather jacket. "Sarah was in love with Enrico and felt humiliated by his ruthless deception."

"You're late," Oliver whispered to Sunil and Maria as he shifted himself on the sofa to make room for them.

"My fault," Sunil replied.

Maria squeezed his arm to show her gratitude.

"Where's Penny and Jason?" Sunil asked.

Maria strained to hear what Oliver was saying. A feeling of guilt crept up on her. Of late she had been a terrible friend to Penelope. She was so consumed by her own problems.

"Penny said she isn't feeling well, but if you ask me it's a cover-up for what's really happening in her life," Oliver said.

"And what *is* really happening in her life?" Maria asked in hushed tones.

"Someone I know in admissions told me Jason's left."

"University?"

"Try England."

"No way," Sunil said a bit louder than he should have, making two girls in front of him turn around and sneer. He mouthed an apology.

"That's not possible!" Maria said under her breath. "Jason would never have left." Maria was the only member of their group who knew Penelope was pregnant. Maria couldn't say she knew Jason well but she was certain that he was not one to shirk his responsibilities.

"Do you have a contribution?" Lawrence glared at Sunil and Oliver.

"Err, no sorry," Sunil said sheepishly.

"Well, what did you think of Sarah's love affair with Nicole following Enrico's brutal murder?"

Sunil tried to look engrossed in his copy of *Darlington House* so as not to attract any further attention from Lawrence, but the silence that followed unnerved him. He had no choice but to look up; first at Maria and then at Lawrence. "I think that… like the young lady in the corner said… Sarah was glad that Enrico betrayed her so it gave her an excuse to murder him and carry on with Nicole. Sarah had always loved Nicole from a distance. She just didn't know that the object of her desire would return her love until that night by the river. Once Nicole and Sarah discussed their feelings, her marriage was exposed for the sham and pretence that it was."

"I suppose…" Lawrence started.

"Love can be like that. It can bring out a different facet of your personality. It can make you do things you never thought you would do. It comes out of the blue," Sunil added, interrupting Lawrence.

Oliver raised his eyebrows. Sunil was normally so shy.

"It does indeed. Ah, you, sir… at the back. What is your view? You don't look like you agree with the young man," Lawrence said.

"Tell us," Maria pressed Oliver. "Tell us about Jason, what's going on?" For a couple of minutes all her problems had disappeared to the back of her mind. When Maria had been back to the bar with Penelope that day, Penelope had spilled the beans about her baby bump. Sharing with Maria just how scared she was of telling her parents, she had also said that Jason had been more supportive than she ever could have imagined. *Poor Penelope*, Maria thought. *She had mapped out their lives together. How would she manage without Jason?*

"I'll tell you later," Oliver said. "I don't want to piss Lawrence off any further. Look at the poor sod; he doesn't look well at all."

As Sunil sat back in the sofa, his mind drifted off from what Lawrence was saying. If Jason had left the country, without finishing his course, then something must have gone terribly wrong. He knew just how in love Penelope was with Jason and surely he felt the same way. What had happened in just a couple of weeks? He knew that time was precious. Sunil looked at Maria sitting next to him; she was talking to Oliver. How much time would pass before he had the courage to tell her? She had a right to know, surely, and then, what she chose to do with the information, well, that would be up to her.

39

Jason had ordered another double vodka on the rocks. Knocking back the clear, cold liquid in one gulp, he allowed it to line his empty stomach before placing the empty plastic cup back on his tray.

They were halfway over the Atlantic already. The passenger sitting next to him was asleep; the man's eyes hidden by a mask, his head to one side—he faced Jason's direction with his mouth half open. The sleeping man was making small grunting noises, his eyebrows rising above his eye mask with each breath. Jason turned away from the man and looked out of the small window into the dark of the night. He thought of Penelope then. He missed her already. But he couldn't just stay in England and carry on like nothing was wrong. He couldn't live with all the lies.

Jason had been in the air for some time now; flights at such short notice were hard to come by. A stopover in Amsterdam allowed him to catch his connecting flight to New York. From there he would have to take another flight to San Diego. It was the long way home, but he had to leave England. He could not bear to face Penelope again.

Jason reached into the back pocket of his jeans and pulled out his wallet. Just forty-eight hours ago, while packing, he had found an old photo in his sock drawer and he had returned it to where it had belonged. Jason rubbed his thumb over the photograph, remembering the day he had taken it.

It had been a Saturday, a well-earned weekend after a week of late nights and early starts. The only thing Jason had wanted to do was to spend time with his wife and son. Eleanor had carefully placed their baby boy in the red swing as Jason had held up the camera to capture the moment. Alfie was wearing what Grandma had sent over: a blue and white striped polo shirt and sky-blue cotton shorts. Their son had smiled and giggled with delight as Eleanor gently pushed the swing.

A feeling of pride had filled them both. It had been a long struggle for the three of them to get where they were. Finally they were a family and they had everything they had ever wanted.

★

The memory of the fateful morning when Eleanor announced she wanted to try for a baby came back to Jason. That was when it had all started.

"I think we're ready!" Eleanor had said one Sunday morning in June. Jason knew the date well because it was his birthday—his thirtieth birthday. She had thrown him a fabulous Mexican-themed surprise beach barbeque the night before. Jason had walked into thirty smiling faces wearing fake, thick black moustaches, multicoloured ponchos and sombreros. Eleanor had really gone to town and, as usual, she had thrown herself into the spirit of things. There were jugs of margaritas, tortillas, quesadillas and stuffed beef tacos with salsa, guacamole and sour cream. There had even been a piñata. The party had been a success, but he had woken up with the mother of all hangovers. Nothing would have shifted him from his bed that day. Well, not until Eleanor announced her decision.

Jason had always wanted children from the day that they tied the knot, but Eleanor had been reluctant. Her career had been her main excuse, though she had never mentioned it before their big white wedding. For a year, Jason had persistently dropped hints about starting a family so when Eleanor said that she was ready to try for a baby, it was the best birthday present he could ever have expected.

They had started trying that very morning, but the weeks soon turned into months and, with each cycle arriving like clockwork, there was no sign of a baby on the way. Both of them started reading up on different ways to help them conceive, what foods to eat and what to avoid. Their bathroom cabinets were taken over by ovulation sticks and folic acid.

"Let's just stop trying for a month or so, and then give it another go. We eat, sleep and breathe thoughts of a baby and it's wearing us both down," Jason said, his patience waning. But Eleanor was determined to find a way. She was not the sort of person to give up so easily and she was certain that it was within their power to conceive.

Jason was well aware of his wife's stubborn personality. When she decided she wanted something, she made sure she got it. They got married when she was twenty-seven, an age she had predetermined a long time before she had even met Jason. She managed to get a place at her first choice university despite an initial rejection, and she made sure that she got the job she wanted at SeaWorld. Failure was just not in Eleanor's vocabulary. The only letdown Eleanor ever experienced was failing her driving test, and she made sure she passed on her second attempt.

Jason's wife was not used to disappointment and, in Eleanor's eyes, not being able to conceive was the biggest failure ever. Trying to get pregnant began to consume her. It became her reason for being and it had begun to tear them apart.

But after eighteen months of trying, and when sex had truly become more of a chore than a pleasure, Jason finally convinced Eleanor to give up speculating and see a doctor. He was tired of sex-on-demand around what her ovaries were doing. He was tired of his wife, after sex, swivelling her body around and lifting her legs up, resting them on their headboard because she read that it just *might* help her conceive. The whole babymaking process was starting to make him feel inadequate, and Jason treated inadequacy the same way Eleanor treated failure.

"Maybe we're not supposed to have children," a tearful Eleanor had said one morning after her period arrived. She cursed those first spots. How things had changed from her university days when she had prayed for her period to arrive on time.

"Of course we are," Jason said impatiently, quashing his own doubts for her sake. "Do you know how many couples conceive through IVF or other fertility treatments these days? We're all a lot older than our parents generation so maybe our bodies are not as, you know… fertile."

"Blame *me* for waiting till we were older. You wanted kids before we were even married. I couldn't do that. I needed to be ready." Hot tears streamed down Eleanor's face.

"I didn't say that," Jason meekly protested, dropping his face into his hands. He wanted to ban the word baby and all its variations from their home.

"You implied it," Eleanor snapped, her eyes red raw from crying.

Jason looked at his normally calm and composed wife. The decisions Eleanor made were always well thoughtout and generally worked in her favour. Not because she was lucky but because she made things happen for her. Who else would write an essay on modern accounting practices and send it to the dean of a college she had been rejected from thus winning a place at her university of choice? Now Eleanor's anger took Jason by such surprise that he wasn't quite sure if he had implied that it was her fault or not. Had he meant to hurt her? After all, she *had* made him wait. No, he would never do that. Jason walked over to her and held her in his arms, silently vowing never to hurt her again.

"I spoke to Larry at work. He and his wife went through the same situation before they had Sam," Jason said gently. "They used IVF for Sam and Patricia was conceived naturally."

"So now you're telling your entire office our problems." Eleanor stiffened in his arms.

"Ellie, please," Jason said, kissing the top of her head. "I told Larry because I knew he had been through the same thing." He released her and sat down on their bed. Eleanor followed and sat close to him like a frightened child. Her face looked gaunt and her collarbones poked out from under her shirt. Jason stroked her hair as she buried her face in his bare chest but her tears continued to fall. "We're both under a lot of pressure at the moment and one of us may have a problem," Jason uttered the words tentatively. Words he didn't want to believe. "It could be that something somewhere is preventing us from conceiving. We need to see a doctor. It may be something they can fix."

"I just don't..." Eleanor started but tears prevented her from continuing.

"Hey, look, maybe there's nothing wrong," Jason said, brightening. "These things can take time, right? But listen, we can rule out anything medical if we go and see someone about it. We don't want to leave it any later."

40

Eleanor reluctantly agreed to see a specialist. She knew Jason had a point but she was afraid, afraid that she was the one with the problem. A week later they had both arrived at the private treatment centre Larry had recommended. They sat in silence with several other anxious couples in the waiting room of the Asthall clinic. Jason instinctively took Eleanor's hand as he heard their names called out and together they walked into the doctor's office.

Dr Spencer was tall and thin with a receding hairline and an angular nose, but he had a kind smile. "Come in, Mr and Mrs Rupert." Dr Spencer introduced himself as he shook their hands in turn. Then he ushered them towards the two black leather seats that sat opposite his desk and closed the door behind them.

Returning to his seat, he smoothed his white overcoat and clasped his hands together on his desk. "I have read your notes from Dr Cane, but I would just like to hear from you a brief history before we get started." Dr Spencer looked first at Eleanor and then at Jason. "Why don't we start with you, Mrs Rupert?" he suggested, squinting at her.

Eleanor looked at Jason for reassurance before she spoke. "We started trying for a baby about eighteen months ago. We can't get pregnant."

"It's not all that long, you know," Dr Spencer said, as he referred to the notes from their doctor. This was becoming a regular occurrence in his profession, especially with the younger generations. They had no patience.

Eleanor looked at Jason. Tears were welling up in her eyes.

Jason swiftly stepped in. "I know it seems like we're in a bit of a rush but we want a family soon, and we think it's best to rule out any issues sooner rather than later. At least then we'll know our options."

"It's sensible to do that, yes. Your notes are clear from Dr Cane, but let me just ask again. Have any one of you had any medical problems before? Any surgeries? Are you on any medications?" Dr Spencer poised his pen above his notepad.

Eleanor watched him scribble their names and the date on the top line.

"No." Jason responded for them both.

"I will need a full history of your reproductive health, such as any previous abortions, miscarriages..." Dr Spencer glanced up at Eleanor. It was more often the case than not that a woman would lie about previous miscarriages or abortions she may have had with a different partner. He opened his drawer and took out some sheets of paper. "Here," he said, handing them both a form. "Complete these and send them back to me..." he looked at his watch, "by the fifteenth at the latest."

Eleanor looked at the form before she took Jason's from him, folded them neatly and put them in her handbag. "We'll have them to you by then," she said decisively.

"Why the fifteenth?" Jason questioned.

Dr Spencer leaned back on his chair. "I'm going to schedule you in for a couple of tests. Hormone and a uterine cavity test, and, of course, a sperm count and motility test. These tests shouldn't take too long and I can have the results fairly soon, but I need you to complete those forms first. We need to get your full medical histories from your doctor and there are some general lifestyle questions on there as well: if you're smokers, etcetera, etcetera."

"So what happens if there is a problem?" Eleanor asked.

"If, and it's a big if, there is a problem, we will take it from there, Mrs Rupert." Dr Spencer gave Eleanor a reassuring smile. "You know, sometimes it's the pressure of trying to conceive that puts stress on the body."

The doctor stood up and shook their hands again before walking around his desk and opening the door for them. "I'll see you here in a couple of weeks with the results. Linda will schedule the tests for you. Try not to worry. If there is a problem, medicine can do wonders these days."

The tests had been relatively painless but waiting for the results had been agony. When they had finally come through, Dr Spencer had invited the couple back to the clinic to discuss their options.

"You're in the clear," Dr Spencer said, smiling at Eleanor. A broad smile spread across her face—there was nothing wrong with her ability to conceive. For the first time in months she relaxed. But then panic began to set in. It was the way that Dr Spencer was looking at the paper in front of him that suggested something was not as it should be, and Eleanor knew that if she had been given the all clear, then it was Jason who had the problem.

Eleanor knew instinctively just how nervous her husband was by the tiny beads of sweat that had appeared just below his hairline. The last time she saw him like this, they were standing in front of an alter reciting their wedding vows. But he had been smiling then.

Jason didn't look at his wife. His eyes were focused on Dr Spencer, who was studying the test results. Eleanor's emotions were mixed. She was glad that her body had not failed her and that, as a woman, she could fulfil her need to reproduce. Yet her soul mate had a problem and she couldn't take away his pain, nor could she take away the fact that they may never be able to have children together. All of a sudden she felt like she was falling. Her lack of control over what the doctor was saying was making her feel faint.

"I have some bad news for you, though" the doctor said solemnly, after what felt like an eternity. "Jason, your sperm is, in fact, very healthy but…"

Eleanor braced herself. She took hold of Jason's hand and squeezed it in hers.

"It's the mobility of the sperm. It's not good." Dr Spencer lifted up a piece of paper from his file and handed it to Jason.

It meant nothing to him. It was a black and white picture with several red dots and a few green ones on it.

Dr Spencer continued. "The red dots represent the sperm that are not mobile. Fast-moving sperm is paramount for conception. The fast-moving sperm are represented by the green dots."

Jason counted the green dots; there were only three on the page. He handed the paper back to the doctor waiting for more detail.

"The computerised sperm tests that we carried out analyse the movement of the sperm and their paths. You see many of the ones that are moving, the green dots, are moving in the wrong direction."

"So what does this mean?" Jason asked, swallowing his fear. "What does this mean for us trying to have a baby?" He clenched his fist into a ball and dug it into his thigh.

"I am afraid the prognosis is not good. You have less than a five per cent chance of conceiving." Dr Spencer looked at Eleanor. He hated this part of his job, crushing people's dreams. "There are obviously ways that you can still get pregnant," he added, giving them something to cling on to. "In vitro fertilisation has very good success rates."

Dr Spencer walked over to his cabinet and pulled out a couple of leaflets for them. "Here, take these and read through them over the next couple of days. They give you a rough idea of what the process involves. The second leaflet is on intracytoplasmic sperm injection or ICSI, which is part of the IVF process in circumstances such as yours. The sperm is taken directly from the semen and inserted directly into the egg." Dr Spencer saw the confusion in their faces.

Using technology to produce a child often scared people. "You could also look into adoption or many couples use surrogacy," Dr Spencer said. "Take some time to digest this information. If you do decide to go down any of these routes, then you won't be on your own. Thousands of couples go through this and we provide counselling services to help you decide and to help you through the process."

Eleanor took the leaflets and stood up. She took Jason's hand and led him towards the door, thanking the doctor for his time.

"If you do decide on medical treatment, just call me and we will schedule you in for an introduction appointment," Dr Spencer said, before he signalled to his secretary that he was ready for his next patient.

Both Jason and Eleanor were silent on the way home. Jason now realised that the thought of him being the one with the problem had never even entered his mind. Jason had never for one moment doubted the virility of his sperm. Although he had unprotected sex on several occasions, he had always just assumed that the girl was using some sort of contraception. Now it all made sense—he couldn't have children. He had pathetic, slow-moving sperm, and the fast-moving ones he *did* have were moving in the wrong direction.

At first Jason avoided Eleanor. She excused his behaviour, saying that he needed time to digest what Dr Spencer had told him. But as the days passed, a feeling of inadequacy gripped him and pulled him down into a depression. It bore on him that he was holding his wife back. Jason knew that Eleanor could have easily left him and had children with someone else. Jason could never have a child of his own.

Jason began to distance himself, working late and using fictitious work dinners to avoid his wife. Their lovemaking became more and more infrequent and, instead of confiding his deepest and darkest fears to his wife, Jason found the allure of strip bars something he could no longer resist. The women in g-strings and suspenders didn't know his inadequacies. They still thought he was a man. For a couple of hours each night, they made him feel invincible and reminded him of his sexual prowess before he guiltily crept back into bed and felt inadequate again. As he lay next to his wife, the thought of not being able to father a child crept into his mind and scared him to the core of his being.

Eleanor, ignorant to Jason's misdemeanours, knew that it was her turn to be the strong one. She believed Jason was drowning his sorrows with a friend in a bar most evenings. Not knowing what to say to him, she felt that the only thing she could do was to make sure there was a pot of fresh coffee in the mornings before work to clear his fuzzy head. Eleanor knew her husband well enough to know that he needed space, and only when she could see him start to confide in her about his feelings did she approach him about the leaflet

Dr Spencer had given them all those weeks ago. She wanted him to see for himself that they could have children together.

It had taken them nearly two months to make an appointment with Dr Spencer after deliberating whether they were ready to go through with IVF. It was an expensive process, there was no doubting that, and even then they could be unsuccessful. Eleanor's parents had given them a large chunk of money to get the process started and the rest they used from savings. If IVF didn't work the first time, Jason and Eleanor would have no choice but to remortgage their house.

The appointment had taken about a half hour. Jason had studied the doctor's certificates that hung in the doctor's office along with pictures of the male and female reproductive organs as Dr Spencer explained the process to them both. The feeling of guilt resurfaced. It was Eleanor who would have to take a hormone suppressant. It was Eleanor who would have to take drugs to stimulate her ovaries and it was Eleanor who would act as a petri dish for the embryo that the doctors would manually fertilise with his slow-moving sperm. Worst of all, it was not a quick fix solution. They would have to be patient and it was all his fault.

41

Jason ordered another double vodka as the airhostess pushed the drinks cart through the aisle. He sipped it slowly this time, still holding the picture of Eleanor and Alfie in his hand. How could he have left them after what they had been through together? They had been lucky, on their first attempt, two weeks after the embryo had been embedded in Eleanor's uterus. They had gone back to the clinic for a pregnancy test and Eleanor was pregnant.

Alfie arrived nine months later to parents who had vowed to love him and each other until the end of time. "You are my rock, Ellie," Jason had told his wife as she held their newborn. But Eleanor soon began to change.

"Her hormones are all over the place," Jason's mother had said to him when he first confided his feelings. "It takes a long time to settle in. Having this new little creature in your lives. It's always harder for the mother," she said, excusing Eleanor's distant behaviour. Jason had listened. Of course Eleanor would be different, he reasoned. They had tried so hard for Alfie, and they knew that he would be their only child. Eleanor was bound to be precious and he couldn't blame her. They had made love numerous times after the birth of their son, but nothing had happened since, not so much as a scare. Jason had even been back to Dr Spencer for an additional test unbeknownst to Eleanor, but the mobility of his sperm had not changed.

So how then had Penelope become pregnant?

When Penelope first told Jason she was pregnant, he had truly wanted to believe that the unborn child was his. That the five per cent chance Doctor Spencer had told him about had worked. But he could only lie to himself for so long and, as doubt began to creep in, he realised that Penelope's child wasn't his. It was obvious, *wasn't it*? After all, she did work in a strip club—she had her pick of men who were dying to sleep with her most evenings. How had he been so naïve?

Jason closed his wallet and put it back in his pocket. Penelope had duped him so well, playing on his insecurities. He had even considered giving up Eleanor and Alfie to be with her and what he thought was his new baby. Even though she had betrayed him, there was a tiny part of him that still loved her; her beautiful body, her delicate personality. The airhostess wheeled her trolley towards him and took his empty glass.

Jason's mind shifted to Eleanor once more. He had run away from his wife back in the summer and now he was running away from Penelope. He had to stop running. He couldn't live a lie with Penelope and he knew deep down that Eleanor was who he loved. Finally, he had made the right decision.

The sun was just beginning to break as the airplane began its descent into JFK airport. Looking out the window, Jason could see the city beginning to stir beneath him. He smiled. He was almost home.

42

"That means you like him!" Alice said, nudging Maria with her elbow. She gave her sister a wide grin as they walked together down the high street with half a dozen shopping bags between them. Alice was content for the first time in over two years. It had been a lonely existence without Maria in her life because nobody knew her like her sister did, not even Owen. Now they had been reunited. Alice was determined never to let anything come between them again. *I'm going to become a better person*, she told herself as she held on to Maria's arm.

After the tell-all meeting between the sisters, something had shifted. Since then they had met on numerous occasions and were slowly getting back to normal. But the relationship was not the same as it had been before Owen. Before Owen, Alice had been the quiet one living in Maria's shadows but now things were different. Maria would have said that they were on more of an equal footing. Alice knew that she was now the stronger one.

Owen was still an issue for Maria. Alice knew that as the sisters walked together arm in arm. How could they be proper sisters if Maria was still hung up on her fiancé?

It was for this reason that Alice had decided to push the whole Sunil situation so it came to a head. Somebody needed to fill the void that Owen had created in Maria's life and that somebody was Sunil.

"Maybe I do like him," Maria admitted as she stopped to look at a cobalt-blue top in a shop window.

"It's not your colour," said Alice, dragging her away from the window.

"I haven't felt butterflies in my tummy since…" Maria looked into the distance. "Well, anyway," Maria stopped short, remembering who she was with. Alice had made it clear that whatever Maria had told her about Owen, it wasn't going to change her decision to marry the man.

*

The words, "It wasn't my place to tell you," echoed in Maria's head. That was what Owen had told Alice about her abortion, or so Alice had said. Was he right? Maria wasn't sure. But she knew now that she had no control over the matter. Alice had made her decision and she had to respect that. Two years ago Maria would have bet money that Alice wouldn't have stayed with Owen if she knew about the abortion.

Now Maria had her own decision to make. She either lost her sister to Owen or she got over it and carried on with the rest of her life. Maria released her grip from her sister and tucked her hair behind her ear. It had been so long since she saw Owen last, she wasn't quite sure how she felt any more. After patching things up with Alice, her hatred for Owen and the dull ache in her heart that had followed her around for the past two years was slowly beginning to disappear.

Maria tried to imagine the feel of Owen's touch on her skin. She knew she would have to meet him soon and it worried her. Would her tummy flutter when she caught sight of him? Would she feel a shiver down her spine as she shook his hand and kissed his cheek? Or would she feel nothing? Maria sighed. Thinking about Alice and Owen always wore her out.

Maria followed her sister into a designer shop where she knew she wouldn't buy anything. Alice laughed with the sales assistant before selecting a couple of items to try. Maria looked around the minimalist decor and white gloss furnishings that made her feel unwashed, and wondered when her sister had started shopping in stores like this.

As Alice climbed into a skin-tight red skirt, Maria looked at the price tag. "How do you afford this? Modelling must be paying well."

"I don't do all that much modelling nowadays. Owen's not keen on me modelling."

Maria raised her eyebrows. "Since when?"

"Oh, I guess the last year. Owen's business has been doing really well. He's told me I don't need to work. He gives me a pretty good allowance."

Maria laughed. "An allowance?"

Alice frowned at her sister. "Call it what you like, it's money in my bank each month."

Maria bit her tongue. When they were growing up, Alice had always wanted to make her own money. Had Owen pressured her to become financially dependant on him? Was he controlling her sister in the same way he had convinced Maria that an abortion was what they both wanted? Maria shook away her thoughts, pushing the past back where it belonged.

"You know, you should tell him," Alice interrupted Maria's thoughts as the cashier rung through Alice's items.

"What?" Maria asked.

"Sunil. Tell him you like him." Alice handed her credit card to the cashier.

"That's a lot of money for three items," Maria said, looking at the total bill. It would have paid her mortgage that month.

"That's how much clothes cost," Alice said.

"Oh," said Maria, awkwardly covering her high street dress by buttoning up her overcoat.

"So are you going to tell him?"

"I don't know. I feel like Si is hiding something. Something he's afraid of telling me. I don't know what it is."

"But I thought you said you two were spending an awful lot of time together and that you liked his company."

"We *do* live in the same building. And he's just always there. I do like him but, like I said, it's like he's holding something back."

"Maybe he's always loved you from afar," Alice said, giggling. "Or," she said with a more serious tone, "maybe it's the arranged marriage you mentioned."

Maria frowned. "Yes, he mentioned that, but my memory of that night is a bit fuzzy."

"Ask him."

"It's a bit personal though."

"Well, if he mentioned it already. If he hasn't mentioned it again, maybe you got it wrong. An arranged marriage is a pretty big deal—if it was happening, you'd know about it."

"Perhaps…"

"So maybe he does like you then."

"Don't you think he would have said something by now?"

"Tell him you like him."

"I am not sure that I do." Maria blushed.

"Look at your red cheeks!"

Maria smiled uncontrollably. Stopping outside a shop window, she distracted Alice by pointing to some red heels with a large satin bow on the toe. "What do you think of those?" she asked, her eyes fixated on the colour.

"I think you won't be able to walk in them."

43

Maria stopped for a moment, savouring the scene while she enjoyed a lemon cupcake. She was standing with Alice outside the bakery they used to go to with their mother as children. Maria had missed moments like this with her sister. She wanted to forget her stupid abduction and move on with her life, but she couldn't.

After months of therapy Maria had finally been given a date for her hypnosis, and it was fast approaching. Dr Timms had recommended that she bring a close friend or relative with her to take her home and to help her with any revelations from the session. Maria wasn't sure whether to ask Leanne or Alice. Leanne had been with her every step of the way, but Alice was her sister, her flesh and blood. The only issue was that Alice still didn't know about her abduction, and she didn't know about her therapy sessions either.

"Maria, if I tell you something, promise you won't tell a soul?" Alice said, interrupting her sister's thoughts.

"Promise," Maria responded, raising three fingers of her right hand. "Scout's honour." Alice took Maria's cupcake wrapper from her and put it in the bin outside the bakery, wiping her lips with her mitten. They started to walk again.

"You won't tell Leanne?"

"Leanne's cool, you know that. In fact, I was just thinking about our sister pact."

"Mmm..." Alice furrowed her brow.

"What is it?" Maria asked, sensing Alice's apprehension. "Of course I won't tell Leanne if you don't want me to."

"I know how close you are," Alice said, looking at Maria out of the corner of her eye.

"I won't tell. Now spit it out."

"But it's about Leanne."

Maria raised an eyebrow.

"Keep it quiet, okay?" Alice fiddled with her shopping bags. "Leanne called me the other day."

"She did?" It was the first Maria had heard of it and it immediately set her heart beating faster.

"I suppose she was worried about you."

Maria was silent as her concern mounted.

"You promised you wouldn't tell."

"Did I say I was going to tell?" Maria said with a firm voice.

"She mentioned that you were a little stressed and that a bit of sister time would be good."

"Oh!" Maria said, her heart sinking a little. Leanne had never mentioned calling Alice.

"She meant well, Maria. Don't think she was going behind your back or something. I think she was just worried."

Maria was concerned. Were her problems getting too much for her best friend? She hadn't been much of a friend to Leanne at all. She had not asked once about how she was coping after her breakup with Scott. Maria was just glad the cheating bastard was out of her friend's life. But she had made no attempt to see how Leanne really felt.

"Leanne told me to keep it quiet. I just told you because, you know, now that we're sisters again, we tell each other everything. I don't want us to keep secrets from one another." Alice looked at Maria. She was tired of being drip-fed snippets of information from Leanne. She felt like a dog begging for scraps.

Maria hugged her sister but anxiety began to prick her thoughts. "Don't worry. I won't tell Leanne a thing," Maria said.

Maria took Alice's hand and led her through to the shoe shop they had passed earlier. As they walked together over the entrance of the shop a shiver ran down Maria's spine, making her stop cold in her tracks. Alice walked straight into her and Maria instinctively let go of her hand.

"Are you okay? You look like you've seen a ghost," Alice said stroking the goosebumps on the back of Maria's arm.

"Something just..." Maria started, but she couldn't find the words. She sat on the low black suede seats amongst several girls trying on shoes, chattering away. She caught her breath. "I'm fine," Maria said, trying to grasp what she had just seen.

Maria was awake. Wide awake, lying on her sofa, afraid that he would realise she was listening. But it wasn't just one person. She could hear more than one voice. She didn't know who they were, but their voices were familiar. What were they saying? She didn't know who they were, but their voices were familiar. What were they saying? There were two, no, three of them. They were all talking. Maria knew them. She could not see their faces. She could not hear their voices clearly enough. Their identities still remained hidden, but she knew them all. She was certain of that.

"You don't look fine. Maybe we should get something to eat." Alice looked at her watch. "It's almost 2.30 p.m."

Maria rose to her feet. "Let's get out of here," she said, trying to block out the terror rising up within her. Maria squeezed her sister's hand in hers.

Alice smiled. Maria was back in her life. Alice and Owen had both deceived Maria in so many ways. Sleeping with Owen so soon after Maria's abortion had been a painful burden for Alice to carry. But now all that was behind them. Alice had buried that memory along with the other skeletons that had been rattling around.

"Maria," Alice blurted out, "I have to ask you something." She smiled.

"What? What is it?" Maria said, still shaken from the fear she had felt only moments ago.

"I know you don't like talking about him much, but you know we're getting married, and, well, I was hoping you would be my maid of honour." Alice looked at her sister with anticipation. This was what it had all been for. Having Maria as her maid of honour was so important to Alice.

Maria looked at Alice's left hand, the two carats flashing back at her. Maria strained herself to smile. She didn't have a choice. "I'm so happy for you, Alice." She forced the words out, but as they left her mouth she knew she meant what she said. "I would love to be your maid of honour."

Alice embraced Maria, her eyes filling with tears. "I told Owen there wasn't a cat's chance in hell that I would set a date until you were back in my life. I'm the happiest person ever."

Maria swallowed her anxiety. "We should all meet, perhaps, for dinner or something. I haven't seen him in ages and… it's time. After all, he'll soon be my brother-in-law."

"That would be great. Perhaps you could bring Sunil?" Alice said.

Maria took in her sister's beaming smile and moist eyes; she had not seen her this happy in years. It was time she told Alice about her abduction. After all, she would need some support after her hypnotherapy and, as she had just realised, blood was thicker than water.

"Alice," Maria said, "now I have something to tell you."

44

"It felt good to tell Alice," Maria said, trying not to give too much away.

"I told you," Leanne said with relief as she poured a handful of caramel popcorn into her mouth. Her brown eyes smiled at Maria. "Last time a secret split you two up. It was only natural to tell her about your abduction."

"I love having my sister back," Maria said, but then she noticed the sadness in Leanne's eyes. She was thinking about her own sister who she had lost.

Maria tried to find a reason why Leanne would have called Alice. Perhaps, she reasoned, Leanne was genuinely worried. But it concerned Maria that the only reason Leanne had confided in Alice was because she believed Maria was making the whole story up.

"So what did she say?" Leanne asked.

"Alice didn't think I was making it up." Maria gave her friend a cold look. "She was absolutely horrified. She couldn't understand why someone would have done this to me." Maria remembered the look of worry on her sister's face, frown lines on an otherwise flawless complexion. Alice had become quiet after her initial outburst, which had made Maria feel uncomfortable. "Alice was very concerned for me," Maria reassured herself.

Leanne was silent.

"I think Alice knows where her *loyalties* are now," Maria said.

"*Alice,*" Leanne muttered under her breath as her eyes narrowed. Leanne wondered if Alice had said anything to Maria about their conversations. It wasn't usual for Maria to behave so hostile for no apparent reason.

"Alice thinks that something was put into my tea at work. And that perhaps someone else was waiting outside."

Leanne frowned slightly, frustrated that she had not thought of that scenario herself. She was also annoyed that Alice hadn't shared any of her own suspicions, yet had prised all of Leanne's ideas out of her.

"So she thinks there was more than one person involved?" Leanne asked, still annoyed with herself for talking to Alice in the first place. The one thing Maria had asked was to keep her abduction a secret and she couldn't even manage that.

"You look confused," Maria said, cocking her head to one side and looking directly at her friend. "It's simple, really. I can't believe we missed it." Maria refrained from telling her friend about her latest flashback.

Leanne pursed her lips.

"What?" Maria asked.

"Oh, nothing." Alice's new theory niggled at her. She had spoken to Alice recently and she had again brought up the possibility that this whole episode was just in Maria's head. What kind of game was Alice trying to play?

Maria switched the television on and sat on the floor with her back against the sofa. Leanne could feel Maria's frostiness and wondered how to broach the fact that she had blabbed to Alice. Clearly Maria knew something. Alice was no longer the quiet, shy girl she knew when they were growing up, the girl she often referred to as her own kid sister, the girl she showed how to paint her nails and curl her hair. This new Alice was so confident and sure of herself. Had Owen played a part in changing her from a sweet and innocent girl to a manipulative cow, determined to get her own way? Leanne wanted to believe that he had, but deep down she wasn't so sure.

In the past, Leanne had conveniently swept aside memories of Alice pulling the wings off a butterfly, and blaming Maria for colouring their mother's shoes with makeup, when, in fact, Alice had done it. And for mashing a banana in the glove box of her father's brand new Volkswagen. Leanne had excused this behaviour as childhood misdemeanours, but now she couldn't help think that Alice was perhaps a little more calculated than she had once thought, even if it had been Leanne who had confided in Alice and not the other way around. Leanne clenched her teeth. Alice had used her and now Leanne was sure Alice was turning Maria against her.

As Leanne mindlessly watched the flashing images on the television screen, the niggle she had about Alice's personality slowly turned into something much bigger. Venom started to build inside Leanne, and for the first time in months she could clearly see what Alice was doing. Leanne had fallen prey to Alice. In fact, by confiding in Alice she had given her ammunition to cause a rift between Maria and herself.

Guilt lapped at Leanne's feet. Leanne had been worried about Maria, but her reasons had not been entirely altruistic. The sad truth was that Leanne *had* wondered if Maria had made it all up. After all, Maria was a bit of a dreamer; she had withdrawn so much after Owen and then crept even further into her shell after the abduction.

Leanne bit her fingernails. She was reading too much into this. Perhaps Alice hadn't said anything to Maria about their conversation at all. Leanne sighed. How would she react if her sister had been abducted? But Leanne knew she would never have to worry about this. Her sister was dead. Immortalised at fifteen. No matter how much time passed, she still thought about Sarah everyday. Sibling relationships were complex, especially between sisters. *Which was harder*, Leanne asked herself, *losing a sister because of your own actions or losing a sister to death?* She wasn't sure. But she knew that she had to come clean with Maria. The guilt was eating her up regardless of whether Alice had told Maria or not.

"There had to be more than one person involved," Maria said, looking back at her friend. "There would have had to have been two people, at least. If you think about the logistics."

"And what did Alice say about Dr Timms?"

"Well," Maria said quietly, worried that her friend would tell her sister something else. "I didn't mention the Dr Timms part." Maria looked out of the arched window.

Leanne changed channels.

"You see, the thing is my mother always said only sick people go to therapists. I don't want her to think I'm unwell. That this has given me some kind of lasting damage."

"Because you were always the strong one? Your mother's view is very last century, Maria," Leanne said, clenching her fists. She herself had visited a therapist after Sarah's death.

Maria turned to face Leanne. "Just don't tell Alice, okay?" The words were pointed and came out before Maria could stop them.

Leanne's eyes widened. So Alice had spoken to Maria about their conversation.

Tears started to stream down Maria's face.

Leanne walked over to her friend and hugged her. "I'm sorry," she said, "I'm so, so sorry."

Leanne sat back on the sofa. "I wouldn't tell Alice anything private. It was just to tell her to keep an eye out for you. I care about the both of you more than you know. When Sarah left us, well, you two were all I had. You two were my sisters, remember?"

Maria was silent.

Leanne's eyes welled up. "I found your tablets and I wasn't strong enough to take responsibility for you by myself."

"What are you talking about?"

"I had to tell her about the incident. Explain to Alice about the antidepressants."

"What?"

"I found them, Maria. You don't have to pretend."

"I don't know what you're talking about!" Maria's head was spinning. She wasn't on antidepressants. And did Leanne just admit she had already told Alice about her abduction? So Alice knew already and didn't say anything. That would have explained Alice's reaction. How she was so quick to come up with a theory as if she'd had weeks to mull over it.

"Leanne..." Maria started, but Leanne was walking to the bedroom. "Where the hell are you going?"

Leanne came back to the sitting room holding a box of tablets.

"I've never seen them before..." Maria said.

"It's okay, Maria."

"No, it's not bloody okay. Those tablets are not mine!" *Bricks, Bricks, Bricks.* That was the only word that came to Maria. In her mind's eyes she saw a hand, a silhouette in the light of the fridge, a scarf—a yellow scarf. She closed her eyes. Could she picture a face? Remember a voice? The colour in her flashback was vibrant now, the images clearer. But no, she could not recognise a face. Maria stood up and pulled the box of tablets out of Leanne's hands. She examined the packaging carefully through bleary eyes.

"So if they're not yours, whose are they then?" Leanne asked.

45

Penelope slumped further into the sofa. Images of a couple with two children sitting around a dining table sharing a roast chicken appeared on her television screen. Penelope closed her eyes. She could not bear to see happy families. Within two weeks she had lost her old family and what she had believed to be her new family. Now she was all by herself with a new baby arriving in less than six months. She looked down at her tummy and, beneath Jason's old t-shirt, she pictured her sleeping baby. It would be the fifth day in a row that she had called in sick at work but she just couldn't face the world. Not yet.

Her mobile phone rang. It was Maria. Given that Oliver had called yesterday, Penelope was certain the whole book club knew that Jason had done a runner. Of course, they would want to know why he left. Maria would be calling to offer her support; after all, she was the only one in the group who knew she was pregnant. But still Penelope declined the call. She just didn't have the energy.

For the third time that day, Penelope picked up the tear-stained letter from the coffee table and reread Jason's words. She would have to face reality sooner rather than later. With no way of contacting Jason, Penelope realised that she didn't know as much about him as she thought she did. Penelope didn't even know the name of the company Jason worked for in America. How foolish in love she had been.

Penelope dialled Jason's mobile number once more. It went straight to voicemail. She didn't bother leaving a message this time. She asked herself what she would say if she did ever manage to get hold of him. She could prove that the baby was his. In her entire life she had only ever slept with two men. The first had been a mistake, a drunken dare by Ciara and they had used protection. There had been countless times with Jason where they had failed to use any protection at all. There was nothing more to it. Jason had been mistaken. He was the father of her unborn child, she was certain of it. A five per cent chance to conceive was still a chance in her eyes. It was still possible. But she had little choice now. Jason had left thinking she was a slut and a liar. Penelope knew that in Jason's eyes she was some two-bit escort he had picked up in a bar. Someone he had the right to toss aside when it suited him. His letter didn't have to spell it out for her. Penelope knew that Jason would never have left without giving her a chance to explain if he didn't think that way. Jason hated her and it stung.

Tears streamed down Penelope's face. Her eyes red and raw, she fell asleep under the duvet she had dragged into the lounge from her bedroom. But hardly an hour had passed when she woke up, overcome with hunger. She padded over to the kitchen and opened the fridge. It was empty. Penelope rubbed her tummy and again thought of her unborn child. She knew that if she starved herself, she starved her child. And she could not harm the child. Her baby was the only thing keeping her going. Grabbing her keys from the table, she put her camel trenchcoat over her old joggers and Jason's t-shirt. No one would see the mess she was under her big coat. Slipping on her trainers, she headed towards the supermarket. Storm clouds gathered overhead and thunder threatened.

Penelope picked up the pace, wanting to get back before the rain started. As she walked down the street, she felt a slight twinge in her lower abdomen. The hunger pains were getting worse. She knew she needed to get food and fast. As she walked she realised a takeaway would have been a better option, but now it was too late. She was already halfway to the shop. A short, sharp pain pierced her abdomen again. Penelope stopped and sat on a low wall for a minute.

When she had caught her breath she started again, slowly. Reaching the shop, she gathered some essential items, milk, bread, and put them in her basket—enough food to get her through the next couple of days. It was then that she spotted Lawrence. Wearing a dark grey suit with white shirt, his familiar face gave her some comfort, but she didn't want him to see her like this. Penelope looked down at the can of baked beans on the conveyor belt slowly moving towards the checkout girl and hoped he wouldn't notice her.

"Penny?" she heard him say.

"Lawrence!" she said, trying to sound upbeat. The twinge in her abdomen came again. She lifted her hand to wave to him and took her shopping bag with the other.

"Here, let me help you with that," Lawrence said as he paid for his items and walked over to Penelope.

"I'm fine," Penelope said, but she had started to feel faint.

Lawrence noticed her pallor. "Let me walk you home," he said, taking her bag from her. "It's on my way to the lecture theatre. I don't need to be there for at least another hour. I just stopped here to buy some lunch." His green eyes were smiling at her.

"Oh no, there's no need." Penelope tried to put him off. All she wanted to do was crawl back into bed, not have a lengthy conversation with him. But Lawrence was relentless. He would not take no for an answer.

Despite Penelope's apprehension, as they walked back to her apartment, she began to relax in his company. He had not tried to prise any information about Jason out of her and, because she hadn't spoken to anyone in a week, she heard herself wanting to talk about the whole wretched situation.

"I guess you've heard," she said tentatively, taking deep breaths.

"To be honest, I don't know much. One minute you were with Jason, and that was news in itself to me, and the next I hear he's left pretty sharpish back to his wife." Lawrence knew as the words left his lips that it was the wrong thing to say—perhaps Penelope didn't even know about Eleanor. Oliver had told him only yesterday.

Penelope tried to hold back the tears that were threatening but one escaped and slipped down her cheek. The emotion was too high and she broke into an uncontrollable sob as the dark clouds above her opened and the rain began to fall. She gasped and held her side. A sharp pain pierced through her. Before she could hold on to Lawrence, she had fallen to the ground. Her vision blurred before she blacked out.

*

Penelope woke up in a bed not familiar to her. She could hear activity around her, but the plastic cream curtain protecting her from the rest of the room restricted her eyes. Lawrence came into her line of vision.

"Hey," he said, walking over to her side with two plastic cups. "Here, have this." He held the cup out for her. "Sugary tea, guaranteed to make you feel better."

Penelope felt sick. The thought of tea made her want to gag. She adjusted herself in the hospital bed and sat up. Holding the cup to her lips, she pretended to take a sip. Lawrence took the steaming cup of liquid from her and placed it on the bedside table.

A doctor in a white lab coat popped his head through the curtains. "You're up!" he said with a big smile. "Let's have a look at you, then. I'm Dr Aston, Charles Aston." He took his stethoscope and placed it on her chest. "Right, just a couple of questions for you." Dr Aston looked at Lawrence and back at his patient. "I'll need to ask you some personal questions," he said gently.

"Lawrence, do you mind?" Penelope said, hoping that this would not offend the man who had just rescued her.

"Of course not," said Lawrence as he stepped out of the cubicle.

"Right, Miss…"

"Leigh."

"Let's start then, Miss Leigh," the doctor said. "First question. Are you pregnant?"

Penelope nodded, casting her eyes in the direction of where Lawrence was standing.

"I thought so, with the bump, although you can never be too sure. I find it best to ask. Do you mind if I do a quick external examination of your abdomen?" he asked.

Penelope nodded again. Dr Aston pressed his hand against her abdomen while asking her a string of questions. Penelope answered as best she could. It was her first pregnancy; she didn't know if the dull pain in her back and her malodorous urine was cause for concern or if it was a natural occurrence. It wasn't as if she had her mother to ask. The thought of her sour relationship with her parents brought tears to her eyes. Again she glanced through the crack in the curtain. She was mindful that Lawrence could have been standing right outside her curtained bed and could have heard about her unborn child.

"It looks to me like you have a urinary tract infection," Dr Aston said, as he took her blood pressure. You'll need to see the nurse, given that you're pregnant. I want to run a urine test to be sure, and I want you to have another scan. But from, what you said about the discomfort during urination and the tenderness, a UTI seems to be the cause. We'll run some more tests just to be sure. In the early stages of pregnancy, fainting combined with abdominal pains could well mean an ectopic pregnancy and we want to rule that out. Although this would likely have been picked up in your ten week scan and you haven't had any bleeding." The doctor looked at Penelope. "You *have* been for your scan?"

Penelope nodded. It had been the last thing she and Jason had done together as a couple.

I don't think, in this instance, that's the case, but I wouldn't be doing my job properly if I didn't check." He stopped writing and looked at Penelope before adding, "By the looks of it, you're not taking very good care of yourself. When was the last time you ate a decent meal?"

"I haven't been feeling well, that's all," she said.

"That may well be the urinary tract infection making you feel like that, but remember you're pregnant. You have to keep your strength up. You're responsible for another life now." Dr Aston pressed a button by the side of the bed and a nurse arrived a few minutes later.

"Miss Leigh needs these tests," he said, handing the nurse a metal clipboard. "Make sure she gets them and fast track her results."

"Yes, Doctor," she replied, unfolding the wheelchair that had been propped against the wall.

The nurse helped Penelope into it and pulled back the curtain. "Your boyfriend is probably in the cafeteria. I'll tell someone to ask him to meet you in the lobby in about a half hour, okay?"

For a split second Penelope thought the nurse meant Jason, but then she remembered it was Lawrence. The memory of Jason having a wife back in San Diego suddenly hit her again with full force, and a lump formed in her throat.

Penelope saw no reason to correct the nurse's mistake. She would only have to explain who he was and she wasn't in the mood for talking. "Okay," Penelope responded under her breath, trying to eliminate Jason from her mind. How could Jason have lied to her so blatantly? He never mentioned in his letter that he had a wife. All he said was that he was infertile, that he had had tests done when he was in a previous relationship.

Penelope buried her head in her hands. If Lawrence knew about Jason's wife then everyone must have known. Jason had left her with humiliation and deception, along with his child. *Jason knew what he was doing*, she thought, *and the pregnancy was an excuse, a way out, a way to his wife back home.*

Penelope urinated into a cup, endured having her skin pierced for the blood samples and forced down the juice and biscuits the nurse had placed in front of her. Two hours and one scan later, they let her go. She was surprised to see Lawrence still waiting for her in the lobby, knowing that he had lectures to give that afternoon.

"Lawrence!" Penelope said as the attendant wheeled her towards him. "I am so sorry. I didn't expect you to wait."

"I'll put the lecture notes on the university's intranet tomorrow. The administrator completely understood the situation," he said, as a way of an explanation.

"I'll make it up to you. I promise," Penelope said, biting her lower lip. It was getting dark outside and she didn't fancy going home, alone with her thoughts of Jason. "Perhaps I can make you dinner as a thank you," she added, wanting to prolong their meeting.

"You just had some kind of emergency there, I'm not going to let you slave over a hot stove for me tonight. Sorry." He put his arm around her waist and then quickly retracted it, remembering that she was just a friend.

"You're right," Penelope said. "Let me buy you dinner, then," she said, surprising herself. "Maybe that Greek place on the corner of

Friar Street. Do you like Greek food?" she asked. Her hunger was returning and she was craving red meat.

"You're on," Lawrence replied after a moment of hesitation, "and then you can tell me what that was all about."

"First I must go home and change, though," Penelope said, suddenly feeling unattractive in her old clothes. She needed to get out of Jason's old t-shirt. Penelope smiled. For the first time since Jason had left her, she felt alive. She thanked the attendant, put on her trenchcoat and stood up from the wheelchair. Hooking her arm in Lawrence's, they started for the hospital exit.

"Miss Leigh, you forgot your prescription," the nurse from earlier said, running towards them.

Penelope stopped and thanked her for it as she folded it and put it in her pocket.

"And don't forget, Miss Leigh, the doctor told me to remind you, you must start eating properly. Being fourteen weeks pregnant, you need to look after yourself." The nurse looked at Lawrence. "Make sure she eats well. It's important for your baby." Then she frowned at him, as if it had been his fault Penelope ended up in the hospital the first place, before breaking into a smile. She left the good-looking young couple at the entrance doors of the hospital and went back to her rounds.

46

The Crooked Camel was unusually packed for a Thursday night. As Maria pushed her way through the throng of people all vying for the bartender's attention, she stumbled over a patent black handbag.

"Hey, watch it!" Maria heard a voice. She mumbled an apology and looked for a clearing where she could stand to gather her thoughts. As people pushed, her anxiety began to suppress all her other emotions. Her old demons were coming back to haunt her: Bricks, a yellow scarf, a silhouette in the light of an open fridge. Maria squeezed her eyes shut and tried to block out the past. When she opened them, a tall man in his late-twenties was approaching her. Maria looked around but she was glued to the spot. She wanted to move but her legs wouldn't obey her. The tall man with slight stature stopped in front of her and smiled. All Maria noticed was that he was unshaven and had a tooth missing. He unnerved her.

"Can I offer you a drink, luv?" he asked.

Maria squeezed her elbow into her handbag, pressing it to her side. She politely declined before heading into to the clear space at the back of the pub. Taking a deep breath, she reminded herself that she was in a crowded venue and that no harm would come to her. *Think of blue skies when you feel anxious.* Dr Timms' words came back to her. Maria often did this but it only marginally helped. The unshaven face was still smiling at her from the crowd. Maria desperately wanted him to look away. Why had he approached her? *There are other singles in the bar*, she thought to herself. Was her fear visible to the outside world? Was her vulnerability more appealing to lonely, single men who spent most of their day in the Crooked Camel?

Maria considered her options. She couldn't see Sunil from where she was standing but the thought of walking back through the gathering at the bar made her feel queasy. After deliberating what to do for a couple of minutes, she eventually decided to stay put, where there was more space to breathe. Reaching into her bag, she retrieved her mobile phone. There was no signal and it set her nerves even further on edge. Maria closed her eyes again and pictured blue skies once more—this time with puffy white clouds.

"Maria…"

Maria heard the familiar voice from a distance. She opened her eyes and let out a sigh of relief. Sunil was frantically waving at her from a corner of the pub. Maria dropped her shoulders as a warm feeling quelled her nerves. She headed in his direction, invited by his smile and the open bottle of red wine.

"You were lucky to get a table," Maria said as she stepped into the alcove.

Sunil immediately stood up while Maria took a seat. "I came here straight from work. It was pointless heading back to King's View. Sangiovese, I hope that's okay," Sunil said, pouring Maria a glass.

Maria nodded. She was eager to let the first sip glide down her throat and hit her empty stomach. Red wine was so much better at dissipating her anxiety than thinking of blue skies.

Maria drank her first glass a little too quickly, and Sunil promptly refilled it. She fought the urge to tell him the real reason why she had not let him past her front door, and why she nearly jumped out of her skin just now, when an innocent man offered to buy her a drink.

There was something holding her back. Was it because she didn't trust Sunil? Or because she knew that once she confided in him, she would want to depend on him? Truth be told, she was tired of having to deal with this situation all on her own. Leanne had been great, but she too had doubted Maria, and had broken her trust by telling Alice. And even if Leanne's intentions were good, Maria had been hurt by her friend's actions. Of course, there was always Alice, but Alice had known about the abduction before Maria had even told her and she had kept quiet about it.

Maria knew that her nearest and dearest were only trying to protect her. She could hardly blame them for that, but she was tired of people from her past trying to second-guess her. Sunil was different—he didn't know about Maria's past. He was new and, to Maria, he seemed like just what she needed: a new beginning. But still there was all that drama from that Wednesday night, before her abduction. Something had happened between them, Maria was sure of it—she just couldn't remember what it was, and the gaps in her memory scared her. Was it just the effects of alcohol that night or had Sunil been part of her abduction as well? The fact that he had now moved into her apartment building was a red warning, surely? If her life were being played out in a movie, would she be shouting at the heroine on screen to grow a brain and leave the pub *now*? The mystery surrounding Sunil wasn't something Maria could just sweep aside and pretend didn't happen.

Sunil's hands shook. This wouldn't have been noticeable to most people, but Maria had become an expert in body language since that weekend in September. What was on his mind? Sunil loosened his collar and sank back into the deep red-velvet sofa.

Maria reached for her lip salve from her bag and dabbed the clear pink sheen on to her lips. They began to talk first about frivolous things, then about Penelope and Jason, and before Maria knew it, another bottle of the red wine had arrived. Maria looked out from the alcove they were sitting in. She knew it was nearing eleven by the few people left at the bar.

"Hey," Sunil said quietly, wanting Maria's full attention. Maria looked up at him and he held her gaze. "Maria, there's something I need to tell you." His hands were still trembling, but more obviously now.

Bricks, a yellow scarf, a silhouette. Maria remembered. *Their lips close together—Sunil's and hers.* She closed her eyes momentarily her palms moist with sweat. "Tell me," Maria said, her heart racing. She needed to know what had happened between them. But a small part of her didn't want to hear it. Her knee began to tremble. Her mouth was dry.

"I was so scared that day..." he began. "I shouldn't have said it, but I did... since that day... that terrible day... it's not been the same between us."

"I..." Maria started, but the words would not come. She felt dizzy. What was he saying? There was a ringing in her ears. She needed fresh air. Grasping for the glass of water on their table, she took a huge gulp and knocked over her glass of wine. The red liquid spilled onto the table and dripped onto her handbag.

Sunil quickly mopped it up with a white napkin.

Maria moved her bag and dabbed the wine off with a tissue.

"Are you okay?" Sunil asked.

Maria nodded. Claustrophobia started to engulf her. She looked around for a familiar face, even the man with the missing tooth, but saw none. Maria realised just how bad her judgement was. Just minutes ago she was debating telling Sunil about her ordeal and now he was telling her. Was he going to tell her that he was behind it? He said "that terrible day." He must have known. But why? Why was he confessing to her?

"That evening in September… it was a terrible day," he said again, avoiding Maria's eyes. "I remember it had been raining so hard." Sunil took a sip of wine.

Maria looked away. A shiver ran down her spine. Her pulse was racing and nausea rose up within her, accompanied by a surge of adrenalin. She fiddled with the strap of her handbag as it all began to slot into place. How Sunil suddenly moved into the King's View apartments. How he always seemed to be around when she was there. She had been so naïve to think that he liked her. How foolish. She had even confessed to Leanne and Alice about her true feelings for him. She should have listened to Leanne, who had been right all along; her abductor had been someone from her book club. Maria shuddered, but as she looked back at Sunil, there was that warm, genuine look that he always had; a look that comforted her. Confusion replaced her anxiety and her head began to spin.

"I blame my brother Omar. It was all his fault," Sunil said, anger penetrating his voice. He lifted his fist towards his jaw.

Maria wanted to leave. She didn't want to hear what he had to say. What did he do to her? She focused on the candle wdged into a green glass bottle, burning in front of them. Wax melted down its sides. Picking off the white solidified pieces of wax and closing her eyes, she tried to digest what he was saying.

"He ran off with this Mexican girl who refused to take on our religion and our culture, so my parents emotionally blackmailed me; they were pushing me into an arranged marriage. I backed out at the last minute." Sunil's voice began to calm. "It was Omar's fault. But how could I blame him? He was in just as bad a position."

"How does this…" Maria started.

"Please let me finish," Sunil's said. His voice was gentle.

"We invested heavily in high-risk stocks and shares. We had often dabbled in the past, but this time it was serious money. If we lost it all, we'd be broke. But we needed to invest big to make the kind of money we needed. So that's what we did. We borrowed money. We bought high-rising stocks and we sold when they hit the target we were aiming for. We did it, we made what we needed. Enough to get out from our parents' grasp. People say money is power, and they're right."

"I just don't see how this involves…" Maria tried again as Sunil interrupted her.

"Once Omar released my share of the money, I had financial independence. I was able to stand up to my parents. They didn't react like I thought they would when I refused the marriage. Of course they were upset, threatened to cut me out of the business. I said I would go with nothing. After all, I could now support myself, even if it was only for a couple of months. Then they came round. I couldn't enter into a marriage I knew was going to fail, not when I was in love with someone else. Arranged marriages work for some but not for Omar and me. We wanted to find love on our own. And I think I've found it. There, I've said it. This time sober-ish." Sunil relaxed his shoulders and looked up at Maria with a smile.

"I don't get it. What? Why are you telling me this?" Maria asked, her brow furrowed.

"Err… I… that night. That terrible night."

"What night?" Maria wrung her hands together.

"That night in September. I told you this at Marconi's. I was drunk, but I remembered and then you were so different with me the next time we met. I had poured my heart out to you and told you about my feelings for you and I figured that you just didn't want to know. I realised that you didn't want to complicate our group. And, until today, I didn't have the courage to say anything.

"We've been getting close lately… well, I thought we were, and so I thought I would tell you again. Come clean with the whole story this time." Sunil's look of relief was quickly replaced with dejection. He realised that Maria was not expecting what he had just told her. Or maybe he had not been clear. He sighed. "Maria, it's you. I like you. I want to be with you! It's why I broke off my engagement to Sushmita, the girl my parents had arranged for me."

Maria looked at Sunil incredulously. She let out a laugh, and then it was Sunil's turn to be confused. She quickly put her hand on his arm. "I'm relieved," she said, unable to conceal her broad smile. "So relieved."

"I…" Sunil began, but Maria stopped him.

"I thought you were going to say something else. This smile is relief," Maria pointed to her lips, "pure relief that you're not a stalker."

Sunil gave her an uncertain look. "That sounds like a backhanded compliment."

Maria took his hand in hers and her fingers began to tingle. She knew it was the right time to tell him. The uncertain feelings had now passed. Fragments of what Sunil had just told her jigged her memory, and she remembered that Wednesday evening in Marconi's more clearly now. Their lips touching after he had confided in her, the passionate kiss they had shared. How could she have forgotten?

"Let's clear this up. I probably had more to drink than you did that evening," Maria said, with a new lightness in her voice. "I remember you telling me about having to go through an arranged marriage and that was it. I completely blanked out the rest. I wasn't sure if I dreamt up the kiss or if it was part of another dream." Maria looked down at the floor. "Now I remember it," she said, looking back up at him. "Nothing else about what you just said, though. Just the kiss." Maria squeezed Sunil's hand in hers. "I felt the distance the next time we met as well, and I thought it was you who was being distant."

Sunil gave her a genuine smile. "Is that how you remember it? And there I was thinking you didn't want to acknowledge that

I liked you. You seemed to be in your own world at the next book club meeting, whispering with Ollie. In fact, you looked scared of me. I've spent the last two months trying to regain your trust. I'll never forget the day I saw you in the lobby of the King's View. I had just moved in and I thought you would be pleased, but you looked at me like I was the last person you wanted to see. My heart sank."

"It's a very bad case of crossed wires, I guess. I didn't remember, Si. I promise." Maria leaned into him, taking in his familiar aftershave. He turned towards her, placing his hand on her thigh. Their lips touched momentarily, but Maria pulled away—her anxieties began to circle her again.

Sunil pulled her in towards him. He wanted to feel her lips on his. Maria didn't resist. She fell into his embrace and the warmth of his body and allowed her heart to take over, savouring every second of their kiss.

As they pulled apart, they were silent. "I guess we've both been fools," Sunil said. Maria felt her eyes filling up with tears, and she rested her head on his arm. Breathing deeply, she realised they were the only couple left in the bar. Sunil put his arm around Maria and pulled her towards him again.

Finally Maria spoke. "It's my turn now," she said, breathing deeply. "I can tell you why I looked so scared when I saw you in my apartment building. I can tell you why I was so distant that week at the book club. The week of *The Sinner*."

47

"It's me," Maria said with enthusiasm when Alice answered her phone. Maria was finally in a good place. She accepted that Alice had pretended not to know about her abduction and had forgiven Leanne for betraying her trust. In both instances she knew her sister and friend were just trying to protect her. Leanne was the one person who had stood by her through her abortion and the black hole of grief that came with it. She was also the one person who had silently kept an eye out for her when Alice went off with Owen, the man who had meant the world to her. Maria knew that she just couldn't cut Leanne out now. It would be like losing a limb. Instead Maria accepted that there was some friction between Alice and Leanne. Perhaps one was jealous of the other, but either way Maria wasn't going to let herself get bogged down in worrying about that. After all, life was too short. The important thing was that, for the first time in over two years, she was happy.

"Oh," Alice said.

"You sound disappointed. Who did you think it was?"

"Owen," Alice said.

"Your other most favourite person." Maria smiled. Just a few weeks ago she would have smarted on hearing Owen's name, but things were different now. In fact, tonight, for the first time, she would let Sunil through her front door.

"Good mood? Heard from Leanne?"

Maria clenched her teeth but she didn't take the bait. Despite the sisters nearly losing each other, Alice couldn't help but have a dig. She thought about telling her sister Leanne's side of the story and she thought about telling Alice that she had never been on antidepressants in her life. But Maria didn't want to bring that up again. The last thing she wanted was to be stuck in a "he said, she said" battle between Leanne and her sister. It was best to leave it alone for now. She ignored Alice's remark. "Things have progressed with Si," she said instead.

Alice smiled momentarily, forgetting Leanne. She had been waiting for this moment for a long time, the moment when Maria would forget about Owen. But a stab of jealousy overshadowed her sense of relief. In some ways it was similar to the feeling she had all those years ago when she had first met Owen. Alice shook her head, ran her fingers through her hair and pushed the thought to the back of her mind. "Is it about the dinner on Saturday?" Alice asked, as she began to drum her fingers nervously on her laptop.

"Well, yes and no. Yes, as in, can Sunil come along too?"

"No problem," Alice said, frowning into the phone.

"And another thing. I wanted to borrow your scarf, the red one with white birds on it. Would that be okay?"

"Of course," Alice smiled, remembering how glad she was to have her sister back.

Alice noted the happiness in her sister's voice. "I'll drop it around to yours later."

"I can come to you, Alice. I don't want you to come all the way into town when you're up in Oadby."

Alice hesitated. "I need to pop out. I have a yoga class later. I'll drop it round about…"

Maria blocked out Alice's voice. A shiver ran down her spine. A flashback skirted on the periphery of her mind. The glimpses into what happened that weekend in September were more frequent now. Maria could feel a memory coming back. She could see a black and white image before her. It was hazy, the brick wall, a stainless steel fridge. *Her* fridge. In *her* apartment and the yellow scarf on the floor. It wasn't her scarf. The fridge was open and a man was standing in front of it, the light from it shining on him. He turned around to say something. He was talking, talking to someone else. Another man was present. Who were they? If only she could see their faces. She tried to concentrate harder but the memory was slipping away.

"Maria? Maria."

"Sorry Alice, I…"

"Are you okay?" Alice interrupted.

"Yes, just lost in thought," Maria said, her heart racing. She had almost seen a face, *his* face. Should I tell Alice? She wanted to tell Alice. No. Dr Timms had told her not to reveal too much about her flashbacks to her friends or family. He wanted her to wait for the hypnosis. "Why?" she had asked him. He had spouted off something about the power of suggestion and other psychobabble jargon. "We don't want people to give you ideas as to what you could have seen. So keep your flashbacks between us from now on," Dr Timms had said. The hypnosis was this Friday. Maria knew that she didn't have much longer to wait. She had been patient until now. Another couple of days wouldn't hurt.

She had seen the silhouette more clearly now. It had a thick, muscular frame. She tried to think of everyone she knew but nobody fitted the mystery silhouette. The smell of cedar wood filled the air. Maria quickly looked around her; a young couple walked passed, unaware of her existence. Had the man been wearing the same aftershave? The smell made her feel sick. Maria clenched her fists as she ground her teeth together. Why was it taking so long for her memory to come back to her? She took three deep breaths just as Dr Timms had told her. *Clear blue skies*, she thought. Maria walked on as anxiety and excitement swirled inside her.

"So, I'll drop the scarf over at three-ish?"

"Yes, that's fine," Maria said, realising she was still on the phone to Alice. Maria relaxed, remembering her date with Sunil.

Alice disconnected the call. It must have been the mention of Owen that made Maria go quiet like that. How dull Maria had become over the last two years. Alice slowly discovered over the last month that Maria was not going to let go of the past so easily. Alice had certainly put the past behind her and she couldn't see why Maria just couldn't do the same. But Alice was lucky like that; she had the ability to forget things as quickly as required. The past was where it belonged, in the past. Alice smiled. She was safe in the knowledge that Maria savoured their reunion as much as she did. They were sisters again and, more importantly, friends. Neither of them wanted to change that. They were too afraid of losing each other again.

48

"Cheers." Lawrence raised his glass to Penelope as the waitress brought over a bowl of kalamata olives.

Penelope touched her glass of juice to his bottle of beer. "What are we celebrating?" Penelope asked.

"I heard from Langford and Sons today. My novel is going to be published. The contract should be in the post."

Penelope raised her hand to her mouth. "I've ruined your day. You should have been celebrating, not waiting at A&E with me."

"The celebrations will follow." Lawrence winked at Penelope.

"Langford and Sons are one of the best."

"I was lucky. Thanks to Oliver, really. He had the contact," Lawrence said, taking a sip of his beer.

Penelope looked longingly at the green bottle. She could almost taste the alcohol. "Oliver? He must be more connected than we give him credit for. You don't just get your foot in the door that easily."

Lawrence shifted in his chair. Oliver had never once before mentioned Langford despite knowing that Lawrence's main aim in life was to find a publisher for his manuscript. He sighed. The opportunity that Oliver provided was too good a chance to go looking for faults. Lawrence put his scepticism to the back of his mind. He was finally sitting in a restaurant with the woman of his dreams and a freshly signed publishing contract. When would he ever learn to just accept it when something was going his way?

"I never thought about it before," Penelope said, "but I knew a Langford once and I bet he's one of the sons. There can't be two unrelated Langfords in Leicestershire."

"There must be hundreds of Langfords," Lawrence said, admiring her enthusiasm. He stopped himself from reaching over to tuck a loose strand of hair behind her ear.

"Maybe. But I think I remember something about publishing or editing… mmm, maybe not. It was a while ago. We were at university together… oh, what was his name?" Penelope rested her chin on her hand and looked into Lawrence's eyes as if the answer was buried deep inside them. "Chris!" she exclaimed suddenly. "Yes, Christopher Langford. We were friends in first year. He had an older brother who lived closer to their family home, some village in Harborough, I think. He used to come to visit for the odd weekend. I remember him well, but what was his *name*? Oh, that's going to really bother me all evening." Penelope popped an olive into her mouth and furrowed her brow. "It's on the tip of my tongue."

Lawrence took another sip of his beer, enjoying the sound of her voice. He watched her lips move as she spoke.

"He was a big guy. Quite tough. The Langford brothers. Funny, that, I wonder which one of them Ollie knows," Penelope said, putting another olive in her mouth. She leaned back in her chair. "Perhaps we could meet up," she said, raising her eyebrows at Lawrence. "It's such a small world."

"Well I guess that would explain quite a bit. Oliver did say he knew this contact from school. Like you said, small world." Lawrence relaxed a little in his chair and let out a sigh of relief. He had been foolish to be apprehensive about how his cousin knew a Langford.

Penelope took a sip of her juice, conscious that she was dominating their conversation with her pointless meanderings about her university days. "So, tell me more about your book," she said, tilting her head to one side. "When will it be published?"

"I haven't been given the finer details yet but they have agreed to a publishing date to make the *Langford Big Summer Read*. It's something they push every year. With any luck my book will take that spot and the rest will be history." He winked at her and laughed.

"Don't be so negative. You should be elated by this. Do you know how many struggling authors there are out there? They would kill to get an opportunity like this."

"A back-door opportunity." Lawrence looked down at the empty plate in front of him.

"It doesn't really matter that you got in through the back door. Millions get in that way. It's who you know, after all. Why do you think celebrities publish under different names when they decide to branch out into the world of fiction? It's so they know it's the quality of their writing that sells, not their name."

"You're too kind," Lawrence said, covering his face with a menu. "Now, what would you like to eat? I can recommend absolutely everything. It's all good." Lawrence rested the menu back on the table and looked at Penelope.

Lawrence thought about what the nurse had said to them, about Penelope being pregnant. He had hoped she would have mentioned it by now. Almost two hours had passed since the nurse had said the words that shook his world. How could Jason have left her? Surely he would have known about the child? Lawrence wished that Jason was still in England—he would certainly have reminded him that you don't just walk out on a beautiful woman like Penelope.

Lawrence watched Penelope purse her lips as she decided what to eat. He wondered if his instincts were correct, but deep down he knew that he was trying to create something out of nothing. The light caught on her silver earring and cast a reflection on her face. Again, Lawrence refrained from reaching out to her. He took one last look at her before turning his eyes back to his own menu. But his thoughts were not of food. He knew underneath Penelope's long black dress there was a slight baby bump.

"What can I get you?" the waitress asked, eyeing up Lawrence.

Penelope looked up at her and smiled. "Another couple of minutes?"

"Take your time," the waitress said, placing her little notepad and pen back in her pocket. She walked over to another table to clear plates.

"I think I'll have the kleftico," Penelope said, looking directly at him.

"Snap," Lawrence said, closing his menu and placing it on the table. He drained his beer and looked at Penelope through the flickering candle. Lawrence had never seen her with such little makeup on. It suited her. He gave the waitress their order and ordered another beer.

There was a silence as they waited for their food. Penelope was the first to break it. As she sipped her juice, she started to tell Lawrence about her work as a research assistant. She wanted to talk about anything but the baby. She could not bear Lawrence's pity. But she was aware of a tension growing between them. Lawrence had been kind not to mention her pregnancy again but she knew she could not avoid the subject the whole evening. How she wished that the nurse had kept silent.

As Penelope's words faltered, Lawrence could not stop himself from speaking. The words that had been dancing on his tongue from the moment they sat down now fell out of his mouth. "You didn't tell me," Lawrence said empathically.

Penelope smiled. "I haven't told anyone really."

"So that was why you've been avoiding the book club then. I was wondering why you missed the last one."

"That and Jason," Penelope said, her eyes filling with tears. She looked into the distance and focused on the candle, hoping that a tear would not fall. She missed Jason and wondered what he was doing right now. Was he with his wife?

Lawrence played with his fork pretending not to notice her watery eyes. The waitress arrived at just the right time, placing their meals in front of them.

"The father is…?" Lawrence asked.

"The baby is definitely Jason's." Penelope frowned, clutching her napkin under the table. *Of course Lawrence knew this, how could he even think…*

"You're certain?" Lawrence asked, not realising how this would sound to Penelope.

"Of course." Penelope's face fell.

"I just think that… fourteen weeks ago… you know?"

Penelope closed her eyes. What did he want from her? What did he think of her? Just because she worked as a stripper, everyone thought she was easy. She had only ever been with Jason.

Penelope questioned his green eyes, which were staring back at her. His eyes were kind but he had no right to degrade her like this. She was about to tell him what she thought of men like him when, all of a sudden, she remembered. *Yes, it was about fourteen weeks ago.*

Lawrence waited.

"It's definitely Jason's," Penelope said, her breathing quickening. *It has to be.* Penelope's mind flicked back to the night Ciara had pushed her towards the good-looking man at the bar. The night she lost her virginity. Lawrence had been her first. But her one-night stand had been a trial run for the real thing with Jason. It didn't count. And they had used protection, for all that was worth.

Penelope hadn't been completely ignorant over the last three months. She knew that Lawrence had worshiped her ever since she walked into that book club. At the time she wondered if she would be better off leaving the club. The last thing she wanted to be reminded of, while reading literary classics, was of her fumbling one-night stand. But, as time passed and Jason became more permanent in her life, she forgot about Lawrence and what they had shared, despite seeing him on such a regular basis. She knew he was too much of a gentleman to say anything, and she regarded him as a friend.

Penelope's recollection of her night with Lawrence did not change that feeling. She still loved Jason.

"I just thought…"

"I know," Penelope said, reaching her hand out to him. Lawrence let Penelope take his hand; he felt her warmth as she entwined her fingers in his. "I know how you feel, Loz, but I'm certain the baby is not yours." Penelope looked at Lawrence for a second longer than she should have.

"I want you to know that I am going to be here for you every step of the way," Lawrence said confidently. Penelope pulled her hand away from him grasp.

"I can manage." She didn't want charity.

"I know you don't need me, but…"

"I'll get through it just fine."

"Will your parents…"

"My parents don't want to know."

Lawrence touched his lips.

"I can look after myself," Penelope said, looking away from him.

"I get the message." Lawrence laughed. "I'm just offering my support."

Penelope played with the untouched meal in front of her.

"I care for you a great deal. I always have. From the moment I saw you that evening. That night we spent together, for me it meant something."

Penelope was silent.

"I never said anything because, well, first, I guess, like the rest of us, I was afraid of rejection, and then I heard about Jason."

"You should have said something," Penelope said, although in her heart she had known how he had felt. She had turned away from his gazes during the book club and had made her excuses when she found herself alone with him, afraid of what he might say, worried she might feel something for him. She had been so wrapped up in Jason, the idyllic boyfriend who turned out to be a snake. She wondered if things would have been different if Lawrence had actually told her about his feelings. No. She was certain they wouldn't. Jason had been everything to her.

"Should I have?" Lawrence asked, as if reading her mind. "You were with Jason, and I could hardly compete with that."

"Well at least you're not a liar!" Penelope smiled, masking the pain. It felt good to feel wanted again.

Lawrence didn't want to say he agreed. He could feel her hurting. "What do you say we give it a go?"

"What do you mean?" she asked hesitantly, leaning back in her seat. The last thing she wanted was another relationship.

The waitress walked over to their table to ask them how their meal was. "Good. Thanks," Lawrence said, even though he had hardly touched it.

Penelope noticed the way the waitress looked at Lawrence; her eyes followed her as she headed back to the kitchen. Penelope turned back to Lawrence. She had never looked at Lawrence in that way before. She had never stopped to appreciate his looks. There was no doubt about it, he was good looking. Most girls would love to have someone like Lawrence in their arms. Penelope stopped herself. It was too soon—her tears for Jason had barely dried.

"I don't mean… we could just start… spending time together. I could take you to hospital appointments. We could go for dinner occasionally. Nothing serious, just see how it goes." Lawrence raised his eyebrows at Penelope.

"I guess. Would that not be weird?"

"Isn't that what good friends do for each other?"

"I don't mean for this to sound cruel, but we aren't good friends. We had a one-night stand and we're in the same book club. That's all. This… today. It was just a coincidence."

"I'm of the philosophy that sometimes things happen for a reason."

"You think?" Penelope asked, running her finger around the rim of her glass. She couldn't believe that theory, given her run of bad luck lately.

"I'm sure of that. You're not sure about this baby, but you've made the decision to keep it. You have no idea why Jason did what he did, but perhaps you're better off without him. You want your parents to forget their high morals for once in their lives and be real parents. Am I right?"

"Am I that easy to read?"

"When you hold that little child in your arms, I think it will all be worthwhile. Jason has missed out on something amazing, and for his actions, I cannot speak. But your parents, I think in time, will come round."

Penelope gave him a wry smile. Lawrence clearly didn't know her parents.

"They'll come round if they want to see you again, and who wouldn't want to spend time with you?" Lawrence raised his drink to her and smiled. "You have to be positive now, for the sake of the baby, at least. From this day forward things could be better."

Penelope was silent as she considered what Lawrence had just said. She thought of the tiny being growing inside of her. For the first time in a long while she felt a sense of calm come over her.

"I think you're right," she said with a broad smile. "Things do happen for a reason."

"So shall we give this friendship a go then?"

Penelope grinned at Lawrence "Okay, but remember this baby isn't yours," she said, relieved that she would not be having this baby all on her own. She would have a friend if nothing else. But no sooner had Penelope agreed than her face fell; a sudden thought crossed her mind and Penelope's eyes widened. "But what if, once you get to know me, you realise I'm not the person you think I am?"

"Well, I'll just have to take that risk!" Lawrence winked at her. He knew deep down in his heart that he would spend the rest of his life with her.

49

"So, Maria, are you ready?" Dr Timms asked.

"Yes," Maria said. There was no going back now. She had been waiting for this moment for the past two and a half months. Regressive Recollection Therapy had delved into Maria's past and dragged out her secrets about her abortion and her turbulent relationship with her sister, kicking and screaming. But now, sitting in front of the doctor, Maria was glad that he knew about her troubled past and the complexities that the relationships around her had brought.

Maria would have to admit that she would not have been ready had Dr Timms hypnotised her before now. The last couple of months had been a whirlwind of discovery. Never before did she realise that by being the elder sister she carried the unspoken burden of responsibility, unwittingly thrust upon her at Alice's birth. She had carried this weight throughout her young adult life. Being the older, more responsible sister was a fact of life, something all eldest siblings go through. Maria had been in no harm of falling under the load she carried until she had her abortion.

In Dr Timms' office, waiting for her hypnosis, Maria remembered a conversation she had with her sister just a week before her termination.

"You're quiet," Alice had said to her.

Maria lay on her bed with her hand on her tummy.

"Tummy ache?"

"No," Maria snapped. Alice had been so inquisitive of late. Maria narrowed her eyes at her sister. What would Alice think of her? Would she run and tell their mum and dad that her irresponsible older sister had gone and gotten herself pregnant. What would they say? Would they tell her it was okay? Maria's parents were modern enough to accept when she dyed her hair purple and when she drank too much, but they wouldn't accept a baby. She could hear her mother's voice in her head: "You're too young, you haven't finished your degree, do you know how much responsibility it is, having a child? You can't bring a child into this world without a stable home." Maria turned on her side. She wasn't ready to become a mum.

"I'm only asking because I worry about you. You're so… I don't know… distant lately," Alice said.

Maria rolled her eyes at her sister and looked away. Maria was desperate to share her inner turmoil with her sister, but she was scared that Alice would blab to their parents and so she had to keep her at arms length.

"Show me that thing you do with your eyeliner to get that gothic look," Alice said, looking in the mirror holding the makeup pencil up to her eye.

Maria looked back at Alice. A feeling of guilt crept up on her. She had fallen pregnant instead of studying for her degree. What kind of role model was she for Alice?

A tear fell from Maria's eye. She discretely wiped it away hoping Alice hadn't noticed. "I'm a failure," Maria said under her breath, "I've let everyone down."

"Did you say something?" Alice asked.

Maria was silent.

"I'll ask once more: are you okay?"

Maria opened her mouth. She wanted to tell Alice then, but she remembered Owen's words. "Don't tell anyone," he had instructed. "You know we're doing the right thing," he said, kissing her gently on her forehead.

"I'm fine," Maria said to Alice.

The noise of the old filing cabinet in Dr Timms office woke Maria from her memory. He was retrieving her file. Maria watched him as he fiddled with the lock. She had grown fond of Dr Timms. Before him, Maria saw the abortion as just an episode in her past, something she had to get over. But now she realised it was much more than that. Maria had begun to see that it wasn't just her pregnancy that had made her believe she had let everybody down, but the decision to have the abortion had cemented this belief.

All along Maria believed she wanted an abortion, but she could see clearly now it was Owen who had forced her into it. "It's what's best for us," he had said so many times, over and over again. "We can't afford a baby right now. We need to finish our degrees." When he saw the pain in her eyes, he tried a different tack: "I want to have children with you, Maria, I do. But I want it to be right. I want us to have a big house with a garden where our kids can play. Don't you want that? Do you really think we can give a child a stable life right now?"

Maria accepted his words. But she now knew that having that child would not have been the end of the world. Her parents would have come around and she would have learned to cope as a mother—millions do. But hindsight couldn't help her now. She had failed herself again by allowing Owen to manipulate her, like a puppet on a string.

Maria adjusted her watch. Dr Timms had been right about a lot of things, and she had realised that Owen had a controlling nature, but she refused to believe that Owen was a borderline narcissist who wanted complete control over her life.

"Your relationship with Owen may not have started like that, but from what you've told me, that was the way it ended," Dr Timms had said at one of her most recent sessions. "Telling you he loves you in front of your friends and putting you down behind closed doors is not love, Maria. It was Owen's way of making you dependent on him and submissive. Owen was controlling you. You just couldn't see it."

"I loved him."

"And he abused that love," Dr Timms said confidently.

"I thought he loved me," Maria said. She remembered the touch of his skin and how kind and generous he was with her. Yes, he called her useless once or twice, and more often than not she was at his beck and call, but every man has his faults, Maria reasoned.

The whole wretched episode had made Maria the person she was today: an introvert who had little self-confidence. Maria could clearly see why she had accepted the role of a travel agent's assistant, and not completed her Master's like she had always dreamed of doing.

Maria looked at her drab black jeans and grey jumper as she appreciated how far she had come under the guidance of Dr Timms. Was the abortion and Owen's continual degradation also the reason why Maria had started to wear dull colours and flat shoes?

Leanne had tried to tell Maria that she was becoming a different person, but she didn't want to listen. She was so blinded by guilt and hatred.

"Maria, I know this is hard for you but you have to start going out. Come on, I've got two tickets to the uni carnival this Saturday," Leanne had pleaded with Maria two months after she had seen her sister and Owen together.

"I feel like this abortion has burned a hole inside me."

"Maybe you should see someone," Leanne said.

"I'm not crazy."

"But you're grieving. I know what that's like. You think nobody understands."

Maria shook her head. "I'm fine."

"You're not fine. What happened to the old Maria? The one with short spiky hair and red shoes?"

Maria ran her hand through her long dark hair. Owen had preferred her hair like this. She no longer had energy to dye it or style it. Leanne didn't understand.

"Come out with me," Leanne said. "You'll get back into the swing of things. You'll never forget but at least you can carry on with your life."

"What if I see Alice and Owen together?" Maria asked.

"We'll go somewhere they don't know about, then."

"If I see Alice with Owen again, I don't think I'll be able to breathe," Maria said. Just the thought of them together made Maria feel faint.

"I bumped into Alice yesterday," Leanne said, playing with the hem of her dress. "She wants to explain."

Maria opened her mouth to say something. She wanted to speak to Alice, desperately. She wanted to know if she had pushed her sister into Owen's arms by not confiding in her. Maria was silent.

She knew that this ultimate betrayal was proof that she didn't deserve any happiness in her life. Maria swallowed back the lump in her throat. "I hate that bitch," she said.

As Maria's life had begun its downward spiral, Alice's life had taken off. Alice had relied on Maria so much growing up but had been abandoned as Maria lost interest in life. But Alice wasn't going to let that hold her back. Years of living in Maria's shadow had taken its toll on her. She was tired of being described only as Maria's sister, the quirky one who never did well in school or sport. Maria going underground was like an unexpected gift for Alice; it was finally her time to shine. Starting university was a catalyst in creating her new persona. Almost simultaneously she was offered a modelling contract. No longer did Alice need her older sister for guidance and protection. People now looked up to Alice and she revelled in all this new attention. As Maria's self worth declined, Alice's grew stronger and stronger, as if she were feeding off her sister's unhappiness.

The idyllic childhood Maria shared with her sister had not prepared her for the harsh reality of adulthood and the fact that her younger sister had become her own person. Maria had been so keen to preserve the memories of years gone by that she failed to notice how much both she and Alice had changed. Maria had Dr Timms to thank for helping her realise this and, armed with this knowledge, she now knew that she was much stronger. But could she handle remembering those stolen hours from that weekend in September? Would she be able to cope with the truth her mind was desperately keeping from her?

An uneasy feeling nudged Maria in the pit of her stomach. The question that had nagged her from the day she woke up with hysterical amnesia surfaced again. Had she made it all up? The question lingered in her mind. Dr Timms had told Maria, in one of her sessions, that she was clinging to the idea that she was a daydreamer. But he believed Maria was no longer a fantasist; he believed she had shed that skin long ago and was now a realist. But was he right?

Maria lifted the glass of water in front of her with trembling hands. Much had changed since her abduction: Alice was back in her life and Maria wouldn't have it any other way. If her abduction had taught her anything, it was that life was too short to hold grudges. What her sister did was hurtful, but it wasn't the end of the world. Maria had also come to terms with her sister's impending marriage to Owen, and had agreed to be her maid of honour. The hatred had dissolved. Whether Owen had controlled her or not, it was in her past. Maria was ready to move on. After all, she had met Sunil and had allowed him into her heart.

Maria looked at the door leading out to the waiting room. She had deliberated on who to bring with her for her hypnosis and now, having made up her mind, she wondered if she had made the right choice. Alice still didn't know she was seeing a therapist and Maria knew she was no longer required to be the strong older sister. But the shame she associated with therapy still burned to an extent that she couldn't bring herself to tell her sister about it. Bringing Alice along to her hypnosis had not been an option. Maria had been torn between asking Sunil and Leanne to accompany her. Recently she had broached the subject with Leanne.

"I get that you like Si, but take me with you. What if Sunil isn't who you think he is?" Leanne said.

"I think he'll be fine."

"The fact that he moved into your apartment building is slightly suspicious."

"He wanted to live in town."

"I don't trust any of your book club sorts," Leanne said. "I don't mind calling in sick. It can be my leaving present."

"Leaving?"

"I've decided I want to go travelling!"

Maria laughed, not sure if Leanne was being serious.

"Please, Tia Maria. Take me for your hypnosis," Leanne said one final time.

Maria smiled remembering Leanne's words. Maria now looked at Dr Timms, who was lowering himself into his armchair. Had she made the right decision? Maria took in a deep breath. She would know everything in just one hour. *Bricks, Bricks, Bricks.* Those words came to her again. She now knew they were the bricks in her apartment, but who was the man taking a slice of pizza out of her fridge, and who did the other two muffled voices belong to? Had they blindfolded her with scarves and bound her wrists? Maria banished the fear from her mind.

"You've come a long way," Dr Timms said. "I think it's apparent, by the number of flashbacks you have had, that hysterical amnesia is the main cause of your memory loss, not the drugs. You do realise what this means?"

Maria sighed. She had heard this enough times already. "That my brain has blocked out an event because it couldn't cope. We've been through this and I know that what I find out could be something really terrible."

He shuffled the papers in front of him. "Okay then, let's run through your list again."

Maria took a deep breath, and for the second time that day ran through the possibilities of what the hypnosis could reveal. It was called her "fear list," as Dr Timms had put it. During Maria's last RRT session she had written down all her conscious fears, and next to each one had handwritten in capital letters: I CAN COPE. Since the meeting, she had studied her inventory of dread so that if any item on her list surfaced during her hypnosis she knew she would be prepared. In theory this method seemed helpful, but Maria was not allowed to show her doctor her list, and this was slightly worrying.

"I can't see the list," Dr Timms said as Maria searched his eyes for hope. How would he help her overcome her darkest fears if he hadn't seen her list?

"If I see the list, I could subconsciously imply something to you within the hypnosis. It would render it inaccurate."

Maria had protested at first, but when she realised her pleas were getting her nowhere, she conceded. Rape was the first item on her list, the most feared and prominent of the ten. It was something she could define. Snakes and rats, her two big phobias, were right down at the bottom. In between was a mixture of crimes against her, ranging from those sexual in nature to more psychotic ones that she had gleaned from crime dramas and books. It was a medley of implausible scenarios involving degradation, humiliation and pain. Had she been bound up and subjected to torture? Were implements used? Anxiety made Maria's heart beat faster. Why had she blocked out these two days? What could have been so bad that she couldn't remember? She gripped the armrests of the chair, mustering up as much strength as she could. She knew she had to find out the truth today.

"Remember Maria, this may not work. I don't want you to get your hopes up. If you had been drugged to a greater extent than we can assume, you may recall very little."

"But you think that's unlikely," Maria said, confirming their previous discussions, "given the extent of my flashbacks."

"Your mind has to be open to this technique, Maria. Regressive Recollection Therapy takes time. "

Maria was silent. Why did he always have to sit on the fence?

"Are you thinking about something positive, Maria?" Dr Timms asked.

"Yes." Maria replied playing with her fingernails. Her mind swiftly moved from her irritation with Dr Timms to Sunil. Sunil was a positive in her life. With his support she had started to move on. And then, of course, there was Owen and Alice's wedding to look forward to. That was now a positive. She would be meeting Owen on Saturday night and she was excited because Sunil would be with her. She knew it would be difficult seeing Owen again after all that had happened, but she was convinced that she was stronger now. Maria took a deep breath and looked at her therapist.

"I will explain once more how you will feel, okay?"

"Hypnosis is almost like a daydream. I should remember everything when I wake," Maria said, anticipating what Dr Timms was about to say.

"You should unless I feel it is unsafe for you. Relaxation is the main premise of hypnosis. In fact, hypnosis is derived from the Greek word for sleep." Dr Timms smiled at his patient. "You will be mentally alert, though. To get us started, once you are under the hypnosis, I will use the power of suggestion to get you back to those missing days in September. For example, I will mention the aftershave we have discussed. And keep in mind you will not remember everything in sequence. You may only remember fragments because it is highly likely that you will have been unconscious for the majority of the time. You would have had to be conscious to remember anything."

"I have someone waiting for me outside," Maria said, interrupting the doctor. She had already heard about what would happen to her once she was under. "You can let them know if there is a problem," Maria said.

"You don't know what you will remember. You may be in shock. We'll discuss whatever it is you see before you go out to your friend." Dr Timms looked towards the closed door.

A lump formed in Maria's throat. Leanne's words of warning came back to her. Maria had not put Sunil's name on her fear list, but perhaps she should have.

"Ready?" Dr Timms asked.

"Ready," Maria said. She crossed her fingers as Dr Timms began.

50

"It's fixed with Maria, drinks and dinner. She wants to see our new place and meet you, I guess," Alice said, stroking Owen's hair.

"Fine." Owen played with his new phone. "I guess the day had to arrive at some point." He moved away from Alice and sat down in front of his computer.

"It's about bloody time," Alice said, looking towards Owen, trying to gauge his reaction. His eyes were fixed on the screen. She could sense Owen's frustration. "Don't worry about it," Alice said trying to reassure him.

Owen shrugged.

"It'll be harder for me." Alice walked over to his new black leather armchair and put her arms around her fiancé. "We've been through a lot this past year."

"Uh-huh," Owen responded without taking his eyes off his computer.

Alice frowned at him. Was he concerned or did he just not care? He could be so aloof sometimes. "At least look at me, Owen. I deserve that."

Owen raised his eyebrows. "Sorry, hun." He turned towards her and gave her his full attention. "Why do you look so worried?" he asked. "Having your sister around will be great. You know I want us all to be friends. I'm busy with work, that's all. So long as you're with me, everything will be fine." He put his hand on the small of her back and pulled her towards him, drawing her onto his lap. He began to play with the two-carat diamond on her finger.

Alice smiled. "A wedding to plan and Maria as my maid of honour. I never thought it would happen. I never thought it would be like the old days. It worked out just perfectly."

"Just like I said it would. When you want something, Alice, I will always make sure you get it." Owen kissed her on her forehead.

"Nothing ever phases you," Alice said, playing with her engagement ring. "It was a huge risk and…"

"And nothing." Owen put his finger on her lips. "Maybe we can go shopping later, get something for you to wear tomorrow evening, but now I need to work."

Alice smiled. Owen usually said something like this when he wanted space. She stood up and walked over to the kitchen as her mind drifted to the new designer boutique that had recently opened in Stoneygate. "I'm fixing myself a sandwich. Do you want one?" she asked.

"Yep," Owen said.

"Ham or chicken?"

"You know I hate chicken, Kitty."

51

Maria fell back into the comforting sofa, allowing herself to be enveloped by it. Her eyes closed. Calmly she answered questions about her apartment and her parents. In the waiting room, sitting only meters away from the mousy secretary, Sunil's breathing began to quicken. The secretary looked up disapprovingly and cocked her head at Sunil as he started to crack his knuckles. He stopped when he saw her face and nodded an apology. He tried to think of something else, anything to take his mind off what Maria was going through behind the oak door. Tiny beads of sweat formed on his brow and he tapped his foot methodically on the dated carpet. There was nothing he could do now. All he could do was wait.

★

"So, Maria, on Friday the 26th of September you are at your workplace in Leicester in the town centre. You are at your desk and you receive an email. What do you see?"

"Nothing," Maria said, hesitating. But then she added, "I'm at my desk, uhh..." Her voice was shaky but her face was serene.

"It's okay, Maria. Now tell me, what do you see?"

"Nothing. I'm on my chair. It swivels," she paused. "My yellow mug has camomile tea in it."

"Does it taste nice?"

"It's bitter. More bitter than normal. I finish it. It can taste bitter sometimes if you leave the bag in for too long."

Dr Timms asked Maria again about the emails she received. Maria carefully described her feelings from when she opened both emails right up until she passed out. Her voice was shaking and her brow furrowed.

"Okay, okay, remain calm. Not to worry, we are taking this very slowly, okay?" Dr Timms said, writing on his notepad.

After a few moments, Maria's breathing began to calm.

Dr Timms knew that it would be better to start Maria off with a familiar smell. It was often smells that evoked cognitive recognition in patients suffering from amnesia and dementia. "Aftershave," he said looking directly at Maria, "do you smell something straight away on the Friday evening, or perhaps the next day, the Saturday?"

Maria lifted her head as if she was straining to hear or smell something. "I can't smell anything."

"You are in your apartment, remember your kitchen, your bedroom and the bare walls. The bricks," Dr Timms tried.

"Wait... the bare walls. *Bricks*, *Bricks*, *Bricks*..." Her voice turned into a whisper before trailing off.

"Okay, the exposed bricks, can you see them?"

"Yes, I can see them." Maria's hands started to shake.

"Is there a hand?" Dr Timms asked, looking at his notes, hoping that the flashback would jog her memory. He was so certain the aftershave would bring some good results, but nothing. Perhaps Maria had been drugged so much so that she had no memory of what happened. Dr Timms made some more notes, giving Maria some time to take in her new surroundings. "What else can you see?" he asked gently.

"I can see the walls and my kitchen. I am in my own apartment. There's a piece of black cloth on the floor and some scarves."

"Gently look around you," Dr Timms said, encouraging her.

"My hands they are tied... not tightly... they're tied with something... something soft, like a silk scarf," Maria paused before continuing. "There are noises, people are talking," her voice began to strain.

"Okay Maria, relax. Nothing bad will happen to you. Take your time, deep breaths."

"It sounds like two men... but the voices are muffled. I'm weak. I feel weak... I think I've been drugged." Maria nestled further into the sofa, the pitch of her voice increasing.

"Take your time. Is there anything familiar in the voices? Do they mention anything familiar?"

Maria was silent.

★

Outside, Dr Timms' receptionist offered Sunil a glass of water. Sunil accepted without hesitation; his mouth was so dry. Gulping the water, he looked at his watch. Time was moving slowly and the waiting area was stifling. He reached for a magazine and stared at it aimlessly.

★

Maria twisted her head as if she was trying to listen. "I can hear them more clearly now. They're talking about me. One of them has opened my fridge and is eating something, a slice of pizza, I think. I can't see his face."

"What are they saying?"

"Wait, a woman has walked in. She's shouting at them."

"What is she saying?"

"She's saying something about me. I know her!" Maria said with panic in her voice. "Who is she? I know that voice."

"Maria, think about what she is saying, not who she is."

"'I thought this would be over, it's been two days already.' That's what she said. The men are telling her to lower her voice. They tell her not to speak. They're all talking, but so quietly. 'We should never have done this,' one man says. 'It'll work. I know it will,' says the other. 'It better work,' the woman says." Maria looked scared and confused, her face red and puffy.

Dr Timms looked at the watch he had taken off before the hypnosis. He would have to call Maria in for another session. He was concerned Maria had been under for too long. The doctor looked over his notes. In his eyes, the session had been successful but he knew Maria would feel differently. Maria had remembered where she was, but had no recollection of who her kidnappers were.

She was only certain that three people were involved, a woman and two men.

"Her memory will come back," Dr Timms said to himself. There was an eerie silence in the room as Dr Timms made a few more notes. Just as he was about to end the session, he heard Maria stir. He looked up at her. "Maria, are you okay?" he asked tentatively. There was a pained look on her face, as if she had seen the devil.

Maria let out a distressed cry.

On the other side of the door, Sunil's heart missed a beat.

Dr Timms walked over to Maria to bring her out of her state of hypnosis. "Calm down," he said, as tears streamed down her face. As she came out of her state, she looked at him, her eyes red.

"I heard their voices again. All three of them, much louder this time. I was awake. I heard the two men. They called the woman Kitty," Maria said, amid sobs. "I know who they are, all three of them. I know who they are."

52

The first time they met it had been chance, or so Oliver thought. As Oliver saw Langers' bulky frame enter the Layton bar that day he shuddered at the sight of his childhood tormentor. Even though twelve years had passed, the hurtful words Langers had chanted at Oliver back when they were at school rose to the forefront of his mind. Oliver's sexuality had been the butt of all his bully's jokes.

Langers was the bully who had given Oliver the name 'Shirty,' derived from another frequent nickname he used: "Shirt lifter." The name had stuck with Oliver like a bad smell throughout his schooling days. Oliver looked into his drink, avoiding his past. Would Langers pick on him again now that they were grown men?

Oliver smelled Langers' musty aftershave as he put his pint glass down on the table.

Langers introduced himself to Oliver, squinting at him from where he stood. "We were at school together," he said. The bully hadn't asked if he could sit down; he just pulled out a chair at Oliver's table.

"Years ago, mate. Sorry, I don't remember," Oliver said, suppressing the feeling of hate and anguish that were stirring inside him. What use was Langers' friendliness now? If Oliver did tell him that his young existence was made miserable thanks to him, would Langers really repent? Oliver doubted it and he wasn't going to waste his breath by telling him. He didn't want a pitiful apology that didn't have an ounce of honesty in it.

"I remember you," Langers said.

Oliver was silent. He wanted to ask him to leave but the words wouldn't come. He hated this man sitting before him; the way he made him feel even after all those years had passed, after all those years Oliver had spent trying to bury his childhood.

"I was a bit of a bully back then. Not the same person I am today," Langers said, taking a sip of beer. "I'm not proud of my past. I did and said some horrible things." He looked at Oliver out of the corner of his eye. "I'm sorry if you were one of those people."

Oliver's heart began to race. *One of those people.* The words echoed in his head. There had been a time in Oliver's life, not so long ago, when he had dreamed of meeting Langers. He had rehearsed a soliloquy of what he would say if he ever met his tormentor again. Sometimes he practiced his speech whilst making dinner, sometimes whilst taking a shower. Oliver vowed that if he ever saw him again, he would let him know just how much he ruined his life. Oliver's daydream had always finished with his fist smacking the pulpy flesh of Langers' cheek. Yet here Langers was, sitting right in front of him, and Oliver felt no desire to harm him. He didn't want to give Langers the satisfaction of accepting a meaningless apology. He just wanted his bully to go back into the hole he had crawled out from.

"Ah, so you do remember?" Langers said, smirking at Oliver.

"I've blocked out that part of my life. I haven't kept in touch with many people who used to go to the Glen." Langers hadn't changed.

"Let me buy you a drink at least, for old time's sake." Langers looked up at the bartender and nodded. Minutes later the server came over with two pints. Oliver noticed that no money was exchanged. In all Oliver's years of visiting the Layton, there had never been any floor service.

For a good half hour Langers talked at Oliver, who pretended to listen. It wasn't until Langers mentioned that he owned one of the biggest publishing houses in England, Langford and Sons, that Oliver's ears pricked up. When Langers asked Oliver for his help, he knew the tables had finally turned.

That night a sense of relief washed over Oliver. Without any harsh words exchanged, for the first time, Oliver felt as if he could leave his past behind. The hours he had spent reading self-help books had been worthless. All it had taken was for his bully to face him and ask for his help. And it wasn't just the money—of course, a Langford could pay well and Oliver couldn't deny that he desperately needed the cash—it was the publishing deal Oliver could get for his cousin that would make it all seem worthwhile. Lawrence had bailed Oliver out financially and emotionally ever since his parents had cut him off, and if there was one good thing Oliver wanted to do, it was to help Lawrence. This part of the deal was priceless.

"It's simple," Langers said, as he explained his master plan to Oliver a couple of weeks later. Enough time to let the greed seep into Oliver's soul.

"She'll be kept in her own apartment and will wake up there with not so much as a hair out of place," Langers said sadistically, as he smiled at Oliver.

Oliver had opened his mouth to object but Langers had silenced him.

"No harm will come to her, of course. Nothing at all. It's just going to be a little scary. That's all."

"So we make her think she's gone mad?"

"I know her," Langers said. He looked around him, making sure that no one else was within earshot. "She can be a bit of a fantasist. Few people will listen to what she has to say. I mean, after all, we're not stealing from her. No physical harm. Where's the proof?" He raised his eyebrows at Oliver and smiled.

"It doesn't matter if you don't do anything with her. You violate…" Oliver stopped himself, noticing Langers' sour expression.

"It's a fool proof plan," Langers said. "I came to you because we have history. I know I can trust you."

Oliver sucked his teeth, examining the scratched wooden table between them.

"I know you need money," Langers said. His expression softened as he stared at his acquaintance. "And I like helping out friends. I have the money. I could give you cash today." He paused. "If you help me out, we're even. Call it a business transaction. Now where's the harm in that?"

Oliver closed his eyes. The kind of money Langers was talking about meant that this wasn't going to be just a harmless *business transaction*. This was the guy who Oliver knew back in school. Langers knew what he wanted and he was going to get it at any price.

Oliver was sceptical. It was not in his nature to go around harming other people, even if it was just a prank.

"There are other people I can ask," Langers said, nodding a hello to the barman. "I came to you because, like I said, we know each other and I can help you out. But believe me, if you don't take this opportunity, there will be others who will."

Every day was a financial struggle for Oliver and he knew this would be an end to his problems. Lawrence, too, deserved a break. With just one action he could make his cousin's dreams come true.

"The money and one other thing."

Langers eyed him carefully. "What I've offered is more than enough…"

"Your publishing business. I have a cousin who's a writer…"

Langers interjected. "I didn't get Langford and Sons to where it is today by signing up any Tom, Dick or Harry."

"Then I'm not interested," Oliver said, with some conviction. Although the thought of having to walk away from that kind of money was painful, Oliver stood up from their table in the corner of the Layton.

"Wait," Langers said, looking up at him. "Fine. Sit down."

Oliver did as he was told and a small smile formed on his lips. Now he was in control.

"Who are we talking about?" Oliver asked.

"Once I tell you, you can't go back on your word."

"Try me," Oliver said, as an air of confidence filled his chest.

"Let's shake on it. Once we shake on it, the deal is done."

Oliver offered his hand to Langers apprehensively. He knew there was no going back now. No one ever went back on a handshake deal with Langers.

"Okay, just remember I know…" Langers stopped himself but the threat was already made. "Her name is Maria. Maria Schroder."

The colour drained from Oliver's face. Now he knew why he had been chosen for this task. It wasn't because they had history. It wasn't because Langers trusted him. It was because he knew Maria. Oliver had accepted the deal blindly thinking it would be someone completely unknown to him. How had someone as sweet as Maria been tied up with someone as callous as Langers? This would be harder than he had initially thought.

"Why Maria?" Oliver couldn't help but ask.

"I want to scare her sufficiently. Make sure she knows that life is just too fucking short."

"Why?" Oliver asked again.

"So that she turns to her sister for help."

Oliver frowned. "And how is that your business, Langers?"

Langers was not in the mood for answering anymore questions. The deal had been done. "And stop with the Langers crap, we're not in school anymore. It's Owen Langford, Shirty. Owen Langford."

53

Sunil steered his grey saloon car up London Road towards Oadby. Maria sat next to him in silence, tears still streaming down her face. He had refrained from asking her any questions even though he was desperate to know what happened during her hypnosis. Of course Maria must have remembered something, but he held his tongue as she had previously asked. Sunil turned the car into a new private development of houses. The personalised number plates on a white Range Rover instantly told him he was at the right house.

As soon as he stopped the car, Maria leapt out and walked up the path, passing beneath the arch of a red and orange bittersweet vine. The vine sprawled along a trellis covering the porch. "Truth," Maria mumbled under her breath.

"Did you say something?" Sunil asked as he kept up with her.

"The bittersweet vine represents truth," Maria said, her voice devoid of any emotion. She remembered the pictures of the plant in her Victorian Age textbook at school. How ironic, she thought as she walked under the sprawling climber. Maria stepped up to the front door and started to bang methodically on the white paint. Sunil noticed a couple of curtains twitching. It was such a quaint street, with white picket fences and perfectly manicured front lawns, like something out of *The Stepford Wives*. He stood bold behind Maria. As the front door opened, Maria forced her way inside.

"What the matter?" What's happened?" Alice asked, but as the words left her mouth she caught a look of pain in her sister's eyes. Silently Alice prayed that Maria's visit was unrelated to the memories that were flooding her mind. Alice looked at Sunil. *He must know. Who else knows?* Owen had sworn to her that Maria would not remember, partly because of the drugs they had used and partly because she was blindfolded. Alice had seen Maria stir that day, but she had believed

Owen without questioning him, like she always did. And Owen was never wrong.

"What's the racket?" All three of them heard Owen call from upstairs. *His voice.*

Alice opened her mouth to speak. She saw Maria's steely eyes bore into her and closed her mouth again. The words would not come. Maria was making Alice feel uneasy. *How dare Maria barge in here like this without warning?* Alice crossed her arms in front of her chest and faced Maria.

Sunil put his arm around Maria and pulled her towards him. He wanted to be alone with her to find out what she had remembered so he could help her. But he was just as much in the dark as Alice was.

Alice turned away from Maria and attempted a smile at Sunil. It was the first time she had met her sister's new boyfriend but, given the situation, there was no time for introductions and pleasantries. Alice didn't have to look twice at Sunil to know that he was good looking. For a moment it annoyed her, but within seconds Alice convinced herself that Owen was a much better catch than Sunil would ever be and her irritation subsided. Alice decided to be happy for her sister, and she realised it was a relief to have Sunil here now, catching her sister's tears. *Did Sunil know what he was getting himself into? It's all in Maria's head. It's all in her head.*

"Come down to the sitting room," Alice called back to Owen, keeping her voice as calm as she could, even though she was shaking with fear. "Maria and Sunil are here." Alice looked at her sister, whose eyes were fixed in the direction of the staircase. *Of course, Maria has not seen Owen in years.* Alice began to collect her thoughts. Owen had been clear on what to do if a situation like this arose. "Do not be the first to speak. Don't give her anything to work with," Owen had said. Alice was desperate to say something but she refrained. She couldn't betray Owen like that. He knew how games like this were played.

Maria walked into the lounge holding on to Sunil's arm. She sat on the white leather corner sofa and scanned the room. Photos of her sister and Owen in exotic locations jumped out at her.

Seeing the happiness and love between Alice and Owen hurt. Still, after all this time, even with Sunil at her side. It hurt.

Maria heard a thud from upstairs and braced herself as she heard Owen descend. She wasn't sure of what to expect. It had been over two years since they last met, since they aborted their baby. Maria smelled his aftershave before she heard him. "Cedar wood," she whispered under her breath as he stepped into the room. But along with the scent that Owen carried came the memory again. This time it was obvious, not hazy and blurred like it had been under her hypnosis; the flashback was clear as if it only happened yesterday.

54

The sofa came into Maria's line of vision as she tried to figure out why she felt so sick and drowsy. Unable to lift her head her gaze dropped to the floor. Several scarves: yellow, blue and orange were around her feet. Her arms were loosely tied behind her back with something soft. She heard a noise and tried to look up. Tilting her head to the right she saw the silhouette of a man standing in her fridge eating something. It only took her a moment to realise it was her boyfriend. She smiled then. Had it all been a bad dream? Maria was about to say something but then realised there was something covering the top of her eyes. She could only see him though the slight gap just beneath whatever it was around her head. She took in her surroundings for several minutes. She had been propped up on a sofa and she could smell male aftershave on her skin. Her heartbeat quickened as Maria realised that she was being held captive. Her head slumped back down.

"Hawaiian, Maria. I got it especially for you. You see, I remember what you like," Owen said, waving a slice of pizza about.

Maria closed her eyes. Owen's voice wasn't how she remembered and he was so muscular, like he had spent years doing weights at the gym. There was something different about him. *What's happening?* Maria wanted to ask, but it was as if her mouth was paralysed.

"Not long," Owen said casually, "Ollie will be here in a moment for the final shift." Owen walked towards the sofa and sat down next to Maria. Confusion engulfed her; being tied up and blindfolded didn't make sense. Why would Owen hold her prisoner? Fear encouraged Maria to stay silent and not to move. She heard Owen swallow his last mouthful of food. The aftershave was so overpowering. It was a mixture of cedar wood and lime. The intensity of the perfume mixed with the smell of the doughy pizza base, pineapple and ham made Maria want to retch. Aware that her breathing had quickened, she wondered if Owen knew she was awake. A feeling of dread circled her. Owen was more than capable of doing whatever he wanted with her. But he had never hurt her before. There was one time when he had pushed her. He had bruised her arm but it had been an accident. Owen had said so, but now, with his bulky frame towering over her limp body, Maria was beginning to realise he could do a lot of harm.

The whole situation did not make any sense to Maria. The last thing she remembered was being at work… The thought of it jogged her memory. Her life was different now. Owen wasn't in it anymore. He was no longer her boyfriend. The last time Maria saw Owen was over two years ago, and he looked less like a bodybuilder then. So why was he in her apartment talking to her and helping himself to pizza? And who was Ollie? Was it her Ollie? Oliver Sanderson from her book club? What did Ollie have to do with Owen? As far as Maria knew, they didn't know each other. Confusion overpowered Maria and made her sleepy.

"You look helpless," Owen said, stroking Maria's hair. "You look so weak like that," he sneered at Maria, tired of her lifeless appearance. "You make me feel so guilty." Owen reached towards her and flicked her cheek. Maria was too weak to flinch and she realised then that her reflexes didn't work. Owen smoothed her hair again and the black cloth tied around her eyes came loose. It fell to the floor.

Owen propped Maria up with some cushions and stared at her. "That's better," he said looking away from her. "I'm not doing this to cause you any harm. I'm doing this for your own sake," he said, standing up and fidgeting with the remote control. "Alice and I are getting married, but she won't marry me unless you're her maid of honour. You see, Maria, I had no choice. I guess you could say I've spoilt your darling sister. But I drove you two apart. It was up to me to bring you two back together. And I make things happen." Owen dropped the remote to the sofa and cocked his head again, looking at Maria. "Are you bloody awake?" he asked.

Maria was silent. Her mouth was dry with fear.

He pulled her head back and opened her right eyelid as far as he could.

Maria mustered enough strength to roll her eyes back into her head.

Happy with what he had seen of Maria's eyes, Owen shook his shoulders and told himself to get a grip.

"Are you talking to yourself?" Maria could hear another voice from somewhere behind her. The voice was recognisable. It was someone she knew. Maria saw this as her chance. She knew she had to say something. The scarves around her wrists were only loosely tied, she could easily set herself free. Maria tried to move her arms but it was no use. She tried to speak but then stopped herself. If Owen knew this second person then it was likely that he was in on her abduction. And what would they do to her if they knew that she was conscious? Her breathing quickened again, making the blood rush in her ears. She tried to calm herself so she could listen to what the two men were saying.

"What took you so long?"

"You shouldn't talk to her, you know. She might be awake! And look, her blindfold has come off. What have you been doing to her?"

Maria recognised Oliver's voice. It *was* her Oliver, from the book club.

"I gave her another sleeping pill," Owen said, flicking Maria's face again. "See? Knocked out."

Oliver shut the front door behind him. "Let's move her to the chair. I don't like seeing her like that. She looks like a corpse!" Oliver said.

Owen stood up and lifted Maria. Her body was dead weight. She tried to move her arm, and this time there was a slight feeling in her limb.

"I think she moved," Oliver said.

"Stop being so paranoid. I'm the one carrying her. I would have noticed if she moved. Don't just stand there like an idiot, help me put her down in that chair. I don't want her to wake all bashed and bruised."

Oliver slowly moved towards Maria, his hands trembling. He didn't want to touch his friend's body.

"What the fuck am I paying you for?" Owen snapped.

"Okay," Oliver said, putting his hands under Maria's arms as he tried to position her lifeless body in an upright position.

"Do you really think this will make her want to get back in touch with her sister?"

"Of course."

"They haven't spoken in over two years. Why would she call her sister after this?"

"Family is important to Maria. She'll forgive and forget after this. Maria isn't callous like *us*, Shirty. Maria has a heart. Anyway, who else has she got to turn to?"

Oliver thought about his own family for a moment. Would his father start speaking to him again if his life was threatened? For a fraction of a second, Oliver understood what Langers was trying to do. "How do you know her, Langers?" Oliver asked, tightening the scarf around Maria's wrists.

Owen ignored him.

Maria drifted in and out of consciousness. She was beginning to feel drowsy again. Her head was propped against the back of the chair. Despite Oliver's concern, he had not replaced Maria's blindfold. If she opened her lids just slightly she could see what was happening around her. Cautiously, Maria did so. She had a clear view of the kitchen. Maria quickly closed them again. Then, silently taking a deep breath, Maria gently opened her right eye, just a fraction, and caught a glimpse of Owen standing in her kitchen drumming his fingers on the worktop.

Maria heard a key in the door. *Another person had a key to her flat.*

"I thought this would be over by now. It's been two days already!" Maria distinctly heard her sister's voice and her palms began to sweat. *It couldn't be. Why would Alice have anything to do with this?*

"Kitty, keep it down," Owen growled. "She'll recognise your voice."

Maria opened her eyelids just a fraction as she felt her sister walk past. Owen put his arm around Alice and she rested her head on his chest. *Where was Oliver?*

"Owen, you said it would be over in a day. It's been two days," Alice said, pouting and playing with her fiancé's collar.

"We had to be sure, Kitty," Owen said.

Oliver came into Maria's focus; he was looking in Alice's direction, away from Maria. No one was looking at her.

"She'll be fine for work tomorrow. We'll put her in her bed in an hour's time, clear up and get out of this place," Owen said.

"No more tablets," Oliver said, looking at Langers. "Let her sleep off the last of the drugs. I don't think it's safe to keep someone sedated for so long."

Alice shot Owen a concerned glance.

"Bittersweet and sleeping tablets are fine. I've checked," Owen said, stroking Alice's hair. "I wouldn't hurt her."

"No, of course you wouldn't," Alice sneered.

"Let it go," Owen said.

Maria tried lifting her lids further. She wanted to see her sister's expression. She wanted Alice to know that she was awake. What would her sister do then? Maria tried, but her eyelids were too heavy and she couldn't open them. As her eyes closed, she saw Oliver's hand flicker in front of her with the bare brick wall behind it. Standing behind her, Oliver gently wrapped the blindfold around her eyes, taking away her sight.

Oliver tightened the scarf.

"Careful," Alice said as Oliver tugged at the scarf. "We don't want to leave any marks."

"Your voice, Kitty," Owen said.

"Oh, puh-lease."

"I'm trying to protect you, Alice," Owen said.

Alice narrowed her eyes and looked from Owen to Maria and back again.

Owen kissed Alice's hand. "We'll be married next summer, I promise."

"We should have just left it to Oliver, though," Alice said, looking at Oliver fussing over Maria's inert body.

"I don't think Shirty could have managed this on his own," Owen said.

Alice looked at Maria and back at Owen. "I don't like the fact that you've been here alone with her," she whispered, giving him a frosty look.

Owen frowned. Sometimes Alice could be totally absurd. He thought about defending himself but he didn't want to have an argument. What had prompted his fiancée's little outburst? She was impossible when she was in one of those moods.

Oliver gritted his teeth. Langers would never change. All he wanted was his money and book deal and to get out of there. Then he never wanted to see Alice and Owen again. "I'll make it up to you," Oliver whispered under his breath. "I promise, Maria. I promise."

"I thought I saw her eyelid flicker," Oliver said, although he had seen nothing of the kind. How could Maria's sister do this to her own flesh and blood? Did Alice have no feelings at all? "You should keep quiet. If it's one voice she'll recognise, despite her state, it will be yours. After all, you are sisters. Sibling bonds and all that."

Alice shrugged. "Don't worry, my sister is such a fantasist. She has the wildest dreams. Don't you know she's on antidepressants?" Alice said, taking a box of tablets out of her bag and walking towards the bedroom. She suddenly stopped in her tracks and turned around. Smiling at Oliver she said, "We may be blood sisters, Ollie, but Owen was the father of Maria's aborted child. If she recognises one voice, it could just as well be his." Alice raised her eyebrows and gave her lover an icy look before leaving the room.

55

"Maria? Maria," Sunil said as he gently shook her shoulder. She looked at him with tears in her eyes. Then she turned to Alice and Owen who were sitting on the sofa opposite her. Owen took Alice's hand in his and smiled.

Maria stared at her sister. Alice knew about the abortion and the abduction before Maria had even told her. It had been Alice who had planted the antidepressants for Leanne to find, right next to her sleepover bag. Slowly Alice had worked her way into Leanne's favour and poor Leanne, without a malicious bone in her body, had been taken in by Alice's charm. Maria now knew just how cruel Alice was, trying to isolate Maria from her only true friend so that she would have no choice but to turn to her younger sister. Dr Timms had been right. There was a reason why Maria's mind had chosen not to remember what happened to her that weekend in September. It was because of her sister.

Maria's mind started to spin. On the one hand she was relieved. Finally she was certain that she was not a dreamer and she had not made up the whole episode. On the other hand, Maria wasn't sure if she could cope with the truth. Before now Maria had been happy that her sister was back in her life. Just over an hour ago she had been blissfully unaware that her own flesh and blood was responsible for violating and deceiving her so ruthlessly. How could her sister and her ex-boyfriend, who she had loved so completely, betray her like this?

And Oliver. Maria had trusted him so much she had even let him into her apartment just weeks after her abduction. Was that why he was being so empathetic the week they were given *The Sinner* to read? Is that why he had a look of utter sadness in his eyes? Maria felt foolish now. She had been concerned for Oliver over the past couple of months and he was the one who had been part of her abduction.

Maria felt as if her whole world was falling apart. The people she was closest to had violated her so terribly.

It felt reassuring to have Sunil by her side. He gave her confidence. Maria looked at her sister and ex-lover. Her fists were clenched but she held them between her legs. It was their turn to suffer. They couldn't just get away with what they had done. She wanted them to feel her pain. "You kidnap me from my workplace, tie me up and drug me, and you sit there in silence. Have you nothing to say?" Tears pricked the back of Maria's eyes as the reality of what they had done hit her once again. It was the first time she had said it out loud. Tears streamed down her cheeks.

Alice looked at Maria in silence. Maria looked away. She couldn't bear to look at what her sister had become. Was Alice's look of disbelief because she realised what she had put Maria through? Or was she just surprised that they had been found out?

"I told you about what happened and you acted like you knew nothing," Maria said. "You knew about the abortion, about the abduction. You were *part* of the abduction." Maria shook her head in disbelief.

"You were always a dreamer. Is this a plea for help? Attention seeking?" Owen said nonchalantly.

"I remember," Maria said.

"How?" Alice mumbled under her breath.

"How? You're asking me how I remember?" Maria said in disbelief. Her hands clenched to her chest.

Owen laughed.

Sunil stood up in front of Maria. How dare they treat Maria like this after what they put her through. He started to walk towards Owen.

Owen stood up but Sunil didn't back down. He matched him in height, if not build.

"Wait," Maria said, holding Sunil's arm back. He turned towards her, about to protest but then sat down.

"I know what happened," Maria said.

Owen sat back down. "Stop wasting our time. You may still have feelings for me but I can tell you those feelings…"

"We didn't mean any harm by it…" Alice interjected, her face solemn, but Owen cut her off.

"Alice, don't," Owen said, staring at his fiancée.

"She knows," Alice said, her voice beginning to crack.

Owen placed his large hand on his girlfriend's knee. "Perhaps it was just to give you a fright, make you realise what's important," Owen said, and then, looking back at Alice, added, "She had nothing to do with it." Owen put a protective arm around his fiancée.

"I remember Owen. Alice was there with Oliver and you. She planted the antidepressants," Maria said. How could Owen think she was upset because she still had feelings for him? The man was deluded.

"Oliver Sanderson?" Sunil asked in disbelief.

"Yes," Maria said. "Did you really think I wouldn't remember? That I was passed out the entire time? Alice, you did this to make me realise that life is too short not to forgive and forget. You were right. Life is too short. And an hour ago I was happy that you were back in my life. Your little plan worked. But did you really think I would want anything to do with you if I found out what you did? You disgust me."

Sunil took Maria's hand in his as he desperately tried to piece together the little bits of information. "It isn't your right to take away someone's freedom. You wanted your sister back in your life? Well you certainly went the wrong way about it!" Sunil said.

Maria let Sunil speak as the memory returned to her: the brick walls and the yellow scarf, her sister and Owen holding on to each other, Oliver propping her up. She would never have put the three together.

"You've hurt your sister more than you know, and for what?" Sunil directed his words at Alice. He didn't have anything more to say to Owen.

Alice raised her knees up to her chin and, hugging them, rocked back and forth on the sofa. She looked at Sunil through her tears.

"So why the emails?" Maria suddenly asked. "If the premise was so simple. You were just playing games by sending those emails."

Alice's eyes widened. She'd had no idea about the emails.

"An email would set the scene," Owen said, more for Alice's benefit than for Maria's. "It was Oliver's idea."

"And how do you know Ollie?" Sunil asked.

"I went to school with Oliver."

"He did it for money," Maria said to Sunil, looking around their living room filled with expensive technology.

Maria caught Owen's smile. It was just a game to him. She wondered how she ever loved him. A man who was so determined to be right all the time. A man who wanted control over her and her sister more than anything else. There wasn't even a hint of remorse on his face. Owen looked at Maria as if she deserved it, as if she deserved what they did to her.

Alice and Owen exchanged looks. "You okay, Kitty?" Owen asked.

Kitty? Maria thought. It had been Maria's pet name for Alice when they were younger; she had been obsessed with a toy cat called *Hello Kitty*. Maria hadn't used that term of endearment in years. How had Owen come to call her that?

"Kitty?" Maria said, looking for a reaction from her sister. But instead Owen put his palms together and glared at her. It sent a shiver down her spine. Owen certainly wasn't the person she had fallen in love with back in university. Alice was going to make the biggest mistake of her life by marrying this evil man. Minutes ago, as Owen descended the stairs, Maria had wondered if she would have any feelings for him. She didn't. Maria could truly put that episode of her life behind her now. Owen would never be a part of her life again.

Maria knew she wouldn't get anything more out of Owen and Alice. It was time to leave it to the police. But there was something else lurking in her memory that was slowly coming back to her. Suddenly, as Owen twisted his signet ring on his little finger and grinned at Maria, she gasped. Her face turned white as another splintered memory came to her.

"Are you okay?" Sunil asked, putting his arm around her and pulling him towards her. He held her hand, which had turned ice cold. "Let's leave, Maria. Let's go to the police."

Maria bit her cheek, hoping the physical pain would take away all the other feelings she was experiencing. The metallic taste of blood touched her tongue. She looked at her sister as the colour slowly returned to her cheeks. Did her sister deserve to know?

★

Alice leaned back on the white sofa, releasing her knees. Only yesterday her world was perfect; her sister was back in her life and Leanne was slowly disappearing. She had actually thanked Owen for making it happen.

Alice's life had been just how she had pictured it: Owen on her arm and her sister as her maid of honour. Alice was so confident that Maria would not remember a thing. Owen had made a promise. And Owen was never wrong. Months had passed and Maria did not have any recollection of what happened. How had Maria found out so abruptly? Had Oliver said something to her? Alice had spoken to Maria only yesterday and there was no suggestion that she even had an inkling as to what had happened.

★

"So what happens now?" Alice asked.

Maria shrugged. She could not think.

"The police will deal with it," Sunil said.

"Don't you think they would find it a bit odd that you hadn't reported the incident after the actual event? Tell me, Maria, if it was so much of a trauma, why didn't you report it straight away?" Owen looked at his ex-lover and took Alice's hand. He played with her engagement ring and smiled. Maria couldn't hurt them. Nobody could hurt them.

Maria swallowed back her tears. She realised Owen was right. Who would believe her now?

"Shock," Sunil said. "Sometimes people don't report crimes for years due to shock and fear."

Owen looked at Sunil with piercing eyes. "Really?" he asked, raising his eyebrows somewhat defiantly.

Alice cut through Sunil, who was about to speak. "Please, Maria. I never meant to hurt you. Nothing happened to you. You were just sedated, that's all. I promise. We only did it so that you would…"

"Would you really want to hurt your sister?" Owen asked Maria. He knew just how to play her.

"Like the way she hurt me?" Maria asked, but she was met with silence. *Alice, if you only knew. If only I could have the courage to tell you. But you hurt me. You hurt me so much.*

Alice was saying something to Maria but she could not hear her words. Her eyes closed. *Did it happen?* Yes, she was certain. The smell of cedar wood was suffocating her. Maria's final memory returned.

*

It happened minutes before Maria woke on the sofa. Some time before Owen was eating pizza from her fridge and before Oliver had arrived. Perhaps it was what had woken her. Maria could see it clearly now. Owen had forced a glass of liquid, perhaps water, down her throat and had helped her walk in a state of semi-consciousness towards the bedroom. Maria didn't know who he was then. Tired and lethargic, she drifted in and out of consciousness. When she woke again, she was naked. Propped on the edge of the bed, her knickers pulled down and her hands tied with the yellow scarf. *Bricks.* The bare bricks of the spare bedroom looked down on her. "No!" she tried to scream, but her attempt was feeble, drained from the drugs and lack of food. "No!" she tried again, louder, but her protests were barely audible. The smell of the cedar wood and lime, *Forever*, was upon her along with Owen's crushing weight. She could hear him struggle with the buckle of his belt and she heard his trousers fall to the ground. She saw his face. He entered her then and she had screamed. But not for long. He placed his large hand over her weak mouth as he thrust himself against her. She had closed her eyes then and drifted into unconsciousness.

★

Alice was still speaking to Maria, but she didn't want to hear her sister's excuses—her mind was preoccupied. When Maria woke on the 28th of September, her nether regions were sore. Why then did she pretend that nothing had happened? Why did she only believe that it was her wrists and neck that were tender? Why had she walked away from the police station and doctor's afterwards, when they could have examined her? Maria couldn't answer those questions and she knew that they would stay with her forever.

Maria knew her sister did not deserve to know that she was marrying a monster. Alice and Owen deserved each other. Maria opened her eyes and leaned back into Sunil, needing his warmth.

"I think we should leave, Maria," Sunil said gently to her. "Let the police deal with them."

"I wouldn't bother if I were you," Owen said as they stood up to leave.

"You know, Owen, you're not the only one with contacts in high places," Sunil threatened.

Owen rose to his feet. "Oh, I am sure you have contacts. But there's not much you can do with a watertight alibi and not a shred of evidence. In fact, go ahead. Please, take it to the police. It'll be interesting to see what happens," Owen said with a grin.

Maria tugged at Sunil's arm. She wanted to leave the house of deception shrouded by the bittersweet vine. As they stepped out through the door, Sunil asked one last question. Something he was curious to know. "And what would your alibi be?"

Owen gave them both a wry smile. "Our alibi? Well that's simple. We were staying with my family in the Lake District."

EPILOGUE

The following summer, Maria and Sunil pulled up to a small cottage in Kibworth. Maria pushed her hair behind her ears, still getting used to her new cropped style. They rang the bell and waited patiently. The door opened to reveal a baby boy, with brilliant green eyes, in the arms of his father.

Penelope stepped forward from the recesses of the cottage to greet her friends and quickly ushered them inside offering a spread of tea and cakes.

"I love your hair!" Penelope said, hugging her friend.

"What a beautiful home," Maria said.

Penelope smiled. "I don't know what I would have done without Lawrence," she said. "This past year has been tough."

Lawrence walked around to Penelope, and with Alex on one arm, he pulled his girlfriend towards him.

"The perfect family!" Maria said. She noticed the emerald on Penelope's left hand. "Congratulations!" she exclaimed.

Penelope blushed. "Lawrence and I are getting married next spring. My parents are attending."

"Nothing like a bit of fame, eh? To bring the family back together," Lawrence said.

Penelope scowled playfully at Lawrence, throwing a tea towel at him.

"Your book is causing quite a stir among the local book clubs," Sunil said. "Just released and already a top seller."

Lawrence grimaced. "The Big Summer Read. I hope it hasn't been too hard for you Maria. I feel bad…"

"Don't." Maria warned quickly, cutting him off mid-sentence. She swallowed a lump in her throat. "What happened was terrible. I'll never forget what they did, and definitely never forgive. But your book, *The Silver Shoe*, well… that was the only good thing about the whole wretched mess. At least something good came of it."

Maria noticed a framed picture of their book club group on the side cabinet. After she regained her memory, she never returned to Du Jour again. "Do you see much of Ollie?" Maria asked, not knowing if she wanted to hear the answer. Oliver was Lawrence's cousin, after all, and she couldn't expect them to cut him out of their lives.

"Now and again," Penelope answered. "Lawrence sees him. But after what happened, when Oliver found out that you had remembered, he couldn't live with himself. And Leicester was such a reminder of what he had done. He transferred to the university of Lisbon and completed his course over there. He writes to us occasionally," Penelope said with a smile forming on her lips as she recalled that Oliver still referred to her as the Siren.

Maria was glad Oliver was no longer in the country. She didn't want to have to endure bumping into him somewhere. He had written Maria a long letter explaining his motivations and repenting for what he had done. Maria had hidden it in the bottom of her bedside drawer.

She thought that, one day, she might find it in her heart to forgive Oliver. He was the only one who seemed to realise that what he had done was wrong and, more importantly, he was sorry for his part in it. But Maria knew she didn't have to think about forgiveness right away. The wounds would have to heal first.

Alex started to cry and Lawrence took him out to the garden. Sunil followed.

"How are you doing?" Penelope asked, taking a seat as the men left the kitchen, her head tilted to one side. Maria noticed Penelope's hair was not as blond as it had been. She had gone back to her natural colour.

"I'll live with it. Time is a great healer. Ask me in a couple of years and maybe I won't remember!" Maria laughed, but they both knew that what happened would stay with her forever.

"And Alice, do you ever see her?" Penelope asked her friend cautiously.

"Even after what she did, I called her. I couldn't let her marry that monster. After I had time to think about what they did, what Owen did, I had to tell her. After all, she is my sister."

"And her reaction?"

"She didn't believe me," Maria said, her voice catching.

"No!" Penelope said, putting her hand to her mouth. "Why would she think you would lie about something like that?"

"Because I'm apparently still in love with Owen, because I crave attention, because I'm a fantasist. She desperately thinks I want to ruin her life as payback for what they did."

Penelope's jaw dropped. "And you would have every right to."

"I tried to tell her, Penny," Maria said. "She wouldn't listen and it hurt. It really hurt that she didn't believe me. Owen has her brainwashed. "

"Have you spoken to her since?"

"She sent me a couple of messages saying that we should leave what happened in the past and move on." Maria took a sip of tea that Penelope had placed in front of her. "You know what? I think I would have forgiven her if she had believed me."

"But she didn't."

"I hear they're getting married next month," Maria said.

Penelope sighed. "You haven't told your parents?" Penelope asked.

"No. I haven't and I won't. It will only end up hurting them. I don't think Alice will ever change. She'll just deny it. Mum has tried to get us talking again but it's not going to happen. She doesn't know the story. Alice has made her choice. She's always done what she wanted. It's amazing what a pink diamond and a holiday home in Los Angeles can do," Maria said sarcastically. "Looks like *The Silver Shoe* helped Owen's bank balance as well as Lawrence's." Maria shrugged her shoulders in defeat.

Penelope put her arms around her friend.

Maria looked at her friend tentatively. "Can I ask you something?"

"What? Anything. Just ask."

"Well… You knew Jason and I wondered if he ever mentioned *The Sinner* to you. The reason he stayed so quiet about it. It's the one thing I can't figure out. I never asked Alice and Owen, and, well, after that confrontation, I don't think I would have believed anything they had to say."

Penelope flinched on hearing her ex-lover's name. There were too many secrets that Jason had kept from her to ever forgive him. "Yes. I do know about it. The one bit of truth he did tell me."

"Oh, Penny, I didn't mean…"

"Shhh," Penelope said, placing a finger on her lips. "I can talk about it." She took her friend's hand in hers. "When Jason was growing up, his parents hit a rocky patch. They were constantly rowing and never had time for their son so he ended up staying with his uncle, J Rupert, for quite some time. Jason thought of him like a father. Later, when Jason's parents had sorted out their differences, they moved away and Jason rarely saw his uncle.

"When his uncle died so tragically, he left all his royalties to Jason. Jason was determined to make his uncle successful, to give him the credit he so deserved and craved when he was alive. He was the one who managed to get Langford and Sons to publish it. But when he heard the book was a recommendation at the club, it really floored him. He didn't want me to mention the author was his uncle.

"I thought he was paranoid at the time and I didn't know his story. I didn't see what the big deal was about. Now I know it was because he thought someone knew about his past, his wife and child perhaps, and was using his uncle's book as way of making him squirm."

"So it really was a coincidence. I'd like to say poor Jason. But we both know he doesn't deserve any pity. I wonder if the *The Sinner* was aimed at scaring me or Jason."

Penelope sucked her teeth. "Lawrence thought it was Oliver, and after some emotional blackmail, Oliver admitted it. He wouldn't say why, though. I don't know if he was trying to get at you or Jason, but if you ask me *The Sinner* served two purposes."

"Have you spoken to Jason since…"

"Not once."

"Rustle?"

"Not since Lawrence."

Sunil walked back into the kitchen. "We must be getting off," he said to Maria, kissing her gently on her forehead.

"Stay for tea," Penelope said.

"We can't. We have a flight to catch," Maria said, brightening.

"Ah, so you're finally using some of your travel vouchers, Maria."

"Yes, I am."

"Still at the travel agency?" Lawrence asked.

"My talents were clearly wasted there. You are now looking at a trainee surveyor at Alcott's."

"Well done, you!" Lawrence said, shifting his son to his other arm.

"I am starting at the bottom, but I love it and they're paying for me to complete my Master's in Real Estate."

"So it's better than being a travel agent's assistant?" Penelope asked, laughing.

Maria smiled, remembering the look on Tina's face as she handed in her notice just a couple of months ago.

"So where are you going?" Lawrence asked.

"Leanne, believe it or not, is still travelling. We're going out to meet her."

"Anywhere nice?" Penelope asked.

Maria instantly remembered the picture of the perfectly manicured beach and lunging palm tree that hung in her office just over a year ago. She looked up at Sunil and smiled.

"Raratonga!"

AUTHOR'S NOTE

The Bittersweet Vine is a work of fiction. The names and characters portrayed in it are fictitious. Any resemblance to actual persons, living or dead, is entirely coincidental.

Regressive Recollection Therapy, *The Sinner* by J Rupert, *Darlington House* and the fragrance *Forever* are references of complete fiction.

ACKNOWLEDGEMENTS

Thanks go to my husband, James, for his continual support throughout my journey and to my family and friends. In particular my mother, Audrey, for providing me with continual motivation for *The Bittersweet Vine*, and Urmi Kenia, who has been a great sounding board for my ideas. Thanks also go to Debbie Riley for her immense knowledge on medications, and to Subrina, Neha and Anna for always being there.

A big thank you to the members of Abingdon Writers for their continuous help throughout the seemingly endless drafting process. And, of course, to my agent, Darin Jewell, and all at Thames River Press, in particular Caelin Charge for all her hard work in editing *The Bittersweet Vine*.

ABOUT THE AUTHOR

Marissa de Luna spent much of her childhood in Goa and moved to Leicestershire to complete her education. After working for several years in property management, Marissa took a career break in 2007 to travel. Her writing career started on her return to the UK. Marissa now lives and works in Oxfordshire. www.marissadeluna.com